Mollie Kendrick lives in the North East with her partner, two teenagers and a dog. Her mum visits sometimes to tell her that her house isn't tidy.

Praise for *Middle Rage*

'Mollie Kendrick's debut is written so engagingly, it's hard to believe you're not one of the women on the retreat. I wanted the cacao, the massage, I wouldn't even have minded the naked dancing. Fascinating company that keeps you entertained with every turn of the page.'
Melanie Cantor

'I loved this compulsive novel that is moving and funny, and a reminder of the journey women have taken - and the lives that still need to change. The characters and their stories slowly wrap themselves around you and hold on oh so tight. A must-read for *good girls* everywhere.'
Samantha Tonge

'A call-to-arms to recognise the power of what happens when women come together, this is a relatable story for women of every age and experience. Warm, wise, funny and moving, these are women who dare to face and forgive their darkest shadows, to strip back the layers to reach back into who they truly are – and to step fully into how they want, and deserve, to live.'
Jenny Knight

'I laughed out loud at times and also felt the prick of tears at others, definitely recommend!'
Reader review ★ ★ ★ ★ ★

'I did not expect to love this book as much as I did and was crying by the end . . . A big recommendation from me.'
Reader review ★ ★ ★ ★ ★

'Fascinating, and often laugh out loud funny. I didn't want it to end.'
Reader review ★ ★ ★ ★ ★

Middle Rage

MOLLIE KENDRICK

ONE PLACE. MANY STORIES

HQ
An imprint of HarperCollins*Publishers* Ltd
1 London Bridge Street
London SE1 9GF

www.harpercollins.co.uk

HarperCollins*Publishers*
Macken House, 39/40 Mayor Street Upper
Dublin 1, D01 C9W8, Ireland

This edition 2026

1

First published in Great Britain by HQ,
an imprint of HarperCollins*Publishers* Ltd 2026

Copyright © Mollie Kendrick 2026

Mollie Kendrick asserts the moral right to be identified as the author of this work. A catalogue record for this book is available from the British Library.

ISBN: 9780008754778

Set in Sabon LT Std by HarperCollins*Publishers* India

Printed and bound in the UK using 100% Renewable Electricity at CPI Group (UK) Ltd

This novel is entirely a work of fiction. The names, characters and incidents portrayed in it are the work of the author's imagination. Any resemblance to actual persons, living or dead, events or localities is entirely coincidental.

All rights reserved. No part of this publication may be reproduced, stored in a retrieval system, or transmitted, in any form or by any means, electronic, mechanical, photocopying, recording or otherwise, without the prior written permission of the publishers.

Without limiting the exclusive rights of any author, contributor or the publisher of this publication, any unauthorised use of this publication to train generative artificial intelligence (AI) technologies is expressly prohibited. HarperCollins also exercise their rights under Article 4(3) of the Digital Single Market Directive 2019/790 and expressly reserve this publication from the text and data mining exception.

For Amy, Alice and Catherine
and
Fi and Naomi
Thank you.

This is a safe space for brave women to tell their stories

PART ONE

1

Maggie

Maggie stood in front of her open wardrobe and checked the packing list the retreat leader had sent her.

1. Journal and pen
2. Coconut oil
3. Warm clothes
4. An outfit that expresses your dark feminine essence
5. Swimsuit
6. Kimono
7. Torch
8. Item(s) for the altar
9. Water bottle

She'd been hoping items 4 and 8 might have disappeared this time when she looked, but they were still there: white letters against a silver background. The design looked as though it was meant to conjure images of moonlight, but all it did for Maggie was cause eye strain.

An outfit that expresses your dark feminine essence.

She should email the leader. *Sorry, I only have gardening clothes.*

What even was a dark feminine essence? Maggie had no idea. Something bold, probably. Something wild.

She turned her attention back to the wardrobe. It was mainly full of jeans. Her mind slipped to that old get-up she'd put together at art college in the Sixties. A black leather dress with a belt of Barbie dolls tied round her waist. She'd picked the dolls up at a jumble sale for two shillings each and tied them together with string. The outfit had been an artistic-political statement, although she couldn't remember now what the statement had been. Something to do with second-wave feminism. Something to do with fighting violence against women.

'And here we are,' she said to Bill. 'Still dealing with the same old crap.'

Bill licked his paws and didn't look up.

'What should I take to express my dark feminine essence?'

Bill looked as though he didn't give a shit. It was one of the things that made him so agreeable. The original Bill would have gone on for hours. She could almost hear him now. Any of her friends' husbands would simply have said, 'You have no darkness, darling,' and returned their attention to the TV. Bill would have given her question passionate consideration, mistaking 'dark essence' for 'Things You Do That Annoy Me' and reeling off a list of her flaws so comprehensive she'd have to spend weeks plotting her revenge.

'Dark feminine essence,' she said to herself, then decided she was overthinking this and grabbed something black. A dress with some slightly suggestive decorative lace around the neckline. That would do, though she wasn't entirely sure what she was suggesting with the lace. She could just about assemble a cleavage if she pushed and shoved enough, but when she took her bra off these days, it was like an avalanche.

Once she'd added the dress to her bag, the list was almost ticked off. But there it still was:

8. Item(s) for the altar

Maggie didn't have a clue what the altar would be for, or what they were meant to bring to it. She was going on this retreat because her friend's daughter had been on one last year and everything about it sounded hilarious and intriguing. 'She looks amazing,' Caroline had told her. 'Seriously, she looks ten years younger. She said it was because of the meditation and forest bathing.'

Maggie liked the sound of that. A bit of meditation was bound to be cheaper than the moisturizer she used. It was designed for A-List celebrities. Maggie couldn't really afford it, but a sales assistant had given her a sample pot and, despite thinking of herself as not at all stupid, Maggie had fallen for that particular ploy and become addicted. Still, she wasn't the only one. A top actress whose name she couldn't remember had even written a love letter to it. Maggie thought that was going too far, but she understood. It was difficult to have skin that only reminded you of your proximity to the grave.

To Bill, she said, 'Shall I take my moisturizer for the altar?'

Bill was asleep and didn't answer.

According to the website, the purpose of this retreat was rebellion and harnessing your dark side. The idea of it had alarmed Maggie at first, but then she remembered how the darkest sides of most people she knew meant failing to share a sharing-sized bar of Dairy Milk, so she signed up for it. She felt like rebelling. She'd felt like rebelling for years. When she and Bill used to take Richard to the beach, she'd look out from beneath the privacy of her wide-brimmed sunhat and wonder what it would be like to launch herself over the sand and into the sea, to keep on swimming and not come back. Bill had never noticed. He'd never noticed all those times she'd been lit from within by a dream of freedom, how often she'd sat beside him, energized, poised for flight.

It frustrated her sometimes, how he hadn't known. How on earth had he managed when it was such a strong force inside her? But then he died, and the thought struck her suddenly that maybe he'd always known and simply pretended not to. Maybe he'd spent their entire forty-five years together expecting to wake up in the morning and find her gone. The thought filled her with almost unbearable guilt. 'I'd never really have left, Bill,' she said out loud. 'You drove me mad but I would always have come back.'

Bill went on sleeping.

Her husband's death three years ago had been unexpected and everything about it was shocking. The circumstances (cardiac arrest), the suddenness, the depth of Maggie's grief. She'd always known he would die before her, and privately she'd make plans for the next stage of her life: one of cool, independent widowhood. Bill had never liked train journeys or cities, so she'd pictured herself touring Europe with her senior-discounted Interrail pass, travelling by night from Paris to Venice, re-establishing herself as an artist, perhaps even becoming renowned and important in her eighties.

But then Bill really did die and she couldn't bear the thought of Europe without him. After that, the cat moved in and that was the end of her freedom anyway. It was odd, how it happened. Bill had always said that if he was going to be reincarnated, he'd want to come back as a cat. The pampered laziness of the cat's life appealed to him. He'd probably be a big ginger tom, quiet and slightly overweight. Six months after he died – which Maggie supposed was enough time to have tried the afterlife and made a decision about it – a bedraggled black cat arrived on her doorstep, miaowing so loudly and passionately that Maggie felt sure it was trying to form words. When she opened the door, it looked at her with plaintive eyes. It had no collar, nothing about it to suggest an owner, so she gave it some water and thought that would be it.

That night, there was a storm. Maggie woke at 2 a.m. She could hear the howl of the wind and the pounding of rain against the windows, but in among it she could also hear the wailing call of the cat.

She could hardly leave it out there to perish. And what if it wasn't a cat? What if it was Bill?

She went downstairs and opened the door. 'You'd better come in,' she said, and gave it a tin of tuna. Bill had loved tuna. The cat gobbled it in less than two minutes. She laid a blanket on the sofa and carried the cat to it. 'Sleep here for the night,' she said, and went back to bed. After five minutes, the cat appeared in her room. It seemed to know its way round the house. It mewled at her for a while, then jumped on the bed and settled in beside her. She fell asleep to the sound of its purr.

After a week, the cat was still there and Maggie accepted

it had moved in. She spoke to it a lot. Did it want food? Did it want to go outside? If it went out, it mustn't bring birds home because her husband had loved birds. When she said this, she was sure it gave her an indignant look. She'd see it chasing balls of paper or plastic bags down the street and it would come home with them clenched in its jaws so she could throw them away. Bill had hated litter, too.

She took it to the vet for a health check. The vet said it was a boy. He wasn't microchipped. There was nothing they could do to find his owners. Maggie was quietly delighted. 'Come on then, Bill,' she said. 'I'll take you home.'

Everyone found it sadly endearing that she'd named him Bill. Of course, she could never tell them the truth. They'd all just think grief had unhinged her again.

Now, she turned to Bill and said, 'I'm not sure why I'm going on this retreat, really. It's not as if I have very much to retreat from these days. There's you, of course, but I don't need to get away from you so much now you're a cat and you're quieter. I'm not exaggerating when I say I once feared I had low-level brain damage just from listening to you go on.'

Bill went on sleeping, but Maggie knew he could hear her. 'I just need to do something, something I've never done before. But this altar business . . . I have no idea what they're expecting. I'm not a religious person. I'm not even sure what an altar is used for. I think it's for offerings to the gods, or maybe sacrifices. It's a retreat for exploring darkness. Should I take images of the people I want to kill, or would that be too much?'

With a jolt, she found herself thinking of Annie and Richard. She pushed it away. Annie was long gone. All

Maggie could do now was try to cherish her memory and allow herself to let go of what happened afterwards, with Richard.

She picked up her phone from where it lay on the bed and started typing a message to the WhatsApp group the retreat leader had set up in advance so people could share taxis from the train station or lifts from further afield. The leader's name was Clover, which made Maggie suspicious. Either she'd made it up herself or her parents had known the minute she was born that this was a child destined to grow up and run dark retreats for wild women.

To Bill, she said, 'It's a cat's name really, isn't it? Would you marry a girl cat if she were called Clover? I don't think you would. I think she'd be all wrong for you. It's pretentious, isn't it? A bit self-consciously alternative. Her parents probably smoked cannabis. They probably called her Clover because Marijuana isn't a socially acceptable name.'

She felt sure Bill was nodding in his sleep. She returned to the message she was typing.

> What items should we bring for the altar? Are these images of the people we want to kill, or should it be something we love?

Maggie had stopped caring what people thought of her when she'd turned 40. Now, at 73, she was in minus figures on the scale of giving a crap.

A reply came back immediately.

> Whatever you feel is relevant for this particular journey.

Okay. She was expected to go on a journey. She'd thought she was just heading off to Bodmin Moor for four days of wild rebellion that nevertheless included eating for deeper health and a laughable attempt to contort her body into some yoga positions while praying no farts escaped. Now the leader was talking about *a journey*. A spiritual journey. A journey into her own unknown darkness.

She thought for a while, then entered the website address of the retreat on her phone and checked the blurb again. *No more sacrificing what it is you truly want. It's time to take up space and create a life that excites you. Come and ruffle some feathers, fuck shit up, trailblaze a new energy. You were born for this.*

Perhaps she hadn't read that properly when she'd made the booking. She mostly remembered promises of woodland walks and meditation. Still, she quite liked the thought of 'fucking shit up'. She hadn't done that for a while. She looked again at the words, *create a life that excites you*.

'Well,' she said to Bill. 'I believe I will.' She opened the box that had been under her bed for years and pulled out her packet of paintbrushes. She hadn't painted a thing since Annie died, and that was forty years ago now.

2

Emma

Forty seemed like a lifetime ago now, another place entirely. But it was when she'd turned forty that Emma had decided to embrace age, rather than let it creep up on her. She wasn't going to become one of those women who woke up one morning alone in an empty house while the world she never realized she'd retreated from spun on without her.

No. She was going to welcome each new year of life, drink champagne on every birthday, delight in the fact that she was still here, growing older. In the three years before she turned forty, two of Emma's friends had died – one from addiction and one from cancer. She owed it to them to see ageing for what it was. A joy. A privilege.

But that was before Oliver. It was in the days before the mere sight of her husband in the same room felt oppressive, made her want to sprint to the front door and fly.

Emma was 53 now. Mostly, life just pissed her off.

'You've been in a bad mood for the last five years,' Ben observed earlier, as he prowled round the kitchen, lifting the lid on the bread bin, opening the fridge, sniffing out breakfast like the muscular hunter-gatherer he saw himself as. 'Is it the menopause?'

'No,' she told him, swallowing a glass of water and

a capsule of evening primrose oil. 'It's because you're an arsehole.'

She felt wild these days. Unrestrained. All her life, a glut of feminine hormones had kept her polite in the face of outrage. Now they were falling away, dropping through her body with the last of her unconceived babies, taking with them the softness and patience she'd needed for maternity and revealing her as she was, with no filter.

Ben said nothing, just raised his eyebrows and shook his head, bewildered. He was nicer than her. He always had been. Emma believed it was acid that ran through her veins, instead of the beautiful, compassionate blood that Ben had. She'd witnessed the deep red beauty of Ben's blood for herself. Every three months, he headed to the whitewashed room at the community centre and allowed a pint of it to be pumped out of him. When she picked him up afterwards, she would see it running into a bag through the line in his arm and was always struck by the depth of the colour. The crimson of passion. Of love and life.

'There's nothing to stop you from doing it,' he suggested once, when she commented with awe on his everyday heroism.

But Emma felt sure her own blood would be nothing like his. Hers would be pale and sharp and toxic, and no use to anyone.

She didn't say that. She said, 'I might, but only if I'm also allowed to give them a blacklist of all the people who've pissed me off over the years, and whose lives I don't want to save. I know that's not really entering into the spirit of the thing, but it really matters.'

That had been before Oliver as well. She'd have given all

the blood in her body to save him, although she could never tell anyone that.

Clara walked sleepily into the kitchen. 'Am I late?' she asked.

Emma smiled at her anxiety-laden daughter. 'No,' she said. 'It's only seven thirty.'

Clara looked relieved. She never seemed to have faith in the clock on her phone, or the clock in her room. It was only when Emma told her the time that she ever really relaxed, as if her deeply flawed and chaotic mother was somehow less likely to lie to her than advanced, twenty-first century technology. Every day, Emma felt the sting of knowing she didn't deserve the magnitude of this trust.

Clara busied herself with the coffee machine and Emma asked, 'Have you remembered I'm going away today?'

Clara lifted the lid of the Aeroccino and poured warm, foamy milk over her espresso. 'Yes,' she said and grinned. 'You're off on an awakening retreat to learn how to open up.'

Emma rolled her eyes. 'Exactly.'

Clara said, 'Do you think you'll have to dance naked round a fire?'

'Let's hope not.'

It had been their therapist's idea. He'd decided they'd reached a point of stagnation because Emma was too reserved. 'I sense a reluctance on your part to open up, Emma,' he'd said. He said it a lot. He probably said it every week. 'We're here to help Clara and, although I know it can be hard, I also know we won't make the progress we need to make unless everyone involved can speak honestly.'

Emma didn't know what to say. What was there to say?

I can't open up because if I do, I'm worried I'll tip her over the edge?

Instead, she raised a hand to her throat and twisted her necklace until the pendant snapped away in her fingers, and said, 'I'm sorry. It's not easy for me to speak from my heart.'

Even that felt like a confession. A confession, for a start, that she had a heart.

He said, 'This isn't something I've suggested before and of course you're free to reject it. But I've worked with a couple of people who've found it difficult to open up before. One of them decided to go on a retreat. Now, before you protest, hear me out.' He smiled. 'They're trendy, I know. They're popular. But it's important not to dismiss something that could be of value just because it's trendy and popular. In my experience, things only become popular because they work on some level. I'm not suggesting that it will create a miracle, but the person I know who tried it found it liberating. It was a safe space, and it was intense, and afterwards she was much more able to speak in therapy.'

Emma looked at him. 'Is this seriously what you're suggesting?'

'It's just an idea. I'm not saying it necessarily fits with any kind of psychological theory or science, but it can do you no harm. What we're aiming for here is for you to open up, and you don't seem able to do that at the moment. It's something that may or may not help you. I'm not prescribing it. I'm not saying you have to do it. I'm simply saying other clients have found the experience beneficial. It helped them to access, in a very short space of time, those parts of them that needed to be explored in therapy.'

'I'm not sure it's really me.'

'Then maybe that's a reason to try it.'

She'd gone home and spent an amusing couple of hours with Clara, searching for retreats on the internet. She'd heard about them before, of course. She actually had friends who'd been on them. They'd all come back rejuvenated and with an aura of tranquillity that Emma envied. What she hadn't known until she started looking was just how many different retreats there were in the world. It was like a sub-culture of escaped women. There were standard retreats involving massage and yoga; then there were those that included meditation; and beyond that were the Wild Women retreats, ones that involved massage, yoga and ordinary meditation but also threw in forest bathing, meditation with horses and ecstatic dancing.

'This sounds hilarious,' Clara said. 'You should do one of these.'

Emma said, 'This isn't something I'd ever do if I were in my right mind.'

Clara gave her a winsome smile. 'You're doing it for me.'

Emma rolled her eyes again. 'That doesn't mean I should just find the most insane-sounding retreat and go for that.'

'I'd love it if you did. It might be amazing.'

'Or it might not.'

They kept on searching.

Wild Fire: embrace your dark feminine divine.

Emma had no idea what that meant. To Clara, she said, 'What do you think this means?'

Clara read out loud from the screen. 'It's time to reclaim the too-muchness of woman. Let your full feminine energy be seen and felt. Learn to express all aspects of you without apology. Take up space, share your voice and be true to your desires.'

'Right.'

Clara went on, 'We live in a world of structures and *should*s, and the wild woman wants out. In this four-day retreat, we will explore the most rebellious aspect of woman: the wild feminine. Join me to explore and embody the dark woman within, to unleash her fullness and reconnect to your wild truth. Explore the ways in which you desire to liberate yourself – and the ways in which you still feel caged. When you welcome the wild feminine into your body and your life, you will walk through the world with more ease, confidence and power.'

'Well. Sign me up,' Emma said.

'Sounds awesome.'

'It sounds bloody mad, Clara. That's how it sounds.'

'But it's only four days. What's the worst that can happen?'

Emma had images of herself being carried off into the darkness by wolves. She said, 'I've no idea. It sounds like anything could happen.'

'Well, if you don't like it, you don't have to stay. You can just come home.'

Emma clicked on the booking form and started filling it in. 'And quite how is this going to help with our therapy?' she asked.

Clara shrugged. 'It'll loosen you up,' she said. 'Stop you thinking everyone's out to judge you.'

That was all it took. She'd signed up.

Now she said to Clara, 'Will you be okay?'

'I'll be fine.'

'You can still ring me if you need me. I'll keep my phone on.'

'Okay. But actually, I'm going to do what Rob suggested. I'm going to know that you're away for four days and that I can deal with any anxiety that crops up without needing to phone you. I mean, I know you say I can call you if I need to, but what can you actually do? You'll be on Bodmin Moor, dancing naked round a fire.'

'I will not.'

'You might be. But anyway, I feel okay about it. I feel fine. And anyway, Dad's here.'

Oh, yes. Of course. Lovely, warm, compassionate Dad. The blameless parent. That, Emma thought, would be the title of his memoir. *The Blameless Parent.* Just imagining its content began to wind her up.

She glanced at the clock on the oven. 'I should get ready. I can drop you at school on my way if you like.'

She pulled herself up from the table and headed upstairs. Ben was there, straightening his tie and draining the last of his coffee. In some other world, long ago, she used to feel a hot rush of desire when she caught him immersed in the intimate minutiae of his day. Now, the way he noisily gulped his coffee made her want to stab him.

She said, 'The way you gulp your coffee makes me want to stab you.'

'You're such a bitch, Emma,' he said.

'I know that.'

Mildly, he asked, 'When are you leaving?'

'In a minute.'

'And what is it you're doing again?'

'I'm going on a retreat.'

He could barely conceal his smirk. Mind you, Emma thought, he probably wasn't trying very hard. She knew what the word *retreat* suggested to him. A load of mad women dancing and sobbing. Possibly he was right. Emma wanted to go because, to her, the word felt so luxurious, so full of promise. *Come here, to this sanctuary where no one will find you.*

Two weeks ago, she'd been told by the leader that she needed to pack an outfit to express her dark feminine essence and some items for the altar. She decided her dark feminine essence was a woman of incredible but woefully unrealized power, so she grabbed a black dress and a long, black velvet coat that swished when she walked and made her feel like she ought to be ruling the world.

She wasn't at all sure about the altar, or what it would be there for. She supposed it must have something to do with sacrifice. Letting go. She watched Ben as he took his jacket out of the wardrobe and wondered if she could haul him over her shoulders and dump him on the altar, in a tragic undoing of the day he'd carried her over the threshold of their first home.

'See you when you get back,' he said.

Her voice in her mind couldn't help itself. *If I come back.*

3

Clover

Clover turned the radio off. The signal had become crackly now she was so remote. She glanced in the rear-view mirror to make sure the car that had been tailing her for the last fifteen miles was gone. She felt pretty sure they'd never find her, but it didn't stop her from being cautious.

She'd read Kevin's blog again today. She couldn't help herself. He was still claiming that Clover's father was gravely ill and needed to see his daughter before he died, but she had no idea whether to believe it or not.

Even now, she still felt the pull of her family. She would love to see her father if he truly were dying, so she could say goodbye and give them both some peace. It would never be enough, though. He wouldn't want her to simply step into the room, talk for a while, kiss him and then leave. He'd want her full obedience.

She turned off the main road at the signpost for Bodmin Moor. Beside her, the passenger seat was full of roses – her gift for the wonderful women she was about to meet. She knew they would be wonderful. They always were. This was the seventh retreat she'd run since her liberation and each one had been full of incredible women, all of them infusing the experience with their own wild energy. She only had three coming to this one. It was enough for now, although six would have been better. She needed six to make any decent money, but hopefully word would spread and in time she'd have a business and be thriving on her own.

She knew all their names already and what they looked like. She'd asked them to upload a photo with their application forms so she'd recognize them when they met. She already knew Fleur. Fleur had been to her January retreat and they'd become friends. Clover tried to hold on to her professional boundaries, but it was difficult with this sort of work, so bound up in the emotional. On her application form, Fleur had written, *My last retreat with you was life-changing. I want to keep experiencing the magical healing you bring to the world.* Clover liked that. It was always useful to have someone in the group she could rely on to throw herself into the experience and show the others they had nothing to be afraid of.

The next one, Maggie, was older than her usual women. At least seventy. She seemed like the sort of woman Clover would like to be when she turned seventy. Her application statement had been mischievous and bold. She'd said things like, *I'm retired and my husband is dead. I want to be released into a new and exciting world but everyone around me is boring.*

Then there was Emma, who she didn't quite have a feel for yet. Her statement was simple, much more reserved than the others'. *I have been advised to come on a retreat to help me open up, something I have always found difficult. I am looking forward to experiencing something new.* Clover expected some resistance from her.

The road became narrower and steeper as the moorland around her grew more expansive. The landscape was wide open, wild and rocky. Her Fiat Panda chugged with the effort of climbing. Ahead of her, a pair of curlews soared into the clouds and then as she rounded a bend she could see it: the stone entrance to the retreat centre, where it was all about to begin.

She shivered with anticipation. Ever since she'd broken free, she'd known this was what she was meant to do, what she was here on Earth for. An awakened woman, awakening women.

4

Fleur

Fleur was aware of the tension slipping further and further away as she walked over the moors towards the retreat centre. It was seven miles from the station, but she didn't care. She felt protected here, among the heath and the peat bogs and the stone circles that carried centuries of mysticism in their granite stillness. She could feel ancient spirits all around her, whispering to her to carry on, to keep going with her journey to recovery and power.

She knew what was waiting for her. She'd been here before, back in January when the landscape was barren and wiry, and the river she swam in ice cold in its embrace. It was late September now, the world sharp with decay. Fleur drew the air deeply into her lungs as she walked. With each breath, she imagined inhaling the changing seasons and letting them shift something inside her, preparing her for her own transformation.

She was ready for this, for the deep immersion in nature, the dive into conquering her toughest memories, and the quiet luxury of the centre where she could consider her future and make a decision she'd be able to live with. She knew she could be entirely herself here, with Clover and the women she was yet to meet. She'd realized last time that only good people were attracted to places like this. It was the first place she'd felt safe for months.

She could see the centre ahead of her now, the single-storey barn spread at the top of the moor, surrounded by some of the last temperate rainforest in the country. Fleur had bathed in that forest before, lying down beneath the trees and feeling the healing power of their 3,000-year-old wisdom deep in her bones. She quickened her pace, knowing Clover would already be there.

Clover. She was like no one Fleur had ever met before, and Fleur felt sure they'd been sent into one another's lives for a purpose. Clover was a part of Fleur's lesson, here to teach her how to claim her divine feminine power and undo the wrongs that had been done to her by men. Clover was just twenty-two, but anyone could see she was an old soul. Fleur couldn't imagine how many past lives she must have lived to have acquired such insight, such poise and grace.

Clover was the only person who knew Fleur's story. She'd taken her aside at the last retreat after Fleur accidentally blurted out her reason for being there. She'd performed an intimate cacao ceremony for the two of them in the barn late at night when everyone else had gone to bed. First, she burned sage oil to clear the energy from the room, then lit candles for warmth and comfort and said, 'Drinking cacao ceremonially has been done by shamanic people for thousands of years. It opens the heart and helps you feel connected to the world. When I give it to you, wrap your hands around the mug and sip it mindfully. Tune into your senses. Allow any feelings you have to come to the surface. Be ready for the unashamed opening of your heart and a greater awareness of yourself and who you are really meant to be. It's okay if you cry. All expression is welcome here.'

They'd sat there into the early hours, in healing silence, and Fleur had never felt anything so powerful.

Fleur saw her as soon as she arrived. She was outside the barn, lugging a box towards the entrance. When she noticed Fleur, she put the box on the ground and her face became lit with a smile of incredible warmth. Fleur walked over to her, and Clover embraced her tightly. 'Welcome back, my beautiful queen,' she said.

'I'm so glad to see you, Clover.'

'The others aren't here yet. Do you fancy a quick catch-up in the lounge? You can check in afterwards.'

'Sounds great.' Fleur looked around her at the fields and woodland stretching for miles. She could hear the rush of the stream as it flowed over the rocks to the river in the forest. 'I've missed this place,' she said. 'I've been dreaming of it ever since I left.'

Together they walked into the barn, under an arch that opened out onto a room the size of a warehouse, its beamed ceiling strung with white lights and hanging plants, and the floor divided into what Fleur thought of as calm spaces. There was a space for lounging around on plump sofas and armchairs; a space for eating at a vast table made from what probably used to be floorboards; and a meditation space with grey floor cushions and white candles. The whole place carried the subtle scent of an essential oil, though Fleur couldn't name which one.

They sat down in the armchairs. 'How've you been?' Clover asked.

Fleur wasn't sure what to tell her. *I was doing okay*, she wanted to say. *I was doing okay until I saw him again and now I'm a mess.*

It was too soon to say that, she decided. There would be time over the weekend for confidences. She said, 'I've been well. You know, when I left here I felt the best I'd ever felt. I tried to hold on to it for as long as I could. I did what you said and actually bathed in the feeling for a week. But then, after a while, it began to wear off. Things became a struggle again. Change hasn't happened as quickly as I'd like.'

'It takes time to rebuild a life, Fleur. Be easy on yourself.'

'I came back because I need a top-up. I think if I keep harnessing my power, one day it will stay. I won't lose sight of it again.'

'That's exactly right.'

'And how've you been?'

'I'm well. I'm building up my work, running more retreats. Things are good.' She looked at Fleur with interest and concern. 'What about Douglas?'

Fleur heaved a deep sigh. 'I don't know. I saw him again a few months ago and . . .' She shook her head at the memory. 'He doesn't know where I am now.'

Clover smiled and rested her hand over Fleur's. 'You're safe here,' she said. 'We're all safe here.'

5

Maggie

Maggie couldn't remember now what she'd been expecting, but it wasn't this. She'd arrived at a barn surrounded by nothing but moorland and forest, and as she walked through the front door, a bright-eyed girl of about twelve smiled at her from behind a rustic countertop and said warmly, 'Welcome to our retreat centre. I'm Harriet and I'm your host for the weekend. Let me show you around. A couple of people are here already, but I think they're relaxing in their cabins.'

The girl led her through to a huge room. Maggie stood and looked around, taking in the dining area and the relaxation area, and in the corner, the wooden cocktail bar.

Noticing her gaze, the twelve-year-old said, 'It's all non-alcoholic. We make our own alcohol-free gin here, and that forms the basis of our cocktails.'

Maggie nodded. 'Are you the retreat leader?' she asked.

'No. I'm just here to make sure you're comfortable and happy. I'll also be doing all the cooking, and making sure you're fed the most nourishing foods to complement what you do here. If there's anything at all you need, or you're worried about, just find me.' When she said *anything*, she made a wild, expansive gesture with her arms, as if no problem could be bigger than her willingness to help.

Maggie followed her through the sliding glass doors, around the pond and over a path towards a forested area dotted here and there with cabins shaped like wooden tents.

Harriet stopped in front of number five and gave Maggie a key. 'Make yourself at home and when you're ready, come and join us for welcome snacks from four. You're sharing with a lady called Emma, but she's not here yet. She's coming from Berkshire, so it's quite a journey.'

'Thank you,' Maggie said. She stepped onto the tiny veranda and unlocked the door. Inside the cabin were two single beds and a wood burner. 'Well,' she said to herself as she dropped her bag and perched on one of the beds, 'I don't know whether I'm at a campsite or a luxury hotel.'

She laid down. The sheets smelled lightly of lavender. She wondered what Bill was doing now and if the neighbour had been in yet to feed him. She could text and find out, but using a phone here didn't feel quite right. She wished she could have brought him with her, but Bill had never really enjoyed travelling. He'd been content to just stay at home, spending hours and hours in the garden and the greenhouse. He was always out there, digging and planting, and yet the garden itself never seemed to look any different and nothing ever grew in the greenhouse. Maggie suspected he'd turned the greenhouse into a bachelor pad, and only went out there to get away from her. After the cat had been living with her for a year, she tested this theory by carrying his bed to the greenhouse and seeing if he'd sleep on it. He did. He spent days in there, lying on his back with his legs in the air, looking as much like her dead husband as any cat possibly could.

'I bloody knew it,' she said to him. 'I won't be bringing your food to you out here. You can eat in the kitchen with me.' She wanted to tell him to make his own dinners, but he was only a cat and she couldn't reasonably expect him to use a tin opener. Mind you, she thought, she'd let him get away with all sorts of incompetence when he was alive, on the grounds that he was only a man. She sighed, and resigned herself to it.

A sudden knock at the door stopped her from drifting off to sleep. It was mildly irritating, but also a relief. She tried to avoid daytime sleeping because giving in to daytime sleeping felt like taking a step further towards death. Whenever she was overcome with daytime fatigue, Maggie would reach for Duolingo. She'd become quite good at French in the last year, just from her desire to stay awake.

She sat up quickly. 'Hello!' she called in her friendliest voice. She definitely had the feeling that friendliness was key here.

The door opened and a dark-haired woman carrying a bright pink overnight bag stepped in. Early fifties, Maggie thought. A difficult age.

The woman smiled and held out her hand. 'I'm Emma,' she said.

'Maggie.'

Emma sat down on the opposite bed and said nothing more. Once her initial smile had faded, she looked glum. What was it they called it? *Miserable bitch face* or something. Maggie was aware of her quietly taking in the surroundings – patting the lavender-scented pillows, sniffing the lavender-scented air. She felt compelled to end the silence. 'Have you been on a retreat before?'

Emma shook her head. 'Never.' Her fingers moved to her throat and started fiddling with the pendant she wore. 'I'm not sure why I'm here, really. It seemed like a good idea when I booked it. You?'

'Me? No, I've never done anything like this before. I don't even have anything to retreat from, to be honest. There's only me and Bill at home, and Bill's just a cat. He's not someone I need to retreat from. Not like a husband.'

Emma smiled briefly. 'Oh, I'm definitely retreating from my husband.'

It was probably too soon to ask why, although Maggie would have liked to know. She said, 'The last time I did anything like this was when I went on a patisserie course in France. That was twenty years ago. I met some great people. There was wine there, though. Do you know if there's wine here?'

'There is now,' Emma said emphatically. She unzipped her bag and pulled out four bottles of Prosecco. 'I had a suspicion it was all going to be water and fruit juice, and I genuinely had every intention of sticking to it, but as I was driving here, I started wondering what I'd got myself into, so I stopped at a service station and found these in M&S. I think I'd have turned round and gone home if they hadn't had any.' She looked around the cabin. 'There's no fridge in here. I'll have to hide it in the bushes outside.'

'It is all a bit monastic,' Maggie agreed.

Emma started unpacking the rest of her bag, laying out her clothes neatly on the shelf above her bed. 'My husband thinks it's a cult.'

'*Bof!*' Maggie said. It was an expression she'd picked up from her French lessons on Duolingo. She used it whenever she could.

Emma pulled a black dress from her bag and held it up. 'This is meant to be my dark essence outfit,' she said. 'Whatever that is.'

'Nice. I had no idea what to bring for mine. I'm not even sure I have a dark essence. To be perfectly honest, I haven't got much of a clue what this is all about. That's why I came. I need an adventure. I've been living on my own with my cat for three years now. I have friends, obviously, and my children visit sometimes, but I used to be so adventurous and I thought *Maggie, if you don't go and do something soon, you'll be ancient before you know it*.'

Emma said, 'That's admirable.'

Maggie felt taken aback. She couldn't remember the last time she'd done anything admirable. 'Is it?' she asked.

'Yes, of course. It's easy to get stuck when you're on your own. It takes guts to throw yourself into something new.'

'You're not on your own, though?'

Briefly, a shadow crossed Emma's face. Then she said, 'No. I live with my husband. My eldest child starts university next week. That's partly why I decided to come away. I need some kind of . . . I don't know . . . I need a burst of new energy.' She paused for a moment. 'I feel bad, though. It's his last weekend at home and I'm not there.'

'I don't expect he minds.'

'He doesn't mind at all. When I asked him, he looked at me as if I were completely nuts. He'll be off with his mates all weekend.'

Maggie knew she was a rare case, but she hadn't felt

that way herself. But then, things had been so bad with Richard for such a long time and nothing she ever did was enough to make it up to him. She just had to let him go and hope the space between them would help heal him in some way. And in all honesty, she'd needed the space as well. It took her a while to adjust to a quieter house without him, but after he'd gone there'd been no conflict any more and the relief was immense. She could breathe again. She could speak without worrying that her words would be pounced on and twisted so they took on new and hateful meanings. Also, as an extra little bonus, she found she had the freedom to choose her own holidays and take them outside peak season.

She said, 'You'll get used to it, then you'll find them irritating when they come home and want their old rooms back, and you've turned them into wine stores.'

Emma laughed. 'Probably.' She looked around the cabin for a moment and said, 'So neither of us really has a clue what we'll be doing here?'

'Not really. The website says we have to "fuck shit up". I liked the idea of it when I was at home, talking to my cat like a mad old cat lady, but now I'm a bit scared.'

'Me too,' Emma said, then pulled her phone out of her back pocket and glanced at it. 'It's nearly four,' she said. 'Shall we go over for those welcome snacks?'

There were only four of them altogether. They met in the dining space, where the table was laid out with exquisite-looking things to eat on wooden boards. 'Vegan canapes,' the twelve-year-old from earlier announced, as she poured everyone a non-alcoholic G & T.

Maggie sipped her drink and bit into a canape. She'd never eaten vegan food before; Bill had been suspicious of people who didn't eat meat. When their vegetarian neighbour broke his collar bone falling out of bed in 1984, Bill was convinced it would never have happened if he'd been a carnivore. 'Weak bones,' he said. 'You can't get a strong body if all you eat is cauliflower.'

These snacks were amazing, though. Dates stuffed with pecans; dainty slices of cucumber topped with cashew cream cheese and smoked paprika; wild garlic puree spread on sea salt crackers. Maggie could taste the promise of something new about to unfold. Without really talking to anyone in particular, she said, 'This is bloody divine.'

Before anyone had a chance to hear her and agree, another twelve-year-old came over and hugged her tightly. 'Maggie. I'm so glad you came, my love,' she said. 'So glad you're here.'

She let her go and Maggie stood for a moment and stared at her. She hoped they weren't all going to be like this.

'I'm Clover,' the girl said. She was waif-thin and serene-looking. Maggie hadn't recognized her because there'd been no photos of her face on her website. The only images were of fires burning, or the figure of one woman taken from behind. She guessed now that woman was Clover. Lithe, tattooed, pert.

'Oh,' Maggie said. 'Clover. Hurrah!'

How on earth could she run these enlightening retreats? She wasn't even an adult.

'You're going to get a lot out of this journey,' Clover promised, and moved to throw her arms round the next person.

'Hi,' someone else said, coming up beside her with a huge smile. Mid-thirties, Maggie guessed, feeling ancient. 'I'm Fleur. Have you met Clover before?'

'No. No, I'm new to all this.'

'Oh, that's beautiful. Beautiful that you've chosen Clover. She's just . . . She's so special. She has such wisdom.'

Maggie nodded. Fleur, Clover. A meadow of wild women. She looked around the room at the guests and the host. They seemed happy enough. Strangers, but part of the same tribe. A tribe who went on retreats to harness their dark feminine divine. There was clearly something bonding about it. Maggie wondered if Emma's husband had been right. Maybe this was a cult. Maybe she wouldn't be allowed to leave until she'd had an inspirational message tattooed across her back, and her buttocks were as rigid as Clover's.

Clover clapped her hands together. 'Right, my queens,' she said. 'When we're done here, we're going to move over to the yoga space and we're going to welcome each other to our weekend and we're going to dance in celebration of our sisterhood.'

Dance? Maggie felt a tight knot of anxiety form in her stomach. She hadn't danced for forty years. She used to, when she was young, but after Annie died, she stopped so many things. Painting, dancing, baking. All the things she'd once loved had lost their meaning.

She raised her hand. 'I haven't danced for many years,' she said. 'I'm not sure my knees will be up to it. I'm not sure any part of me will be up to it, to be honest.'

Emma gave her an understanding smile.

Clover said, 'That's okay. No one has to do anything

they're not comfortable with.' She eyed the uneaten snacks still left on the table. 'Are we ready to start?'

There was an excited murmuring. They all moved to the yoga space and Clover pulled a screen across to separate them from the rest of the room. It was intimate now, suffused with the warmth of candlelight and the scent of bergamot oil burning on the cloth-covered table in the corner. Clover had moved the grey meditation cushions and on the floor she'd lain four sheepskin rugs. On top of each rug were two yellow roses and a slim length of brown satin.

Clover spoke in a soft voice. 'Please choose a sheepskin and sit down. The roses are my gift to you. They represent feminine wisdom and love, for ourselves and for our sisters. This is the energy we want to channel this weekend. We're going to tap into our deep feminine wisdom and explore our most profound desires.'

Maggie hoped she wasn't talking about sex. She might have been to art college, but that didn't mean she was into loving a group of women in some kind of spiritual lesbian orgy.

It reassured her that Clover kept referring to them as *sisters*.

'You will see the table in the corner of the room. That is our altar. We'll keep the candles lit all weekend and if you've brought any items with you that are significant for this journey, please place them there whenever you'd like to. It doesn't have to be now. It can be any time during our weekend together. By placing our items on the altar, we are offering them to our divine feminine ancestors, and they will give us healing and wisdom.'

Maggie felt sure Emma snorted, but skilfully turned it into an attack of fake coughing.

Clover looked at her with concern. 'Are you all right, Emma?'

Emma stopped coughing. 'I think so.' She looked at Maggie, as if to find out what Maggie was making of all this. Maggie gave a discreet half-shrug to say she suspected it was nonsense, but wasn't it also quite amusing?

No one moved, so Clover continued. 'Before we start, let's have our first circle time of the weekend. Can we just go clockwise around the group and can everyone say a few words about how they're feeling?'

Clover nodded at Fleur, who said, 'I'm feeling deep joy and the strength of our sisterhood.'

Emma went next. She blushed and looked self-conscious as she spoke. 'I'm pleased to be here.'

It was Maggie's turn. Clearly, whatever she said needed to be positive and bold. 'I'm feeling the excitement of a new world,' she told them.

It wasn't a lie, although she wasn't sure she'd ever said anything like that in her life before.

Clover smiled beatifically around the circle. 'I'm excited as well,' she said. 'I'm excited about the journey you'll all be taking into releasing the good girls you're used to being and stepping into your full power.'

Fleur whooped.

Clover whooped.

Maggie thought she might as well whoop as well.

Emma didn't whoop. Emma looked bewildered.

'Now,' Clover said, 'before we begin our celebration, let's talk about the dark feminine. She is the spirit, deep within ourselves, that we're here to explore and uncover. What does the dark feminine mean to you?'

Maggie averted her gaze. She had no idea. She just liked the sound of it.

She noticed Emma averting her gaze as well. Neither of them had a clue.

Fleur said, 'Embracing the dark feminine means refusing to submit to masculine control. Usually, feminine traits are seen as light, fragile, nurturing. The dark feminine is the opposite.'

This woman had clearly done her homework.

Clover smiled. 'Exactly,' she said. 'Exactly!'

Fleur looked delighted. She'd pleased the teacher.

Clover looked at Maggie and Emma briefly, but didn't linger to ask what they thought. She could obviously tell she had two women in her midst who hadn't read up on this.

She went on, speaking passionately. 'For thousands of years, women have been rewarded for their softness, their gentleness, their obedience. Of course, there's nothing wrong with some of these qualities, but too many of us get stuck in them. Women who only have contact with their maiden archetype haven't grown into maturity. They haven't touched their full power. When we don't develop our inner power, we can't help but feel unsafe, even if only subconsciously, and this will put us in positions of dependency.'

She raised her voice slightly and looked intently at everyone as she continued. 'We want to tap into the dark feminine archetype that exists in all of us. We need to do the shadow work that will awaken our dark feminine energy and help us become fearless! Fierce! Passionate! The dark feminine doesn't only welcome the tame woman. The dark feminine welcomes the *whole* woman. While you are here, I invite every part of you to rise up and be seen and you will find radical acceptance.'

She stopped speaking and let her words settle on everyone. *Radical acceptance*, Maggie thought, and wondered what on earth it meant. Had anyone ever accepted her radically? Had she ever accepted anyone radically? Her acceptance of Bill hadn't been radical. The way he used to pick his filthy toenails and leave them on the kitchen floor really wound her up. If she'd just accepted it and let it go, would that have been radical? She could hardly think so. It would have been stupid, it would have made her a downtrodden woman who actually swept up her husband's toenails in the guise of accepting him for what he was. She began to feel uncertain of this . . .

She shot a glance at the others. Fleur was wiping away a tear. Emma looked as if she thought it was all nonsense. She had one of those faces, Maggie decided, that couldn't conceal what she really thought. It made her a little intimidating.

Clover started speaking again. 'I'd like us to talk now about what it is that brought us here. We all have reasons for seeking out this retreat. They might be deeply personal, in which case of course you can stay silent. But if you would like to share, please do.' She looked at her most reliable student. 'Fleur,' she said. 'I invite you to start.'

Fleur swallowed hard. 'I want to be in the company of women. I feel that I can be my best and most authentic self around women. I had . . . Well, like many of us, I had a difficult relationship with a man and it left me . . . bruised. I've come here to celebrate the end of that relationship and to take back my power.'

'Beautiful,' declared Clover.

Maggie glanced again at Emma. She looked distinctly appalled.

'Would anyone else like to share their reasons for coming here?'

There was a silence. Maggie had never been good at dealing with silences. She felt compelled to fill them. 'Why,' Bill had asked once, 'do you always have to substitute the sound of our garden birdsong with some right-wing madman they've dragged in to add balance to Radio Four?'

Maggie had no real answer, other than that silence always felt like a gaping hole to her, something she could fall down if she wasn't careful.

She said, 'I came because I've been widowed now for three years. My husband's death was a real shock to me. I used to think I'd enjoy being single again. Sometimes, when I was really fed up with him, I used to dream about my life after he'd died and I made so many elaborate plans for it . . .' She paused for a minute here. She wasn't being entirely serious, but no one so much as tittered. Clover was nodding earnestly, as if she could truly understand the urge to slaughter a man after more than forty years of living with him.

'Anyway,' Maggie said, 'I found I was more upset than I'd expected, and it was hard to adjust to being single again after so long. Instead of taking a train across Europe like I'd planned, I've really just stayed at home for the last three years. I want to stop this now. I want to get out, meet new people, discover the woman I'm sure I still have it in me to be.'

Clover looked delighted at that. 'Excellent!' she said. 'We all contain within us the younger women we used to be, the women we are now, and the older women we will become. We must cherish our younger selves, while also relishing the excitement about what we can grow into. Maggie, I am gratified that you have chosen this retreat as a place to find and release your full potential.'

Maggie nodded. She wondered if this woman might be part-American.

Clover turned then to Emma. 'Emma,' she said invitingly, 'would you like to share your reasons for choosing this retreat?'

Maggie felt sure she could hear Emma muttering 'for fuck's sake' under her breath. It seemed a little harsh. No one had forced her into this. Of course, the whole thing was mad and Clover was likely benignly delusional, but they'd known that when they signed up. She could have gone for a weekend at a spa instead.

Emma spoke at last. She said, 'I wanted some time away and also to find out if I have it in me to . . .' She looked around, then shrugged helplessly and said, ' . . . to do this.'

'I'm sure you do, my queen.'

Emma's eyes went rolling again.

'Okay,' Clover said. 'Tomorrow, we start the work. Now, we celebrate. We're here, we're together, we're strong. Let's dance.'

She picked up the length of satin from her sheepskin and held it up in front of her. 'This is a blindfold. I don't want any self-consciousness here. No worrying about what anyone else is doing, what anyone else looks like. This is your journey, your experience. You are going through it on your own, while being connected to the women around you. I invite you all to stand and put on your blindfolds. Move your sheepskins into the corner of the room. I'll start the music and then I'll guide you into the dance.'

Maggie felt slightly better, knowing she was to be guided. She wasn't sure she could remember how to move her body in dance any more.

The music came on. It was nothing Maggie recognized. She put the blindfold over her eyes and tied it at the back of her head.

'Okay, my queens. Let's start by loosening our bodies. Walking on the spot, slowly at first.'

Maggie focussed on her feet. She let them lift off the ground and back down again. They were fine. They kept on moving. She wondered what the others were doing and adjusted her blindfold slightly so she could peek out through the bottom of it. She saw three other pairs of feet, moving slowly like hers. No one else seemed to be dancing yet. She was glad. She didn't want to be left behind.

'Soften and relax your knees. Feel them bend and release now as you quicken your pace.'

Soften and relax, Maggie told herself. *Soften and relax*. Her knees seemed to know what to do. She was marching now, marching in time to the music.

'And your hips. Let your hips loosen. Give them some freedom to move.'

She let them move from side to side. The music quickened. Her feet went faster.

'Bring your attention now to your arms. Be aware of

them moving by your side. Raise them into the air if you like. Feel the lightness in your whole body. Feel the air in your feet.'

Maggie's airy feet seemed to speed up without her even telling them to. Around her, she could hear other people's feet against the floor and the steady pulse of music. She moved her arms at her side, slowly at first and then faster, until all of a sudden she was no longer marching, but dancing.

6

Emma

There was no electricity in the cabins. They each had a small lamp, charged by the light of the sun during the day and giving them back just enough light to see by in the evening. Emma lay on her bed, listening to the beat of rain on the roof, and wondering what on earth she was doing here and how soon she could get away.

On the table that separated her bed from Maggie's, Emma's phone vibrated with an incoming WhatsApp message. Clover had told them to put their phones away for the weekend, to give themselves what she called 'a digital detox'. At first, Emma was open to the idea but now there was no way. Her mobile phone was going to be with her through every moment of this. Letting go of her connection to the outside world felt dangerous, as though she'd be recklessly trapping herself here, in this world of the voluntarily insane.

The message was from Clara.

How's it going?

Hideous.

Really?

Really. We just had to dance, but it wasn't dancing as you or I know it. It was primitive dancing, like they did in the cave days, with some whooping thrown in. The others all seemed to love it.

Did you join in?

Course I bloody didn't.

They'd looked mad. All of them. Absolutely bonkers. No one watching could ever have mistaken that room for a nightclub. It looked more like a coven of wild things. 'Let your stomachs relax,' Clover kept saying. 'I don't want any sucked-in bellies here. We're proud of every inch we take up in the world.'

Easy for her to say. Her body looked as if it had been sculpted from clay.

Emma tried, briefly. She hid inside her blindfold and moved her knees obediently as Clover instructed. It was just about okay at first, but then the music grew faster and the stomping grew louder and people's blindfolds fell off, and then the whooping started. Emma feigned exhaustion and moved to the side of the room, where she stood against the wall and, from the safety of her stillness, watched the others turning gracelessly across the floor, whooping and sweating. Then, to Emma's horror, they began removing their clothes. Trousers were hurled through the air, T-shirts dropped in a pile, bras triumphantly thrown towards the ceiling. By the end of it, Clover and Fleur were only in their knickers, Clover's taut little breasts barely moving as she leapt in the air.

At least Maggie had kept her clothes on. If she'd unleashed her breasts and forced Emma to witness them, Emma wasn't sure she'd have been able to face sharing a cabin with her any more. The haunting image of two generously sized breasts swinging in time to the music would have undermined any attempt at conversation.

Emma put her phone back down on the table. In the bed opposite her, Maggie was recovering from the exuberant hour of dancing that seemed to have left her exhilarated. She spoke quickly, high on her own energy. 'I never knew I still had it in me to move like that,' she said. 'I loved it. Honestly, I'm going to have to find an over-70s night and start clubbing again.'

Emma closed her eyes for a brief moment. Maggie was harmless, but she talked too much and too openly. She'd even cried earlier when the dancing finished. Emma had no idea why, and she was afraid now that Maggie might tell her. She hated listening to people's confidences. She never knew how to arrange her face.

When she opened her eyes again, Maggie was looking at her intently. 'Did you enjoy the dancing? I wasn't sure.'

'It was all right, but at heart I'm very lazy. I like to spend my evenings drinking wine in front of a fire. Fifteen minutes' dancing is fine. An hour was a bit too much for me. That's why I stepped out of it.' She sat up and reached for the bottle of Prosecco she'd put on the floor beside the bed. It was going to be warm, but in situations like this, warm Prosecco was better than no Prosecco. It hadn't crossed her mind, when she'd stopped off to buy it, that there would be no fridge here to store it in. Nowhere in the literature did it say this was a sober retreat. If it had, Emma would never have come. She'd assumed that getting in touch with her inner wild woman would involve booze, and possibly class B drugs. But that non-alcoholic cocktail bar exerted a strong, silent pressure. There was no way she could openly put four bottles of wine in the kitchen fridge. They didn't even have wine glasses. Emma had been on the prowl earlier and had to make do with borrowing two tumblers.

She poured herself half a tumbler full, then said to Maggie, 'Do you want some?'

Maggie glanced around the cabin, as if she expected someone to come in and catch her. Then she said, 'Yes. Why not?'

Emma smiled. 'Thank God for that,' she said. 'I was worried you were going to be all teetotal. There is no way I can get through this without alcohol. Clover looks as if she never touches anything other than spring water.'

'I wonder what she's got in store for us tomorrow. I hope I won't keep crying. Who'd have thought someone would become emotional just from dancing?'

Emma wondered that, too. She could cope with Maggie's brief tears, but on the whole, Emma turned away from emotional scenes the way other people turned away from blood. It could only be pain that brought people to this place, to do something like this. She could hear her best friend's voice in her head, the only person she'd ever told about Oliver. *You need to recover, Emma. You've been through trauma.*

It was true. Emma had scarcely been alive for the last year.

She tried to steer the conversation to safer ground. 'What do you think of the others?' she asked.

'I thought Clover seemed lovely. I was expecting her to be older, though. At least fifty.'

'Me too.'

'You expect that from a sage, don't you? A few wrinkles, a bit of darkness round the eyes to show they've suffered for their wisdom. All she's got to hint at any suffering is a rock-solid backside. I can't begin to imagine the hours of torture that must have taken.'

Emma smiled thinly. She knew exactly what she thought of Clover. She was on high alert for insincerity and narcissism these days. In Clover, she'd found both.

Maggie carried on. 'She seems to know what she's doing, though. The dancing . . . It was powerful. A release of some kind, I think. It stirred something in me. Reminded me of the time before . . .'

Her voice trailed off and Emma didn't dig around for more. She sipped her lukewarm Prosecco and said, 'Fleur seems to be lodged up Clover's rock-solid backside.'

Maggie looked a little shocked. 'Does she?'

'I think so. Definitely. I'm sure she said she'd been on one of these retreats before. You heard her answer when Clover asked what we thought the dark feminine meant. She's been drinking in the bullshit. Feasting on it, I'd say. She'll be sick if she's not careful.'

'I thought she seemed quite sweet.'

Emma said nothing and drank more wine.

Maggie said, 'Do you think it's bullshit?'

'I'm not convinced that dancing half-naked is going to change my life.'

'So why did you come?'

'I wanted a break. My daughter has a few problems and I felt like getting away for a while. I thought it would be good to try something different, but I'm not sure this is really me. I'm giving it until tomorrow lunchtime.'

'Oh, I came hoping for magic and I'm not leaving until I've found it.'

Emma tried not to roll her eyes. Rob had suggested she come here to try and make her open up. She'd come along dutifully, but she knew now she could never open up, not ever. Not among strangers and not at home, either. Her trauma was buried and if it came up again, it was going to drag her away. She could no more talk about Oliver than she could cut off a limb, but now here she was, trapped among these foolish, over-emotional women who wanted nothing more than to dance and cry and reach deep within themselves to unearth the horrors from their pasts.

She finished her glass and poured another one. None of this felt wild and rebellious. It felt ridiculous.

7

Clover

Clover lit the wood burner in her cabin and sat cross-legged on the floor in front of it. She loved it here. She loved everything about it: the purity of the air, the incredible food, the simplicity of a life focussed only on being well. She loved knowing that all these women were going to leave this place feeling better than when they'd arrived. She could already see it happening. As she expected, the older two were suspicious of her. Older women always were. They didn't even have to say it. They just took one look at Clover and it was there on their faces: *What can you possibly have to teach me?* They loosened up, though. As they'd begun their slow movement towards dancing, Clover had simply said, 'If you're feeling uncomfortable, ask yourself why you're uncomfortable. Try and lean into this experience and work with it.'

Even Maggie, who said she hadn't danced for forty years, began to move with abandon. The blindfolds all fell off after a while. People grew hot and joyful and stripped off layers. They laughed and cheered, and afterwards, when the music stopped, they were happy, rejuvenated. Maggie had wiped the sweat from her face and cried as she said, 'I had no idea I could still do this,' and Clover could see the years fall away from her.

Emma was another issue, but Clover would get there. She always did.

Women were so powerful. They didn't realize it. They'd had it oppressed by parents, or they'd given it away to men. It was Clover's job to help them get it back. If Clover had learnt anything in her twenty-two years on the planet, it was how to regain her power.

8

Emma

In the morning, they took their seats at the table and Harriet explained their breakfast to them. Today, she said, she was nourishing the heart chakra. 'The heart chakra is green. It's connected with love, compassion and empathy. It can be difficult to open this chakra and many of us have blockages, but by eating green food, we can coax the chakra to open up and receive love and light. You'll see you all have a smoothie made with kale, cucumber, parsley and ginger. There's also buckwheat and quinoa porridge cooked in coconut milk with kiwi and gooseberry compote, and scrambled tofu with green peppers and mushrooms.'

Emma stared at the spread before her. She'd drunk almost the full bottle of Prosecco last night because Maggie had only wanted one glass, and now she had a hangover with a mood to match. Everything on the table looked amazing, but she remained unconvinced that the smoothie in her hands was going to transform her into a woman who could receive love and light into her heart.

She held the glass out in front of her and examined it. It reminded her of the magical superfoods she used to feed her toddlers, or used to imagine she would feed her toddlers before she actually had them. Once she had them, she was so tired she often just gave them Shredded Wheat and peas for dinner. Her friends, who either weren't too tired or were more committed to feeding their toddlers magical superfoods than she was, insisted they would confer both genius and eternal life, but then all their children had grown up to be as unexceptional and prone to illness as everyone else's. Emma suspected the same would happen here. She would drink this smoothie and eat this porridge, and the cold-blooded bitch she'd been yesterday would endure.

In fact, she thought she probably wouldn't drink the smoothie. She hated kale, and she could see morsels of it drifting like pondweed around the glass.

Harriet returned to the kitchen and Clover looked round the table at everyone and said, 'Today, we're going to be making space for what you want to welcome into your life, to make way for new energy. I invite you all to drop into silence this breakfast time. While you eat, think about what you want to gain from our time together. Allow yourself to formulate your intention. Who do you want to be on Monday when you leave here?'

Oh, for God's sake. Nowhere on Clover's website had it said she'd have to become a new person. Besides, this was a four-day retreat. They'd have to cram a lot in if they were going to die and be reborn.

She said, 'It seems a little ambitious that I can become someone new in four days.'

Clover looked at her with sympathy and understanding and said, 'Just lean into the experience, my goddess.'

Emma rolled her eyes. She couldn't help it. She'd just

been patronized by someone half her age. My goddess. Oh, do fuck off with your wild rebellion and your rebirth.

She should never have come. All this self-discovery and self-improvement. Emma knew who she was. Her character was fixed. 'I'm too old to be improved.'

'No one is ever too old to work on themselves.'

'Oh, I'm deeply flawed, of course. I'm possibly even awful at times, but I do my best and there are far worse people out there. The world should just accept me as I am.' She pushed the smoothie away from her, to show that she was through with all its promises. 'This green shit isn't going to change a thing.'

Clover smiled serenely. 'Whatever feels right for you, my queen.'

Emma looked around her at the others eating their breakfast in silence, dutifully reflecting on who they wanted to be by Monday. With any luck, Maggie was wanting to become someone who talked less, and Fleur wanted to be less nauseating, and Clover wanted to be a woman who stopped flooding the world with her made-up bullshit.

She stretched over the table and spooned some scrambled tofu into her bowl and wondered who she would become, if she really had a choice in it. She'd like to be someone who was *alive,* she thought – perhaps even someone whose partner spoke to her more often than every six weeks, and for some reason other than to ask if she'd hold the long-haired cat while he wiped away the crap stuck in the fur around her arse. But that was a foolishly romantic fantasy, a dream for people just stepping out into married life and hardly a realistic expectation after nearly thirty years with someone.

Because no one was talking, the sounds of their eating were amplified. The wet squelch of tofu between teeth and the gulping of porridge was unbearable and sent Emma to the edge. She knew she wasn't meant to but she had to speak, just to stop the noise.

She said, 'So Clover, what's your intention for the weekend?'

Clover drank from her transformative smoothie and smiled serenely again. 'My intention is to lead this wonderful group of women on a full journey to the women they want to become.'

'But who do *you* want to become? Or are you complete?'

For just the briefest moment, an expression of unease appeared on Clover's pretty young face, replaced quickly by her usual poise. 'We are all works in progress,' she said, as if Emma had been making a joke. 'I am on this journey with you. I, too, want to loosen the shackles of my past and claim my full power.'

'Right.'

Clover's gaze shifted to take in Maggie and Fleur, who were still sitting in co-operative silence. 'The intentions you form this morning belong to you. I won't be asking you at any point to share them. I only want you to keep them in mind as we move through the weekend.'

Emma felt suitably chastised. Of course Clover was bound to be a master of passive-aggression. Of course she was.

She glanced at her watch – 8.30. She could leave now, catch a taxi to the station, take the next train to London and be home in Windsor by early afternoon. She'd be able to spend Jake's last weekend with him, and this evening she'd drink Prosecco in the garden with Clara and plot how to leave Ben while keeping the house for herself in the divorce settlement.

But then she'd have to explain. She'd have to explain to Clara that she'd failed at this before she'd even started, that the family therapy designed to help her daughter was going to stay at a permanent standstill because Emma was, and always would be, too uptight to peel away her skin and examine the wounded flesh beneath it. She was meant to talk about her trauma and the crap parent she'd been while she did her best to carry on as normal when, really, her heart felt as though it had been set on fire and was burning her to death. She hadn't been able to tell anyone. So many lives had already been shattered. She couldn't shatter them again by speaking up, asking for sympathy.

She formed her intention in her mind. *I want to stop being such a stupid bloody fool.*

9

Fleur

Fleur walked away from the breakfast table, angry on Clover's behalf. Last night, Emma had scarcely joined in. She'd simply stood at the side of the room, watching the others dancing with an expression on her face that suggested she'd rather be anywhere but here. She reminded Fleur of those sullen, aloof girls at secondary school, the ones who considered themselves too cool to join in and instead just stood on the sidelines and smirked, leaving everyone else self-conscious and uncomfortable.

It was the vibe Emma gave off and Fleur resented it. Emma felt like trouble. These retreats were meant to be safe spaces, where women could be themselves without fear of judgement, but Emma seemed to have decided it was all foolish nonsense and everyone taking part was a gullible idiot. Fleur had the urge to ask her why she'd come here, why she thought there was room on this retreat for her particular version of cynical self-loathing. *The world should just accept me as I am. This green shit isn't going to change a thing.*

If she'd been Clover, Fleur would have openly given Emma the option to leave, right there in front of everyone. But Clover was too sensitive for that. 'It can take time for people to let go of their defences,' she'd said once before. 'They resist for a while, but the magic works in the end.' She would probably turn Emma into a project, Fleur thought.

She forced Emma to the back of her mind and headed through the wood to her cabin to gather her things for the day. The sky was bright blue and the moorland stretched as far as she could see. No one could find her here, but still Douglas's presence was everywhere. She could sense him lurking in the nooks and crannies of her life, an ever-present temptation, always dangerous.

She wondered what she'd do if he somehow found her number and contacted her. Would she phone the police? Would she hit him? Would she turn steely eyes upon him and send him far away? Or would she weep and weep, and wrap her arms tight around him? *Oh, my love. Come back to me. Come back. I cannot live without you.*

That was the most frightening thing. Even now, she had no idea if she'd be able to resist.

Once she'd gathered her water bottle and a spare jumper, she went back to join the others in the meditation space. Clover pulled the screen around them for privacy and they took their seats on the sheepskins. Clover said, 'First of all, we're going to take a look at what it is that's holding us back. What is it we're doing that is blocking us from living the full, unapologetic lives we were born for? What I'd like you to do is move closer to the person on your left-hand side and you're going to take it in turns to answer a question I am going to give you in just a moment.'

The person on her left-hand side was Emma. Obediently, reluctantly, Fleur shuffled her sheepskin closer to her and tried to transmit a silent message through the airwaves between them. *Give in. Let it happen. You will feel amazing if you do.*

She had the feeling Emma wasn't in tune enough with her to receive it.

Once they were all settled Clover carried on. 'Now, in a minute, when I give you the question, I want the goddess with the longest hair to go first, and to tell the other goddess their answer. Other goddesses, I don't want you to respond in any way. Your role is just to listen, to let your sister share her thoughts with you and to silently honour her story.'

She looked at the group and smiled. 'Are we ready? Okay, here's your first question: *What is it that keeps you being a good girl?*'

There wasn't a lot in it. Both Emma and Fleur had bobbed hair, but Emma's was about half an inch longer. She shifted uncomfortably on her sheepskin for a moment, then took a deep breath and said, 'I'm sorry, but this is shit. I'm not doing it.'

'What?'

'All this. It's rubbish. None of us here are sisters. We're strangers.'

'I know, but . . .'

'I'm not sharing private things with strangers. I know that doesn't exactly fit with the ethos of all this, but seriously . . . I think if I'd known what this was all about, I wouldn't have come.'

Fleur tried to keep the ice from her voice. 'What were you expecting?'

'I was expecting wild rebellion. I don't know. Alcohol, for a start. People not doing what they're told. So I'm rebelling now. I'm not doing what I'm told. I'm not even a particularly good girl in my real life, so there's no need for me to talk about what keeps me that way.'

'That's fine,' Fleur said, with cold politeness. 'We can just sit.'

Emma made a face Fleur couldn't interpret, but she wondered whether she was using all her facial muscles to keep from rolling her eyes.

They sat in a difficult silence. Snippets of Clover's conversation with Maggie drifted over to them, and Fleur longed to be a part of their circle instead of here, with this woman who didn't belong.

Clover stood up and spoke again. 'Okay, my goddesses. It's time to swap. The one who was previously silent must now speak, and the one who previously spoke must now silently receive the other's words. The question is the same. *What is it that keeps you being a good girl?*'

Fleur looked at Emma, who looked back at her with interest.

She said, 'I realize you don't want to take part, but I'm here to get the most out of this, so I'm going to go ahead and talk. You don't have to listen. You can block your ears if you like.'

Emma had the grace to look slightly sheepish. 'It's fine,' she said.

Fleur tried to consider what Clover would do in this situation. She would probably think of Emma not as rude and obnoxious, but vulnerable, a woman holding hidden wounds. Instead of refusing to speak, she'd be even more honest in an attempt to show Emma how to do this properly.

She took a deep breath. 'Fear,' she said. 'That's what

it is. I'm scared of everything. There was someone in my life for a while . . . He destroyed my confidence, really. I shouldn't blame him. I allowed him to do it. Anyway, he's been out of my life for six months now – apart from that time three months ago – and I still hear his voice in my head sometimes. He used to tell me I'd need him if I was ever going to amount to anything. I know it's not really true, but sometimes it's hard to make myself believe it. I don't have a very good job, but I don't know how to leave it. What I really want to do is help other women, but I'm not like Clover. I don't have the courage to just take a blind leap and go for it.'

She stopped herself there. Emma was nodding in some strange combination of sympathy and awkwardness, as if she needed to be polite but couldn't bear this weird intimacy. There was no way Fleur could tell the truth about what an idiot she'd been.

The gentle sharing came to an end. 'Now we're going to start the real work,' Clover said. 'This is an emotional release exercise. I want you all to find a space. You'll see I've given each of you a nice, thick cylindrical bolster cushion. I'm going to play some music suited to the occasion, and you're going to thrash out your emotions. You are welcome to use your blindfolds if you want to. We're going to start by stamping on the spot.' Here, she stopped for a moment and demonstrated stamping. 'Stomp. Stomp. Stomp. Let yourself think of anyone or anything who has hurt you, upset you, angered you. Stamp it out. Stamp as hard as you like. Shout if you want to. Cry. Scream. And when you're done with stamping, take that cushion and goddamn whack it. Punch it. Grab hold of it and smash it on the floor. Keep shouting, keep screaming, keep crying. Let all your emotions, all your bad energy, flow out of you. Remember, as usual it doesn't matter what anyone else is doing. You are connected to the other women in the room, but separate from them. This is your journey.'

Fleur tied the blindfold over her eyes. She preferred not to see the others as they dived deep into their pain. It was private, and not to be watched.

Clover hit a button on her phone and the music started. The beat was fast and angry, the lyrics something to do with a mad woman. *You say she's mad, but you made her mad.*

That was all it took. Fleur stamped so hard she thought her feet might go through the floor. She stamped and stamped and she could hear herself shouting like a woman in labour. She grabbed hold of the cushion and attacked it with her fists. 'You bastard,' she said. 'You bastard.' She thrashed the cushion against the floor, imagining it was his face. She bashed him and bashed him until she felt sure he was gone, and then she laid down on the floor and sobbed.

10

Maggie

Perhaps it was the new setting; perhaps it was the people she'd found herself with, who'd all come here to be wholeheartedly open and emotional; or perhaps she was finally ready for everything to rise to the surface and overflow, but whatever it was, Maggie found that she was hurling herself into this with abandon.

'What is it that keeps you being a good girl?' Clover asked.

Maggie opened her mouth and could hardly believe what came out of it. 'I don't have any great desire to be bad. I just want to become the person I know I am. You see, I'm a painter at heart. An artist, I mean, not a decorator. I used to paint in oils. Portraits mostly, although I could do landscapes as well. But portraits were what I was best at. The last thing I painted was a portrait of my seven-week-old daughter.'

Clover looked at her with gentle, encouraging interest.

Maggie wasn't sure if she should say the next part. She'd learnt from years of experience that sharing her tragedy made people uncomfortable. They never knew what to say to her afterwards, and she could always see them deliberately trying to avoid the subject whenever she saw them again. They'd start talking about their new baby grandchild and suddenly stop themselves, or they'd turn the radio off if there was tragic news breaking about a child or a baby.

But the words from Clover's speech last night came back to her. *The dark feminine welcomes the whole woman. I invite every part of you to rise up and be seen and you will find radical acceptance.*

She thought she might as well try it. She said, 'My daughter died the day I finished painting her. It was a cot death. Very sudden, and I've never been able to paint again since. I don't know why. It was so long ago. Forty years next month.'

She could feel a hot flush rising in her cheeks. It had been so long since she'd mentioned Annie to anyone but Bill.

Clover took both of Maggie's hands in hers and even though she wasn't meant to speak, she said, 'I hear your experience, Maggie, and I honour it. I honour your daughter, too. Please tell me her name.'

'Annie.'

'Annie,' Clover said. 'I'd like to light a candle for her at the altar, if you'll let me.'

'Thank you,' Maggie said. 'I'd like that.'

Clover went to the altar and lit a new candle. Maggie wondered if Clover was a woman who carried emergency candles in her handbag for unexpected moments of grief, the way normal woman carried tampons. She was grateful for it. A lot of the time these days, it felt as though Annie had never existed and now here she was, her short life being acknowledged in this room.

Then it was Clover's turn to speak and confess. What was it that kept *her* being a good girl? Maggie was interested to know.

'It's always a battle,' Clover said. 'We carry generations of toxic obedience in our female blood.'

Really? Maggie thought. Toxic obedience. That was another new phrase. She tried to remember a time she'd been toxically obedient. The only things she'd ever really obeyed were recipes. God, they were so oppressive the way they told you what to do, and so punishing if you didn't do it. BBC Food once told her to cut a red pepper into 1 cm pieces, and that was the day she finally hurled her toxic recipe obedience to the wind. 'Bollocks to that,' she'd said to her iPhone. 'That is an unnecessary level of work. I am cutting this pepper into whatever sized pieces I like, and screw you, you bright young thing who thinks they have time to waste in life. Before you know it, you'll be seventy, too, and then you'll wish you hadn't spent your youth cutting red peppers.'

Clover went on, 'I'm still learning to overcome it. Sometimes, I doubt myself. I'm following a very different path to the one I was brought up to follow, and there are nights when I wonder if I'm doing the right thing. That's what risks keeping me a good girl. It all comes down to a lack of confidence in my own power. I have to work at that. Confidence is a key trait of the dark feminine.'

Maggie nodded. She felt she was beginning to understand, in a way.

After the talking came the stamping. It felt better than Maggie could ever have imagined to have her eyes covered in silk and feel her feet pounding the floor until they hurt. She wasn't angry any more. She used to be. Oh, she used to be so angry. Her rage had been white-hot and frightening, and it kept her alive.

What she realized now, all of a sudden, was that for all this time, she'd been misunderstanding herself. She thought, after the rage had subsided – and it took years; years and years – that she was spent, that she would never feel anything else again. No joy, no love, no pain. Even sex left her numb, and Bill had eventually given up on her. (She knew how it hurt him, but she couldn't help it.) Mostly, she wanted to be left alone.

And now she was alone. Her husband had died and her son still struggled to be civil to her, even forty years later, no matter what she did.

The days after Bill died were long and awful, and Maggie wished she could have him back again, just for the chance to stop wishing him away. Late at night, when she couldn't sleep, she'd wonder if her thoughts had power and the force of them had caused his heart to shrivel up and then stop. He was the only person in the world who understood what it meant to lose Annie, to keep marking all her birthdays, even into what should have been her thirties. And yet, as Maggie wept her way through that first year without him, she'd somehow known those tears were old tears from way back, the ones she hadn't shed for her daughter and now she couldn't stop from flowing. It shocked her. She thought she'd recovered, more or less.

She'd decided recently that she didn't want to cry any more. It left her with a raging headache and besides that, what was the point in outrageously expensive moisturizer if you were just going to screw up your face with hours of sorrow?

Right now, it was good to be stamping instead. She could feel the might of the grief, which once threatened to crush her, powering into the floor beneath her feet. She hadn't known she possessed this much strength. Close by, someone else was crying, but Maggie had her blindfold on and couldn't tell who it was. *Connected but separate.* They were filling the room with a potent energy. She wondered how long it would linger after they'd gone.

She could hear Clover's voice. 'What is it you're letting go of?' she was calling. 'What do you want to make space for?'

Maggie took her blindfold off, kneeled down on the floor and started punching the cushion. *I'm letting go of sadness,* she said silently. *I'm making space for whatever it is that comes after grief.*

Afterwards, Maggie headed to the dining area feeling exhausted, but also three stone lighter and ten years younger. Any misgivings she'd had about all this being a load of mystical baloney were falling rapidly away. There was power in it. Something unknown and unknowable was shifting inside her and she felt ready to surrender to whatever Clover told her to do. It no longer mattered that the woman was young enough to be her granddaughter. Maggie was impressed by her.

Maggie, Fleur and Emma took their seats at the table. Harriet had decorated it with candles and bunches of white roses. She stood before them and said, 'Clover told me you'd be working hard this morning, so I've made your setting calm and soothing for you. This lunchtime, to continue with healing and opening your heart chakras, I've prepared green lentils with oven-dried tomatoes and dill. There's a fresh spinach loaf just finishing off. I'll bring it over in a minute.'

Maggie helped herself to the lentil dish. She wasn't sure

she'd ever eaten this well before. She could almost feel her body thanking her for it.

She turned to Fleur, sitting beside her, red-eyed and silent. 'How did you find this morning?' she asked.

Fleur sighed. Maggie couldn't tell whether she was in despair or ecstasy. 'Intense,' Fleur said. 'Really, really intense. But powerful. I just . . . I feel like I released things I've been holding on to for a long time.'

'Me too,' Maggie told her. 'They were things I didn't even know I was holding. I thought I'd let them go years ago.'

'Clover is brilliant. She really is. I think a lot of people misunderstand her, but the work she does is so important.'

'She's quite incredible. She has the wisdom of Buddha and yet she can't be more than . . . I don't know . . . What is she? . . . Fifteen at the most?'

Fleur laughed. 'She's twenty-two.'

'Still a baby, really. It feels like a very intense, very sharp form of therapy.' She glanced across the table at Emma, who was eating in silence, and wondered what she'd been through this morning. She looked worn out but there was something about her silence that made Maggie think she was unhappy. Angry, perhaps. Cautiously, she said, 'How did you find it, Emma?'

Emma hesitated for a while before she spoke, as if weighing her words. Then she said, 'I think it's bullshit.'

Maggie hadn't expected that. She could feel Fleur's anger glowing beside her. She kept her voice light. 'Why?'

'It's crap,' Emma said. 'Really. Clover is getting us to do this stuff, but she's not explaining the purpose of any of it. What was the point in the dancing last night?'

Fleur said, 'What do you mean, what was the point? It was a celebration.'

'Of what?'

'Of our sisterhood.'

'Well, I felt like I'd come to a cult. All that releasing of inhibitions. I know I'm probably rare these days, but I quite like inhibitions. I think they're there for a reason.'

'What reason?'

'Protection. Privacy. That sort of thing.'

Fleur laughed with derision, but Maggie had to admit she could see Emma's point. Younger people these days didn't understand privacy. They shared everything on social media. Everything. It had become normal now for the whole world to know the state of everyone else's marriage, or the development of their foetus. Maggie herself was beginning to regret talking about Annie this morning. It had opened something, left her feeling raw and exposed. She'd come here to move on, to embrace her wild self, not fall back into that dark hole again.

Slowly, she said, 'I do know what you mean. It does feel a bit culty. We're meant to become really vulnerable and then be in thrall to our leader.'

'Exactly. I think you've hit the nail on the head there, Maggie. She seems to want us to dig too deep and unleash too much emotion. It gives her a lot of power. A lot of control over us as we become emotional wrecks.'

Fleur said, 'You don't strike me as someone who'd ever become an emotional wreck.'

'I'm well practised in holding it together,' Emma said shortly.

'Maybe you need to overcome your fear of letting go.'

'Maybe. Or maybe there's an argument for keeping it in.'

'Keeping it in gives you cancer.'

Emma laughed. 'Oh, right! I must remember that.'

Maggie felt conflict brewing and had a strong need to put a stop to it. 'Maybe we just all need to be careful not to do anything we aren't comfortable with.'

'You're right,' Emma said. 'Which means I won't be doing any of it.'

Beside her, Fleur lost it. 'Then why did you come here?' she demanded. 'What was the point?'

'Believe me, I keep asking myself that. It's not just that it's nonsense. I also think it could be dangerous. Is Clover really qualified in dealing with people's mental health? What if she goes too far with getting you all to dig too deep? What if one of you cracks up? Will she have the capacity to deal with that?'

Clearly, Emma didn't consider herself at risk of cracking up. Cracking up was for the weak ones, the ones who were in thrall to this mystical power.

Maggie said, 'I won't be cracking up. My days of cracking up are over.'

'I won't, either,' Fleur said.

Emma made a resigned-looking face, as if accepting defeat for now. Maggie wondered how long she would stay.

11

Clover

Clover had spent all morning trying not to think about her father dying. She'd been fine yesterday. Resolute. But then last night, she woke up with a start and realized she'd been dreaming about him. An unwelcome image flooded her mind: her father, shrunken by illness, weak and longing for his stray child to come home and bid him goodbye. In this new image, clouded by impending grief, he was no longer the hard authoritarian of Clover's childhood, but a man of remorse, who'd had time to reflect and understand.

She hadn't stayed in the barn to have lunch with the others. She'd come back to her cabin to be on her own with her thoughts, even though she knew she needed to do some work with Emma to help her gain the most she could from this experience. Clover's intuition was finely tuned. Emma thought the whole thing was a load of wishy-washy nonsense, run by a child with no idea about life and how to survive it.

Clover picked up her phone from the table by her bed and entered the website address for Kevin's blog. It was still there, newly updated just twenty minutes ago. Doctors now believed her father had only days left to live, holding on only so he could see his daughter.

She scrolled as far down the page as she could. The comments section of the blog was empty. Clover would bet every pound she'd earned from this retreat that no one read it. Most members of her congregation had little interest in connecting their lives to the internet. Some even believed the internet – like the Beatles – had unlimited power to corrupt. Her husband was talking into the void.

She looked again at the blog post. What she wanted to see was a photo of her father. There was nothing, and there were no conclusions she could come to about this. It could mean the whole story was a lie, nothing but a ploy to manipulate her into going home; but it could equally mean no one wanted to put a photo of a dying man on the internet. Why on earth would they?

The trouble was, Clover just wanted to know.

She hit the text message icon on her phone and entered her father's contact details.

Hi Dad. It's me. I heard you . . .

What? *I heard you might be dying so I wanted to say thank you for doing your best as you saw it, and it's okay that it was all wrong. I'm fine now.*

She stopped there. She couldn't say goodbye to her father in a text message. Maybe she couldn't say goodbye to him at all. He would only see her if she repented, and she wasn't going to repent. All she'd done was choose life.

She tossed her phone onto her bed. There was nothing she could do, and thoughts of her father were intrusive, distracting her from her purpose.

She was about to head over to the barn and find her

group of wild women, but a knock on the cabin door stopped her. 'Come in,' she said, expecting to see Harriet with arms full of extra lavender-infused towels, or leftover vegan snacks that she could tuck into late at night.

It wasn't Harriet. It was Fleur.

'Hi,' she said, a little uncertainly. 'I wondered if you had time for a quick chat?'

Clover smiled warmly. 'Of course, my love. I always have time for a chat.'

Fleur stepped into the cabin and perched on the edge of the unused bed. She looked like the bearer of bad news.

'Are you okay?'

'Yes. I am. It's fine. I'm sure it's fine, but I thought you should know about a couple of concerns I have about this retreat.'

Clover's heart quickened. 'What concerns?'

'I loved our last one. You know, in January, when there were six of us and everyone got on so well and really bonded and accepted your teachings and your practices, even when they were challenging . . .'

'I remember. I loved it, too.'

'I'm worried this one won't be like that. One of the women here seems . . . Well, she seems like she could be a destructive force.'

'Oh, you mean Emma.'

Fleur nodded. 'Yes. I don't know what she's doing here. We were just having lunch together and she was quite a cynical presence. She said she thinks the practices are dangerous, that they could awaken things in people that ought not to be awakened, and this could cause . . . I don't know . . . some kind of mental health issue.'

Clover laughed.

'I suppose it's fine for her to think that way, and to question it herself, but Maggie seemed to be agreeing with her a bit by the end of it. That's my concern. That she'll turn Maggie against you and threaten the harmony of the retreat.'

Clover said, 'Don't you worry about Emma. I can see how resistant she is. I'm also wondering what it is that brought her here. We'll find out.'

Fleur looked doubtful. 'Will we? She seems determined to keep everything to herself. She was talking about the importance of keeping things in, of privacy.'

'People say things like that when they feel vulnerable, Fleur. I think Emma probably needs this experience more than anyone. She's worried about what she'll uncover about herself, and it's frightening. But I'll work on her. You'll see. We'll find out what her trauma is, and on Monday morning, when we say goodbye, she'll be amazed by her transformation. She'll probably be crying more than anyone.'

Fleur smiled. 'Okay,' she said. 'I have faith in you, Clover.'

12

Emma

After lunch, the sun came out and they had two hours free to do whatever they liked. Harriet, the curiously young host who could cook like a Michelin chef, came over to the table while they were eating and offered to take them on a ninety-minute mindful hike over the moors. 'It's just two miles,' she assured them. 'You don't have to be particularly fit. We take it very slowly. The purpose isn't the exercise *per se*. The main purpose is to absorb the beauty, the wonder, the stillness.'

Absorb the wonder, Emma thought. Wonder was an abstract noun. Deliberately vague. You couldn't absorb something that had no actual meaning. She could imagine what Ben would say about it:

'What did you do on your retreat today?'

'I absorbed wonder.'

'Right.' Here, he would pause, thinking it over. Then he'd say, 'This wonder that you absorbed, did it come in a bottle? Did you rub it over your skin? Where do they sell it?'

In another life, they'd have laughed about the absurdity of all this together. That life was long gone. Now she was here, in the middle of Bodmin Moor, with some benign but nevertheless insane strangers, trying to heal the mess she'd made of herself. She'd come to the wrong place. Choosing a retreat because it sounded hilarious was another one of her foolish life choices. It had looked hilarious on the screen that day with Clara, but in reality, it wasn't hilarious at all.

Maggie and Fleur were responding to Harriet's offer of the guided mindful hike with enthusiasm. 'Emma,' Harriet said, 'would you like to join us?'

Emma could think of nothing more excruciating than spending ninety minutes walking two miles.

She smiled politely. 'I'm quite tired. I think I'll just go back to the cabin and rest. Thank you.' She turned to the others, who were both smiling with joyful anticipation at the thought of shuffling over the moors at the pace of an ageing Labrador.

'That's fine,' Harriet said. 'Do whatever you need to do. That's the whole purpose of this place.' She gazed at 'this place' in awe again, as if it just never stopped surprising her or bringing her joy.

The three of them headed to the front exit together. Emma went back out through the sliding doors and across the woodland towards her cabin. She was desperate to lie down on her own and shut out the morning's experience.

At the entrance to the clearing where the cabins were, she caught the glint of a plastic card on the ground in the sunlight. She picked it up. A driving licence. The photo was of Clover. Emma supposed she should take it to her cabin and give it back to her, but then she spotted the name.

Meredith Slater.

She let the realization settle and found she wasn't surprised. *Here we are*, she thought. *Our wonderful Clover isn't even real.*

She tried to be fair. She tried not to let her mind go off in wrong directions. She imagined lots of people in the hippie nonsense industries used false names. She'd once passed a fortune teller's caravan when she'd taken Jake and Clara to a fairground and the board outside read 'Find out your destiny with Juniper Rose'. Surely no one in the world was really called Juniper Rose, but Anne Gardener didn't have the mystique that people who bought into this bullshit needed.

Clover was a name that suited this woman's work. Meredith Slater sounded like a corporate bitch. But what if . . . Just *what if* Clover had a deeper, darker reason to lie? No one here knew the first thing about her. She could be anyone.

She probably wasn't, though. She just had a business name. That was all.

Emma knew she really ought to take the driving licence back to her, but it didn't seem that there was an easy way to do that. What would she say? 'I found this and now I know you're a complete fake'? Awkward. Even if she took a more subtle approach, a more simple, *I found this*, the rest of the sentence would still sit heavily between them, unspoken but obvious.

She slipped the driving licence into her back pocket. She'd work out what to do with it later.

When she looked up again, that beautiful, svelte figure in leopard-print yoga leggings and a tight black top was heading towards her, smiling and smiling. It made Emma feel as though she was the only person in the world Clover wanted to see. God, everyone around here smiled so fucking much. How could they bear it? How could they manage it?

'Emma,' Clover said.

'Hi.'

'I was just coming to join you all. Have you finished lunch?'

'Yes. Maggie and Fleur have gone for a mindful hike with Harriet. I'm too lazy for that. I was just going to lie down for a while.'

Clover looked disappointed. She said, 'Have you been down into the rainforest?'

'No.'

'It's beautiful there. And it's such a lovely afternoon. I love these bright September days, don't you? It makes me want to make the most of the light before winter settles in.'

She spoke like Anne of Green Gables.

Emma said, 'Did you ever read *Anne of Green Gables* when you were a child?'

She could see Clover's eyes practically lighting up. 'I did! It was one of my favourites.'

'I can tell. You speak like her.'

Clover looked as though she didn't know what to do with that comment. She said, 'It's just such a lovely afternoon.'

Emma didn't give a shit about the weather. She hadn't given a shit about the weather since losing Oliver.

Clover continued, 'I was just going to have a very quick walk down to the rainforest studio to plan this afternoon's session. Why don't you come with me? There's a beaver colony in the river down there. We might see them.'

A beaver colony.

Emma said, 'Is that a metaphor for the divine feminine?'

Clover looked confused. 'What?'

'Never mind.'

'Do you feel like it? I'm going now. It'll only be for

twenty minutes or so. You might find it more energizing and beneficial than a nap.'

Daytime napping was the exclusive preserve of the unemployed and depressed. Emma knew this well. She didn't feel she could do anything other than say, 'Okay. I'll come along.'

They walked together, side by side, across a couple of fields and then down a steep, muddy path that took them into the rainforest. The trees were mostly ancient oaks, still in full leaf but beginning to turn. The air was damp from last night's rain, the sunlight muted but the shade from the trees tinged the whole forest with gold. For the first time in a long time, Emma felt a slight ache in her chest, but found she couldn't name the sensation. Longing perhaps, but for what? To inhabit the forest, to lie down on the ground and spend her life here?

But that would be bollocks.

The path ran by the edge of the river. Clover stopped walking for a moment, waved her hand towards the water and said, 'There are swimming areas here. Three of them. Small pools you can just jump in, or climb down to if you prefer. It's perfectly safe.'

'What, now? In September?'

Clover gave her an amused look. 'Of course.'

'No way.'

'Why not?'

'Because it's freezing.'

'You might surprise yourself. It's incredibly good for you to be immersed in cold water, especially in surroundings like this. It's good for your muscles, for your heart, and for your wellness.'

'A glass of Prosecco in a hot tub is even better for my wellness.'

Clover chuckled, like a grandparent indulging a foolish grandchild. It irritated Emma. She said, 'What's your story, Clover?'

'I beg your pardon?'

Emma rearranged her face into an expression of meekness. She couldn't let on that she had Clover's real identity in her back pocket. 'Sorry,' she said. 'I don't have a very effective filter. Whatever's in my head comes out of my mouth. My son says it's like Tourette's. What I meant was, what is it that brought you to this sort of work?'

They started walking again, on through the forest. All around them, trees cast off their leaves; a few weaker branches cracked and fell, and the flow of the river picked up speed. There was movement everywhere, but Emma was aware of stillness easing slowly into her, and the unknown ache in her chest beginning to bloom. It wasn't unpleasant. Perhaps it was something like awe. But it was more gentle than awe.

For the very briefest of moments, she wondered if it was her heart chakra.

She turned away from the thought.

Clover said, 'It all started for me with yoga. These things often do. Yoga is everyone's gateway drug. I started going to classes at my local community centre to get away from my husband . . .'

'You're married?' This took Emma by surprise. Clover seemed too in love with freedom to be tied into marriage.

Clover waved her arm dismissively. 'Not any more. It was by accident really that I came across yoga. I'd have gone to anything, but yoga was the only class they offered where I lived and it was really cheap. I absolutely loved it. It was a version of light spirituality that worked for me. It was all about the divine but it made so much sense. It involved self-care and emotional balance and seemed so much wiser than anything I'd been taught before. After that, I got into meditation. That's what this afternoon's practice will be. Meditation. Have you ever tried it before?'

Emma shook her head. 'I haven't.'

Clover smiled. 'Anyway, you asked for my story. My aim is just to send you on a journey into your deepest self and guide you towards the woman you want to become. That woman is in there. She's there in all of us. She's bold and powerful, and she needs to be let out.'

Emma looked at this young woman standing before her, the woman with the fake name and the insane passion for bullshit, and Ben's words came back to her. *It's a cult. She'll never let you back.*

She shivered at the thought, then shook the feeling away. This afternoon, back in her cabin, she'd find out the truth about Meredith Slater.

13

Fleur

Fleur was lying on a yoga mat, enclosed by the forest. Above her, the autumn sunlight still burned its way through the shade of the oaks and warmed her skin. The drama and anguish of the morning began to ease slowly away, as the forest reached out its arms and received them from her.

She closed her eyes.

'Feel your body rooted in this place,' Clover was saying. 'Be aware of the ground underneath you, of the sounds you can hear – the gentle murmur of leaves in the wind, the slow flowing of the river. Allow yourself time to bathe in this forest, to feel that you are a part of it . . .'

Fleur was aware of her mind emptying, of every thought that wasn't the forest drifting away from her like a breeze.

She heard Clover say, 'And now . . . come back to the breath. Feel your lungs fill with air as you breathe in. Hold the breath, and then breathe slowly out. Again, feel your lungs fill with air . . . Hold the breath . . . and breathe slowly out . . .'

Fleur was good at meditating. She was good at clearing a space in her mind and inhabiting it, serenely, for just this moment, and thinking of nothing but the steady rhythms of her breathing. It was something she'd taught herself during those last few weeks with Douglas, when the fear of what might happen next became too much for her. She'd downloaded an app, sat cross-legged on her bed and followed the exercises, and after a few weeks she found she could calm her racing thoughts simply by closing her eyes and concentrating on her breath. That was all it took and she often thought now that it had saved her life, in a way.

'Take another deep breath in . . .' Clover said again.

Fleur did as she was told. By this point, she would usually be fully immersed in a meditation, almost unaware of anything other than the peaceful clarity of her psyche. She was struggling to maintain it today, and didn't know why. It bothered her. The content of her mind would drain away and she'd be ready for the next breath, and then all of a sudden a thought would find its way back in, unwelcome and intrusive. *You miss him.*

She tried using the technique the app had taught her – realize the thought had arrived, acknowledge it and then let it go – but it wasn't working today. As she relaxed into the peace of the forest, his face would appear in soft-focus. It wasn't the version of his face she'd known by the end. This was the face he'd shown her at the start, the gentle face she'd loved with a force that took her breath away and had the power to unhinge her. This was the face she wanted now, the one she wished could be permanent. If it was, all her problems would be solved.

But it wasn't him. She had to accept that. That version of himself he'd shown her no longer existed.

She had the sense of him being close by, could almost feel him lying on the ground beside her. With her eyes still closed, and still trying to maintain some sort of focus on her breathing, she reached out an arm and felt around in the dirt for him. There was only empty space. She turned her head to the side and opened her eyes to check. He wasn't there. Next to her she could see only Emma, whose eyes were closed in obedience for once.

She returned her attention to the exercise and tuned into what Clover was saying. 'If it helps, count each breath as you are aware of it in your body. Count one on the inhale, and two on the exhale One . . . and two . . .'

It was no good. Fleur's mind kept on slipping. She couldn't stop seeing that face, or hearing that sensuous voice that used to speak such beautiful, caring words to her. It created a yearning in her heart so strong, she almost sobbed from the pain and frustration of it.

You can endure much more than you think you can, she reminded herself. It was something her mother used to say to her whenever Fleur was going through a difficult time, a cure-all for everything from a broken arm to exam stress to having her heart broken. And she was right. Fleur, like so many people, had endured the unendurable.

She wasn't sure it had done her any good, though. To her therapist, she'd said, 'I know it's made me what I am today, but I don't want to go through stuff that doesn't kill me but makes me stronger any more. I'm sick of it.'

Her therapist had understood. 'You shouldn't have to, Fleur,' she told her. 'No one should have to go through what you've been through.'

It was the first time anyone had ever acknowledged that. It gave Fleur an incredible feeling of relief just to hear it.

14

Maggie

Maggie knew this feeling from long ago. It was the floating, not-quite-present feeling of being mildly stoned. It was the sort of feeling she'd loved when she was younger: serene, unhurried, thoughtful.

The only difference was that she hadn't been smoking marijuana. She hadn't been doing anything except for lying down on the forest floor, looking up at the trees for a while, then closing her eyes and following Clover on her guided meditation. Clover called this experience *forest bathing*. They'd all lain there together and focussed on their breath and then away they'd flown on a journey of the mind, taking in the nearby sounds of the river and the birdsong, and the rustle and shift of leaves in the breeze.

'Imagine yourself walking on a path through this amazing woodland. Breathe in the air, filling your lungs completely. Let your body relax even further. Smell the forest around you. Smell the air filled with the scent of trees, soil and the woodland stream . . .'

Maggie loved it. After the intensity of smashing a bolster cushion against the floor this morning, then suddenly shouting and eventually reducing herself to tears, this long bathe in the golden light of the rainforest was just the revival she needed. Something in the emotional release followed by the deep relaxation was acting like a drug in Maggie, which would have alarmed her slightly if it hadn't felt so damn *good*. She decided to think she'd simply reached a heightened state of awareness, rather than that her mind had slipped its moorings and she'd gone a bit mad.

She sat in the circle and looked around at the others to see if they were experiencing it too. Fleur seemed slightly pained. Emma looked pissed off.

Clover gazed at them as though they were all her children. 'How's everyone feeling?' she asked softly.

Maggie wished she had a bottle of wine beside her, something that would loosen her up enough to speak. She wanted to speak. She felt as if she'd have a lot to say if she could only open her mouth, but it was more difficult now than it had been this morning. The words felt lodged in her throat and uncomfortable. She blamed Emma and all her doubts but, then again, Emma was the woman with the wine in the bushes. Maggie needed to stay on good terms with her.

Fleur was the first to speak. Obviously. She said, 'I found it hard to focus on the meditation today. I don't usually. I've been meditating daily for a long time now, and I'm good at it. But my mind kept wandering. It was wandering back to all the things I was letting go of this morning, and that worries me because it makes me feel I haven't really let go.'

Clover gave her a smile of gentle understanding. 'Don't beat yourself up, Fleur,' she said. 'It's possible that this morning's practice brought things to the surface. That has to happen before we can let them go. Tonight, we'll relax by the campfire and we'll do some more work on letting go. We can't always let go of ingrained issues in one session. What we did this morning was begin the process. Finishing it can take a little longer.'

Maggie shot a glance at Emma, who shrugged. It was difficult to know exactly what the shrug meant. The woman had a cynical approach to all this, and Maggie couldn't blame her for that. She was in her fifties – experienced enough to be deeply mistrustful, but not experienced enough to be desperate for a belief in something, *anything* beyond this daily grind of love and loss.

Clover turned to Emma with another one of her nurturing smiles. 'And Emma, how are you feeling?'

Emma scooped up a small handful of dirt and let it run through her fingers. 'Fine,' she said.

'Just *fine*? Nothing deeper than that?'

'Just fine. You can move on from me now.'

Clover nodded wisely, as if to show she understood that Emma wasn't rude, just strongly defended. 'This morning will have been intense, probably for all of you. That's why we came here afterwards – to come to terms with whatever we released earlier today and to immerse ourselves in the relief that comes with letting go, or least with beginning to let go. I would recommend making space in your lives for a daily meditation practice. Just twenty minutes a day can be life-changing.' She paused for a while, then said, 'Maggie, how are you?'

'Oh, I'm great,' Maggie told her. 'I'm feeling very relaxed. More relaxed than I've felt for years. Actually, I feel as though I've been smoking forbidden substances.'

They all laughed.

Quickly, Maggie added, 'I don't smoke anything. I don't take any drugs, so I don't actually *know* that this is the feeling. I'm just pleasantly tranquil, the way my son used to look when he sat outside in our summerhouse with his friends every night, claiming to be burning incense.'

Clover smiled again and went on in her soothing voice, 'Our practice for this afternoon has now come to an end. We'll be leaving this beautiful space soon and we'll meet again for dinner at 7. I'm pleased with the way you are all embracing your own journeys and I would like us now to look round this circle at each of our sisters, and to acknowledge each of them in turn. Look them in the eye and share some way of understanding without words – perhaps a smile or a nod, or an expression that means something to you. We are honouring our sisters for what they have been through today, and for what they will continue to experience for the rest of this retreat, and we are welcoming the women they will be when they leave on Monday.'

The women they will be when they leave on Monday.

Who would Maggie be? She wasn't sure. She wasn't sure she even wanted to be another person. She'd have quite liked to stay the same person. Or perhaps the same person without the mistakes of her past.

Her eyes met Emma's. She grinned at her, to show she understood the madness of this. Emma made a face. Maggie started looking forward to drinking with her this evening.

She moved on to Fleur. Fleur's expression was serious, of course. She appeared to gaze deeply into Maggie's eyes, and then she nodded. It was a nod of profundity, of wisdom, a nod to suggest she saw straight through to Maggie's soul and understood her.

Maggie smiled at her. She had the urge to take her home, run her a hot bath and feed her some good meals. Fleur carried the air of a waif about her, a fragile woman trying so hard to be strong. Maggie had a well-honed radar for that sort of woman. She used to be one herself.

She wondered what woman Fleur would be by Monday. There was an urgency to this if they were going to make their reincarnation deadline. It was already late Saturday afternoon and Maggie wasn't feeling drastically different. She kept thinking about Bill (the cat) and wondering how he was. She hoped the neighbour was remembering to feed him, and that he wasn't pining for her. Everyone said cats didn't care about their owners, but Maggie wasn't convinced. Bill loved her. He was always bringing her leaves and sticks and things he found on his nightly adventures beyond the house, and whenever she came home from the supermarket, he hung around the car while she loaded her arms with shopping bags, in a way that made her feel sure he wanted to help. Sometimes, he'd mewl at her, as if he were saying, 'I'd carry those bags for you if I could'. There was even a time when she'd accidentally left the door ajar before she went out and he'd walked ahead and opened it for her. It had taken her three years to bring herself to leave him on his own for a weekend. Bill needed her, and she wasn't prepared to take the risk of neglecting someone who needed her again.

They all stood and rolled up their yoga mats and began walking slowly back to their cabins. Maggie fell in step beside Fleur, although Fleur was silent and didn't seem to feel like talking.

Maggie wondered if she should phone Richard. She

hadn't spoken to him for a while. His wife was five months pregnant and Maggie was trying hard not to be too keen. She couldn't betray her desperation to be part of the baby's life. She wanted to be a big part. She wanted to be the grandma who picked the children up from playgroup and school, who had them for sleepovers at weekends, who played endless games of hide and seek, who made cakes and listened to their troubles, who sat them on her lap knowing she smelled of lovely perfume and that the children would grow up saying wistfully, 'Oh, that smell reminds me of my grandma . . .'

She wanted to be everything she'd failed to be as a mother. Wasn't that what grandparenting was all about? A second chance?

The trouble was that Richard still wanted to punish her, even now. He pretended he didn't. He pretended everything was fine, but Maggie had always known it wasn't. There was so much distance between them. He rarely phoned her and when she phoned him, he was always distracted and found a reason to end the call before he'd told her anything about his life. Most of the time, she had no real idea how he lived.

'You've got to give him space, love,' Bill always said.

She guessed he was right, so she gave Richard space. She gave him years of space, and now she wondered whether giving him space had been a mistake. Maybe Richard had taken the space she gave him to mean she didn't care, that she really did hate him as much as he'd always thought she did. Maybe now she should be more explicit – phone him up, say how sorry she was for being such a bitch all through his childhood, how he had every right to hold it against her, but she'd really like the chance to be a grandmother to his child if he would let her.

Oh, but what if he said no? What would she do then?

She thought about it as she walked back through the rainforest. She wouldn't cope if he said no. She also wouldn't cope if he said yes and then carried on as usual. She should wait until the baby was a few months old and they were exhausted, ready to hand the baby over to anyone if it meant they could sleep for a night. That would guarantee a yes.

She wouldn't phone him now. It could spoil this retreat, and she was loving it here, even if it was like nothing she'd ever known before. Or perhaps because of that. Never in her life had she been in a place where the whole purpose was to engage with your emotions. When Maggie was young, emotions just weren't recognized. No one really seemed to have them, or certainly not to the debilitating extent that young people had them now. There was something very freeing about it, about lying down in a circle and saying *I have been wounded, but I will find my way out and I'll get better and be more powerful than I've ever been before*.

Maggie wasn't sure she'd ever really felt powerful, even though she'd had power. She'd had so much power over her son, she'd destroyed him.

15

Emma

Emma lay down on her bed and groaned. Dinner had been another serving of nourishment for her heart chakra – a bowl filled with miso-roasted tofu; broccoli in sweet chilli dressing; sesame cabbage; and smashed edamame beans with lime. Her body wasn't used to it and she felt about four months pregnant. She was going to ask for sandwiches tomorrow, although they probably didn't allow bread in this sacred place. She wondered what would happen to her heart chakra if she consumed carbs. It would probably close up again. Good. She needed uncomplicated food so she could live an uncomplicated life.

She'd eavesdropped around the kitchen while Harriet was taking things out of the oven and Clover was asking her about the meal. 'I want everyone to feel nurtured and cherished when they eat this,' Harriet had explained, sprinkling something that looked like ground nuts over the food. 'I try and put that desire into the food as I cook, even when I'm just adding these last bits that might seem unimportant.'

It was touching, in a way, that someone could be sweet enough to believe this. It was also really annoying that anyone was this stupid. Emma wanted to take Harriet by the shoulders and shake her.

She'd googled Meredith Slater when she came back from the rainforest earlier. There were lots of them, but she found the right one when she clicked on a blog and saw a photo. It was a couple of years old and she'd had her hair cut since then, but that pretty little face was definitely the woman she knew as Clover.

Meredith Slater turned out to be a missing woman with a dying father and a husband desperately looking for her. Emma wasn't sure what she should do about this. She looked on the UK Missing Persons website run by the police and typed in Meredith's name. Nothing came up. The police, as far as she could see, had no record of her. If they had, Emma would probably have felt compelled to report it.

On the bed opposite, Maggie said, 'How long can we lie here before she makes us do something again?'

Emma checked her phone. 'Not long. Fifteen minutes max, I think. Time for a glass of Prosecco if you want one.'

'I'd love one,' Maggie said. She clutched her belly. 'Oh, God. It's all such guilt-free food, so I eat so much of it. I'd never eat this much at home. I think it's going to kill me. I'll be the first person in the world to die a broccoli-related death.'

'You won't,' Emma reassured her.

'Maybe it's the pain of my heart chakra opening.'

Emma poured the Prosecco into two tumblers and said, 'You don't really believe in this heart chakra stuff, do you?'

'I have no idea. It's the sort of thing my husband would have mocked . . .'

'And mine.'

'. . . but since we're here, we might as well embrace it. So yes, I believe in it. There must be a link between the food you eat and how well you feel . . .' She trailed off. 'What's the word I'm looking for? *Spiritually.* How well you feel spiritually. Not just how healthy your body is, I mean. When Bill died, I lost all interest in cooking – not that my interest was ever that high – and I ate mostly rubbish. I once tried to celebrate my freedom by having a box of Quality Street for dinner because he'd never have tolerated *that* when he was alive, but it didn't really work. I just felt awful. I was so tired and sluggish and I'm sure my diet didn't help. But since being here, I've felt really energetic. The way I smashed that cushion against the floor this morning . . . Who knew I had that kind of strength? It doesn't come from eating lard and potatoes, I'm sure of that.'

'Oh, sure. I can see that. But all this chakra stuff sounds like baloney to me. Is your heart chakra opening?'

'I'm not sure. Is yours?'

'Oh, my heart is a lump of rock,' Emma told her. 'It has been for years. It'll take more than some smashed edamame beans to set it on fire.'

Maggie laughed. People always laughed when she said things like that. They didn't believe her, or they at least thought she must be exaggerating. She told people an awful lot about herself that they didn't take seriously. Probably just as well.

Maggie said, 'I don't know about the heart chakra thing, but all this talking and bashing things and lying in the forest has definitely made me feel more . . . Oh, I don't know . . . emotional, I suppose, although I can hardly believe I'm saying that. *Emotional* was a dirty word when I was younger. Only women who belonged in asylums ever spoke about their emotions.'

Emma understood. Apart from her children, the only person who'd ever awoken wild feeling in her had been Oliver. Until him, she'd assumed she had some sort of emotional deficiency that kept her from scaling the great heights of heady devotion, or plunging into the yawning pits of heartbreak and despair. It didn't bother her. She became an observer of other people's lives instead, and thanked God she'd been spared this chaos.

She'd loved Ben in the early days. She had. But it was a tame love, a love characteristic of someone with an emotional deficiency. She was thirty years old by then, time was ticking, and seeing as she'd never experienced the madness of true adoration, she decided she should probably settle for something comfortable. Lots of people did that. She was absolutely sure she wasn't the only one settling for a man who was decent, kind, solvent, steady . . . The sort of man you'd pick out from the CVs of eligible husbands.

Ben was lovely. He was entirely lovely. But life with him was *boring*. Dear God, it was so boring. It wasn't the boredom of everyday life. Everyday life was full. She didn't have a moment to be bored because she was laden with babies, toddlers, playgroups, work, school runs, music lessons, homework, cooking, stories. It was deeper than that. It was an existential kind of boredom. It was boredom of the soul, boredom at the minutest level, as if every cell in her body was about to wither and collapse because it was just so fucking fed up.

Sometimes, in Emma's head, she and Ben went

for relationship counselling to try and do something constructive with the remnants of their marriage. In reality, it was something that would never happen. Ben was entirely private and closed off and would never talk to anyone about his problems. It was part of what had made it so easy for Emma to have an affair. Ben was busy in his own world and didn't notice. All their married life, he'd left Emma to it, and made no emotional demands at all. At first, she'd felt lonely and mildly offended, but after a while she learnt to embrace it. Living with Ben had all the perks of being single, with the additional bonuses of there being someone to share the financial load and bring her a cup of tea in the mornings.

The other reason they'd never go for counselling together was Emma. She wouldn't be able to bear the judgement. She, after all, was the one who'd strayed from her marriage. She'd been with someone else for three whole years, and there'd been nothing casual about it. They'd planned a life together, she and Oliver. It would put Ben safely in the position of betrayed husband, and Emma as the betrayer. 'But,' she'd want to say, and she could imagine the counsellor dealing with her like a strict parent. *There are no buts. You cheated on your husband and he has every right to be angry for as long as he likes.*

Infidelity gave the other partner a free pass. Ben wouldn't have to take any of the blame for the wreck of their domestic life. Maybe that was fair enough. If someone asked her to pin down the reason why she'd gone ahead and slept with Oliver that first time, knowing as she did exactly what she was risking and being undeniably old enough to know better, what would she have said? 'I had an affair because until then, I'd spent most of my time examining the mysterious rashes that were always appearing on the bodies of my children, and listening to Ben moan about his aching shoulders, and I fancied a change from all that. I needed a bit of passion. I needed someone who was going to make me feel buoyant, instead of sapping every ounce of energy I had.'

It was hard to make that sound like a good enough reason, and yet it was the reason, and it had felt massive to Emma at the time.

What do you think everyone else's lives are like? her mother would have asked, and Emma would have no answer to that. Everyone else put up with it and Emma should have done too.

But she hadn't, and now she was here, on the long road to recovery from the sudden and unexpected aftermath, still wishing she could turn back time because she knew there'd be no one like him in her future. Love like that came along once in a lifetime, if you were lucky.

To Maggie, she said, 'What's happening this evening?'

'A campfire.'

'It won't be a normal campfire, though, will it? We won't get to just sit around and drink wine.'

'No. It involves more "letting go" and I heard someone say there'd be dancing. And maybe some howling at the moon.'

'Oh, for God's sake. Howling at the moon?'

'I think so.'

Maggie sounded as if she thought this was completely normal behaviour.

'Why?' Emma could think of nothing anyone could gain from howling at a rock in the sky.

Maggie shrugged. 'I don't know, exactly. It's all to do with the divine feminine.'

Emma sniffed. 'I'm still not sure what that is.'

'I think it's . . . Well, I'm not sure, either. I can't define it exactly.'

'It sounds like a deliberately vague term to me,' Emma said suspiciously. She couldn't help it. She was an English lecturer. She was always telling her students they had to be specific. If you were vague, it meant you didn't know what you were talking about.

Maggie tried again, 'I think we're meant to assume there's some kind of divine power in the world. Not necessarily God, but something more powerful than we are. So I think the divine feminine is maybe just female energy. My husband would have called female energy hysteria, but he's dead so we don't have to take any notice of him.'

Emma nodded. 'But this is the dark feminine divine. Am I right?'

'So this is where we turn our backs on being submissive and nurturing and lovely and harness our dark sides. Instead of being loving, we're seductive. Instead of nurturing, we become powerful. We tell our husbands and kids to bugger off and fend for themselves, and then we take over the world. Something like that.'

'I'm still not sure why we have to howl at the moon, though.'

Maggie lowered her voice and said darkly, 'So the moon knows we're here, and we're rising up and claiming our power.'

'Is the moon meant to feel threatened by us?'

Maggie shook her head. 'The moon is full of feminine wisdom. We need to absorb its messages and its energy.'

Emma looked at her. 'Do you actually believe this?' she asked.

Maggie looked back at her. 'I want to,' she said.

Emma finished her Prosecco and poured another half-glass. 'I'm taking this out with me,' she declared. 'I am not howling at the fucking moon, and if I have to watch you lot howl at the fucking moon, I'll need alcohol.'

'Fleur will disapprove.'

'I'll tell her it's elderflower cordial.'

'I don't think she likes you. She thinks you're a destructive presence on a wholesome retreat.'

'She's a pain in the arse. There's nothing rebellious about her. She came here to worship at the temple of Clover.'

'To be honest, I think I might be worshipping at the temple of Clover by the end of this weekend.'

'I told you,' Emma said. 'It's a cult. It's a fucking cult. Honestly, this afternoon I was ready to drive out of this place, but I can see she's sucking you in, and it's my job now to save you.'

Emma topped her glass up to the brim, then she opened the door and they walked together to the campfire.

16

Clover

Her father had died this afternoon. After the forest-bathing session, she'd come back to her cabin and immediately checked Kevin's blog. There it was, in black and white: *I am sorry to report that Meredith's father has now passed away. If anyone knows where Meredith is, please ask her to get in touch. Her mother would appreciate hearing from her.*

She felt sure now that they knew, somehow, that Clover was following this blog, still keeping up with her family, still silently caring about her ailing father. Why else would Kevin be updating it with every piece of news as it happened? Clover struggled with the realisation that reading this was no longer her shield, her way of keeping herself one step ahead of any attempt they might make to come and find her and try and force her into repentance. It had become a means of communication. Her family sent out their messages, and Clover quietly received them.

She'd lost her control of the situation, after nearly two years.

Also: her father was dead, and she hadn't been to see him. And her mother would be lost without him.

She felt the ache of grief making itself known beneath the

shock, and then the words of the priest from the last funeral she'd been to drifted back to her. *As soon as someone dies, we feel regret. We wish we'd done more, or said more, or been a better husband, wife, friend, son or daughter to the person we've lost.*

Clover was feeling this now, more strongly than she'd have thought possible, and she was angry with herself for it. She put her phone down beside her on the bed and took a moment to remind herself of the man her father was, how he'd have been prepared to sacrifice her life for his cult. She could only have seen her father before his death if she was prepared to go back to the life of a Witness, and she wasn't. She never would be.

She had to harden her heart, to tune into the dark feminine. She needed to honour her inner wild woman, and allow all her female rage to swamp the good girl her father had created. She needed to use the rage to burn down this attempt by her family to keep her small and stuck and guilty. She was going back into the woods, to join the other women and create a dance of fire.

17

Maggie

The temperature had dropped and Maggie was glad of the fire. She'd never lit a fire in her life. Fire-lighting and barbecues were Bill's things. He used to love them and then he'd wax lyrical over the flames he'd created, as if he'd missed his true calling as an arsonist or a caveman. Maggie let him get on with it. She wasn't bothered about lighting fires, and cleaning all the ash out of the grate in the mornings looked like such a bloody palaver. In the years after he'd died, if she'd really wanted a roaring open fire or some charred sausages to eat, she would have learnt how to do it – of course she would – but she'd just never had the urge. She would probably die without ever having lit a fire and she felt okay with that.

Clover was different. Clover probably saw fire-lighting as a crucial skill for women who wanted to embrace the dark feminine. Maggie wondered if she might bring out a cauldron this evening so they could all whip up a spell. She quite liked the idea, as long as she didn't have to deal with any frogs.

That lightly stoned feeling was showing no sign of waning yet.

'Lean into it,' Clover said, when Maggie asked if she

should be worried about feeling drugged without having taken any drugs. 'You're going through a transformative experience. Just let whatever needs to happen, happen.'

It sounded sensible enough. Maggie was still waiting to feel she'd been transformed. She wondered how she'd know when it finally happened. Perhaps this drugged sensation was part of her metamorphosis. Eventually, the pleasant cloudiness of her mind would subside and she'd re-emerge, full of clarity and with a whole new purpose.

The four of them were gathered round the fire in a circle, each sitting on a rock, which Maggie had to admit she felt too old for. There was a time she'd have just put up with it, but not now. She said, 'Are there any chairs? My days of sitting on rocks ended thirty years ago.'

The briefest moment of irritation flashed over Clover's face, but then she smiled. 'I'll go and find you one,' she said.

'I can go, if you just tell me where they are. I'm not the Queen. I just can't sit on rocks. I can feel my back splitting already.'

'Let me do it. It's what I'm here for,' Clover said. She looked round the rest of the group. 'Does anyone else need a chair?'

Fleur shook her head like the young woman she was.

Emma said, 'I wouldn't mind . . .'

Clover, ever-patient, set off in search of chairs. *She might be wise beyond her years,* Maggie thought, *but she has no idea what it's like to inhabit an ageing body.*

The moon appeared in the sky above them, almost full. If she'd been wearing a cap, Maggie probably would have doffed it. The beautiful, feminine moon, casting her silvery wisdom from afar.

Emma picked up a stick from the ground at her feet and threw it on the fire. 'I wonder what she's got in store for us this evening,' she said.

Defensively, Fleur said, 'Something amazing, I'm sure.'

Emma, who Maggie was well aware had just started her third large tumbler of Prosecco in forty-five minutes, said, 'Has it ever occurred to you she could be a crook?'

'Oh, for God's sake. Of course she isn't. Clover is the most compassionate, healing woman I've ever had the privilege to know.'

'Classic sign of a psychopath.'

'I don't know what you're—'

Maggie jumped in. 'Ladies,' she said. 'Enough! Ignore her, Fleur. She's half pissed.'

Fleur looked aghast. 'We're not meant to be drinking here. This is so disrespectful—'

'Oh, for fuck's sake. What is this? A rebellious retreat or a convent?'

'Emma, please!' Maggie said.

'Sorry,' Emma murmured, and the moment of conflict ended.

Maggie couldn't help agreeing with Emma that Fleur seemed to see Clover as some kind of feminine equivalent to Buddha. Perhaps she was right. Perhaps in a few centuries from now, Maggie's descendants would be punching their pillows and dancing topless in worship of Clover and the moon. It was, when you thought about it, no stranger than worshipping God. And maybe it was what religion needed. Something where the divine power was a gutsy, full-blooded woman instead of a limp male who constantly demanded the feeding of his ego. Maggie wondered how long it would take to knock up enough churches to gain a worldwide following, and if it would result in rapid and lasting social change.

'I still feel like I'm off my head,' she confessed.

Fleur smiled at her. 'Enjoy it,' she said.

Clover returned then, carrying a stripy deckchair under each arm. Maggie and Emma both stood up quickly to relieve her of them. Maggie set hers up and sank into it gratefully. 'Thanks, Clover,' she said. 'This is so much better.'

Clover smiled. 'You're welcome,' she said. Then she took her seat on a rock, gazed round at the group again, arranged her face into something ethereal and serious, and started:

'Today, we've been working on what we needed to let go of in order to make space for the women we want to become. Letting go isn't always easy, and I know some of you did some really hard emotional work this morning. We're going to continue our work on letting go this evening, so that tomorrow, we're ready to welcome the future.'

Here, she paused for a moment and when she spoke again, her voice was slightly louder. 'We need to quash the good girls we still can't help being. We need to let go of our feminine guilt – the guilt of generations that has been heaped on us. We need to stop quashing our own desires so we can nurture other people's. Make space for boldness! We are going to become the unapologetic women we were born to be. Forget the good girl and all her shame! She's gone! She's out of here!'

Maggie couldn't help herself. She whooped.

Clover pulled her phone from her pocket and pressed some buttons to make music play. 'Let's dance!' she said, and they did an odd sort of follow-my-leader around the fire pit, with Clover swaying ahead of them and everyone else in her wake. Even Emma joined in. Maggie supposed she was feeling guilty.

They danced like that for a while, sometimes waving their arms in the air, sometimes whooping, sometimes just moving forwards with something vaguely like rhythm. Emma, as they'd come to expect, sat down after ten minutes, but the others carried on. By the time they stopped, they were all breathless and the flames were dying out. They sat down while Clover brought the fire back to life.

Maggie's feet hurt and she knew there were wet patches under her arms. She wondered if she smelled as well, but decided she didn't care. She'd rather stink from the exertion of dancing here than anywhere else.

Clover came away from the fire and said, 'The next thing we do will probably be the most important practice of the whole weekend.'

Everyone looked at her expectantly.

She went on. 'We're going to release our shame. Any shame we've been holding on to, whether recent or from long ago, we're going to let go of. As we do so, we're going to remove an item of clothing – it can be an earring, or it can be your trousers, it doesn't matter – and we're going to throw it on the shame pile next to the fire. As we do this, we will utter the affirmation, 'I release the shame of . . .' and we state the source of our shame. If you aren't comfortable revealing your shame to everyone, simply say, 'I release my shame.' There are no rules. You can be as clothed or as unclothed as you like. You can talk about your shame or remain silent. As always, all expression is welcome here.'

She stopped speaking abruptly and spun round.

Maggie heard it, too. A rustling in the darkness. A feeling that someone was out there, watching.

'Who is it?' she whispered.

Clover turned back round, her face broken with relief. 'It's no one,' she said. 'A fox, I think. Something darted into the bushes.'

'Are you sure?' Fleur asked.

'Absolutely.' Clover looked carefully around the group again. 'Are we all ready? I'm happy to go first.'

She stepped forward, unwrapped the shawl from her shoulders, dropped it on the ground and said, 'I release the shame of walking away from my marriage.'

She stepped back.

Fleur stepped forwards. She removed her jumper, threw it on top of Clover's shawl and said, 'I release the shame of not being able to forgive.'

Clover whooped.

Maggie whooped.

Even Emma whooped. Then belched slightly drunkenly.

Fleur stepped back.

Maggie stepped forward. She lifted her jumper over her head, threw it on the pile and said, 'I release the shame of hurting so many people when I was grieving for my baby.'

The response this time was softer. It was a gentle, sympathetic murmuring, rather than whooping or cheering.

She stepped back.

Fleur stepped forward again. She removed her bra and tossed it on the pile. 'I release the shame of sometimes wanting him back.'

Again, the response was muted.

She stepped back.

Clover stepped forward. She, too, removed her top and threw it on the pile. 'I release the shame of leaving the Jehovah's Witnesses.'

'Hell, yeah! Fuck that!' Fleur cried. This took Maggie by surprise. She thought of Fleur as gentle, not really a swearer.

The others cheered.

Clover stepped back.

Maggie stepped forward. She wasn't wearing much. Either her trousers or her bra had to go. Fleur was already standing there topless and Maggie felt pretty confident that Clover would be soon as well. She unhooked her bra and was aware of the weight of her breasts as they fell almost to her knees. 'I release the shame of never letting my husband know I loved him.'

Muted whooping.

She stepped back.

Fleur stepped forward. She took off her skirt and hurled it on the pile. 'I release the shame of not knowing what to do with the life I have now.'

Slightly confused whooping.

She stepped back.

Clover stepped forward. She took off her bra and hurled it on the pile. 'I release the shame of disowning my parents nearly two years ago.'

Wow, Maggie thought. *That's a big one*. She wanted the story behind it. If only they could convince Clover to drink some wine . . .

Clover stepped back.

Emma was standing in silence, watching everyone.

Maggie stepped forward. She thought of Richard and

everything she'd done to him, everything she'd accused him of. She pulled off her trousers and threw them on the pile. 'I release my shame,' she said.

She stepped back.

The others cheered especially loudly for the shame Maggie couldn't bring herself to speak of. She was insanely, absurdly grateful. 'Thank you,' she whispered.

Clover stepped forward. She stepped out of her leggings. 'I release the shame of knowing my father was dying and not going to see him.' She threw her leggings in the air. They landed on the pile.

Another muted cheer.

Both Fleur and Clover stood there now, dressed only in their knickers.

Fleur stepped forward. 'I release the shame of not knowing if I want what he's left me with.'

Oh, God, Maggie thought as she watched. *Oh, my God. She's going to do it.*

Fleur stepped out of her knickers. She threw them on the fire. The flames grew. The knickers were obviously made of nylon because they melted. Maggie made a mental note to talk to Fleur about yeast infections.

They all cheered.

Fleur stepped back, naked and smiling.

Clover stepped forward. She also took off her knickers and threw them on the fire. The flames rose again. 'I release the shame of not getting in touch with my grieving mother now, when she needs me most.'

She stepped back.

There were some more sympathetic noises.

Suddenly, Emma stepped forward. She removed one

earring. 'I release the shame of adultery,' she said, and dropped the earring into the pile.

Maggie gasped. She hadn't meant to. But *adultery*? What a scandal.

To make up for her hick-like gasping, she cheered. 'Woo-hoo!' she cried. 'Let it go!'

Emma stepped back.

Maggie stepped forward. She took off her knickers and thought she might as well throw them on the fire as well. 'I release the shame of not having lived up to my potential.' Before anyone could cheer, Clover jumped in with, 'It's not too late, Maggie! It's never too late!'

They cheered.

Maggie stepped back.

No one else stepped forward. They simply stood there, three of them entirely naked and one still fully clothed.

Clover gave them all some time to stand in silence. Maggie looked ahead of her, towards the trees where they'd heard the noise earlier. It had been more than rustling, more than just the wind or a fox. Was someone there, watching them?

She shook the thought away. It was the darkness, together with the fact that they were here, in the middle of Bodmin Moor, making her think like this. No one was there. The place was almost impossible to even find.

Clover said, 'We have witnessed our sisters in their shame and we have witnessed the release of that shame. We honour our sisters, both in their shame and in the release of their shame. We celebrate ourselves and our sisters for the work they have done today and for how far they've come. Now, who would like to join hands with me in this circle of femininity, as we make way for boldness and power to take the place of shame?'

They all reached out and took the hand of the woman next to them.

'Connect with your power,' Clover said. 'Feel the power of your divine womanhood overthrow any shame you have ever felt. In this place, you are loved. In this place, you are honoured for everything that you are.'

The music started again. They dropped hands and everyone but Emma danced.

18

Fleur

Before going back to her cabin that night, Fleur took herself into the barn and sat for a while by the altar. She needed to calm the racing of her heart. Earlier, when they'd heard the noises in the darkness, her mind had flown immediately to Douglas. *He's here*, she thought. *He wants me back.* She felt sick at the thought of it.

He didn't, though. There was no way he could reach her here.

It was a fox, Clover said. *Something darted into the bushes.*

For the first time, Fleur didn't believe her. It gave her an uneasy feeling she wasn't sure what to do with.

She relit the white pillar candles Harriet must have blown out when she went to bed. They cast a gentle glow over the strange treasures everyone had lain at the altar on the first day, giving them an air of reverence.

She'd come here to honour the women who were here with her. It was too much, too intense, to go up to Clover or Maggie herself and speak her admiration for all that they'd endured, so she thought if she simply sat among their possessions, some of her energy would be transferred to them.

Someone passing this makeshift altar would probably hardly even notice it, or if they did, they'd see only junk: a few dried roses left from the first night here, old photos, a handful of stones, folded sheets of paper, paintbrushes, a glass. Fleur saw them as private relics from the wounds these women had endured.

She'd brought with her two photos for the altar, one of Douglas alone and one of the two of them together as a couple. She hadn't wanted anyone to see the photos so she'd hidden them in an envelope that she'd laid beside the flowers. Now, she reached over, slipped the photos out of the envelope, tore them in half a few times and placed the pieces back on the altar.

She sat cross-legged with her back straight and turned her attention to her breath, but instead of emptying her mind now, she wanted to fill it. She wanted to fill it with all her memories of Douglas so she could observe him through her new lens and let him go at last. *Stop wanting him to come back. Stop thinking he will have changed.*

In the calming light from the candles, she rested her hands over her belly, and tried to tune into the life inside her. Before she had any hope of making a decision, she needed to accept Douglas for what she knew he was. A bastard. An arsehole. A man who was never going to stand by her so they could lovingly bring up a child. If she kept this baby, he'd always have a reason to come back.

Oh, but she'd always wanted a child and this might be her last chance. Also, she had liberal views about abortion, but she wasn't sure she could do it herself. Abortion was there for other women.

Just as she was about to start, the door opened behind

her. She turned her head and saw Maggie in her red-checked pyjamas, carrying a hot water bottle.

'Sorry,' Maggie said. 'I didn't mean to interrupt you. I was just coming to fill this up. I know there's a wood burner in the room, but I can't light it and I share with Emma. She prefers to sleep in cool air, apparently.'

Fleur said, 'It's okay. I'm going to do a weird meditation. Don't take any notice of me.'

Maggie looked suddenly interested. 'What kind of weird meditation?'

Fleur said, 'I'm not sure it really exists. I've just made it up. But you know how normal meditation is all about emptying your mind and focussing on the moment?'

Maggie nodded.

'Well, I've decided to try and fill my mind and focus on the past.'

'That sounds interesting. And what's your reason for this?'

'There was this bloke . . .'

Maggie came and sat on the floor beside her. 'There usually is,' she said. Her hot water bottle appeared to be forgotten for now.

'And he was horrible, really. Awful. A terrible person.'

'I'm sorry.'

'But the trouble was, he wasn't like that from the start. At the start, for the first few months, he was the loveliest, most sensitive, most amazing person I've ever met.'

Maggie nodded again, as if she knew exactly what was coming next. She said, 'And you kept thinking that version of him would come back if you tried hard enough?'

'Yes,' Fleur confessed. 'Yes. Exactly that.'

For a while, Maggie didn't respond. Then she said, 'And do you still think that?'

'No. I don't think that. I know who he is. I know exactly what would happen if I ever took him back. I just can't persuade my heart. There are times when I still really miss him. He always said . . .' She paused and cleared her throat. 'He always said we were destined to be together and he'd find me if I ever left him. I did leave him. It was six months ago now. I'm okay most of the time, but sometimes I do imagine him finding me. I know him. I know his strategies. He'd be lovely again. He'd be sorry and he'd make me believe he meant it. He's clever.' She paused, then added, 'Or maybe I'm stupid.'

Maggie laid her hand over Fleur's. 'It's not you,' she said.

'Thank you.'

'So what's the meditation going to do?'

'I just want to feel strong enough to resist him. I want to sit here, let the memories come and go and observe them without any anger or sadness. I just want to see him as he is. And then I think maybe I'll be able to really let this one go. It's only when I've let go of the man I want him to be that I'll be able to make a decision about the next step.'

Maggie said, 'It sounds like a good idea. Maybe if it works, you could sell it.'

Fleur laughed. 'Maybe I could.'

'Would you . . .' Maggie began. 'Would you mind if I joined you? I'd like to try and apply this to my own life.'

'Sure.'

They sat side by side in the candlelight for a long time.

PART TWO

19

Fleur

Love had taken her by surprise. She'd sworn off men when she turned twenty-five. Nothing especially bad had happened to make her do that; it was just that everyone she'd ever been out with left her feeling she'd rather be on her own than tied to somebody else. They were all decent and pleasant enough. They just weren't exciting. Fleur wanted adventure. They didn't seem to want anything much, apart from a beaten-up sofa, a few cans of lager and some football on the telly.

Douglas wasn't like that. He was older than her, for a start. Thirty-seven compared to her thirty-one. He was a comedian. A good-looking comedian. She'd seen him at her local arts centre when she'd taken herself to a comedy night after work one evening, and he was the only one who'd made her laugh. Afterwards, she passed him in the foyer and said, 'I really enjoyed your act. Thank you.'

It wasn't mean to be flirtation. She'd said it because she had friends who were trying to make it in the arts world and they spent three-quarters of their time feeling despondent about their prospects. She knew how much one word of encouragement could mean to them.

He smiled at her appreciatively and the force of it made

her look away. He was even better-looking close up than he'd been onstage. He said, 'Thank you. I'm honoured that you took the time to say this to me.'

She looked back up at him.

He said, 'Are you busy now? I'm only in Brighton for this one night. I'm going to Bristol tomorrow, then Totnes. It can be lonely on the road. I'd love to have a drink with someone.'

'Okay,' she said, and they went to The Ship, an old-man pub where a fire burned in the corner and the smell of a hundred years of cigars smoked before the ban still lingered in the carpet.

He had a pint of ale. She had a glass of white wine. They talked a lot. They talked until the pub shut. Fleur was aware of a lightning-bolt connection between them. She spoke animatedly in his presence. They moved easily from sharing the smaller details of their lives to things that were more meaningful, more private. He told her how he'd always wanted to be a performer, but came to it late. 'I succumbed to the pressure from my parents,' he said, taking a slug of his beer. 'They're very mainstream. They have trouble seeing beyond the standard ways to earn a living. I said I wanted to be a comedian and they laughed, but ironically not because they thought it was funny. They thought it was an unreachable goal. I became a drama teacher for a few years. I quite liked it, but I was jealous when I saw students going off to start their degrees in performance, knowing they were going to spend three years doing exactly what I was burning to do. It doesn't feel great, to be jealous of an eighteen-year-old. My sister kept telling me I should ignore the doubters and just go for it. But I didn't.' He lowered his voice and started to fiddle with a beer mat. 'And then she died, and I decided I was going to live the rest of my life in tribute to her memory, and that's when I gave up teaching and started doing this instead.'

Fleur's heart lurched with a surge of emotion – pain, shock, admiration, and a sudden, intense connection. 'I'm so sorry about your sister,' she said. 'I think if she could see you now, she'd be proud of what you're becoming. Of what you've become.'

It was a trite response, but what else could she say? To show she understood loss, she told him, 'My dad passed away a couple of years ago. It's hard.'

His face softened in sympathy. 'How did he die?'

'Cancer. It was sudden, though. They said he might have three months, but he died six weeks after his diagnosis.'

Douglas shook his head. 'That's rough. Really rough.'

'What about your sister? How did you lose her?'

He looked away for a while, then he said, 'She took her own life.'

'Oh, Douglas . . .'

'Yeah. I sometimes think if she'd known what it was going to do to us – to all of us – she would have stayed alive.'

Fleur reached for his hand and took it in hers, her chest bruised with care for this man she'd only just met. How could he be so funny, when he carried such a terrible grief?

He said, 'I'm sorry. I don't usually tell people this the first time I meet them.'

'It's okay.'

Now, when she looked back on that conversation in the light of everything she knew, she saw it as the first red flag. It had put her in her place. *Whatever you've been through, I've been through worse.*

20

Maggie

Richard was her first child, and an only child for eight years. Maggie gave up work to look after him because it was the late 1970s and mothers didn't work back then. They stayed at home, wearing floral skirts and smelling of fabric softener, and devoted their time to baking fairy cakes and making play dough from scratch. Sometimes, they did things today's parents would consider outrageous, like give their toddlers a honey sandwich. The authors of the advice guides back then said honey was natural, and so this made the sugar benign. Now sugar in any form was the gateway drug. If a child was high on honey aged three, you could expect them to be on coke by the time they hit sixteen.

Other terrible things Seventies mothers did included smacking, shouting and a general sort of neglect. In the summer holidays before Annie was born, Maggie would send Richard out on his bike in the morning and be annoyed if she saw him again before tea. She never really knew what he was up to during those hours away from her, although he often came home with wet trousers from wading through streams, and he'd once sprained his ankle when he jumped out of a tree and into a field for a game of football. (The field belonged to the farmer and was strictly out of bounds, separated from the public by some elaborate barbed wire and a few unnecessarily grumpy signs.) Still, on the whole, these adventures beyond the home did him no harm, although Richard had since pointed out that this had more to do with good fortune than a lack of danger, and Maggie could accept that he was probably right.

When she looked back on that time now, Maggie wondered what on earth she'd been doing with all those child-free hours and why she had nothing to show for them. She'd heard of mothers these days who set up online businesses while their babies slept, or did OU degrees, or saved the rainforest, or clocked up other achievements to let the world know that motherhood had not compromised their feminist principles. They were stronger and more driven than ever.

Maggie hadn't been like that. Maggie had spent the first two years of Richard's life in a sleep-deprived delirium, experiencing soaring highs whenever he smiled or laughed or said something adorable, and then desperate lows when she thought the only way she'd ever sleep again would be if a stranger jumped out at her one night, held a knife to her throat and stole the baby. She used to dream of this happening, and feel guilty.

Once he started sleeping, Maggie forgot what it had been like and spent the next five years trying and trying and failing and failing to conceive again. Oh, it was a horrible, wretched business. Heartbreaking. It was also impossible to fight the obsession it created. She marked dates on calendars; she took her temperature; she phoned Bill at work to announce that she was ovulating and he needed to get home immediately; she counted days hopefully;

she plunged into despair to find she hadn't conceived; she pulled herself out of despair and returned to marking dates, taking her temperature . . .

It went on and on, for years. She hated watching Richard playing on his own, knowing that all his friends at playgroup and school had siblings. She didn't want him to be an only child, and her arms ached to hold a baby again. She cried whenever anyone else announced a pregnancy, and friends would offer stupid platitudes like 'You have Richard' as if she should stop moaning and be grateful, while they went on pushing out babies as if the pill had never been invented.

She gave up.

And then it happened. Just after Richard's eighth birthday, she took a positive pregnancy test. Bill was as delighted as she was. She hadn't known, until then, just how deeply he'd been longing for a second child, and realized that every month he'd hidden his disappointment for her sake. She wondered now why she'd never told him how much she appreciated that, how she was sorry she'd ignored his suffering. She must have had her reasons, but she had no idea any more what they could have been. Perhaps she'd just never been very good at loving Bill properly.

Annie was born in September, when Richard had just started his second year in the juniors at primary school. She was truly the most beautiful baby Maggie had ever seen. Bill fell in love and doted on her in a way that was different – softer, more tangible – to the way he'd doted on Richard. 'She's my baby girl,' he said simply when Maggie pointed this out to him, and Maggie realized then that everything they said about fathers and daughters was true.

Richard, at first, had adored her as well. He would sit on the sofa and let her lie on his chest while he watched *Grange Hill*. He'd show her off to his friends when they knocked for him, and once he even refused to go out because the baby was sleeping on him. For a while, Maggie was more blissfully happy than she'd ever been in her life.

She couldn't bear to look back on that time. She avoided it, would do anything at all not to think about it. She couldn't bring herself to try and pinpoint what it was that had triggered her later madness. *Abuse*. It had been abuse, what she'd done to her son, and no one stopped her. They should have stopped her. She was so angry with them for not stopping her.

Before Annie was born, one of her friends had regaled her with those retrospectively hilarious stories about bringing a new baby home when their first child was a preschooler. Her four-year-old daughter had picked the baby up one day, put him in the pram, and then hauled him next door and left him in the driveway. When she went back home, her mother was frantic. 'Where's the baby?' she cried. 'What's happened to the baby?'

'He's gone to live with Olive and Derek,' the little girl said. 'He doesn't like it here.'

Richard had never done anything like that, never shown any jealousy, except for once. There was one day, when Annie was two weeks old, when she caught a cold that Maggie was terrified was going to turn into bronchiolitis. Her nose was stuffy, her breathing laboured, and the only way to soothe her was through endless feeding. Maggie sat, pinned to the sofa for hours each day, while Annie guzzled her milk and drained every scrap of energy Maggie had.

She was exhausted, and worried, and irritable, and so glad she hadn't had this new baby when Richard was younger. How on earth would she have coped with a newborn and a toddler at the same time? It baffled her how anyone managed it.

And then the school phoned. 'Three of our second-year boys have been in a fight this lunchtime,' the headteacher told her, gently but very seriously. 'I'm afraid we have taken the decision to suspend them all for half a day.'

'Was Richard one of these boys?' Maggie asked, her mind foggy with lack of sleep.

'I'm afraid he was. We know this is very out of character for him and we don't know exactly what went on. Everyone involved has a different story about how it started and who caused it, and who punched who. No one has been seriously hurt, but you will understand, of course, that we cannot even begin to tolerate violence. Would you be able to come up to school and collect him?'

Maggie sighed deeply, and agreed.

She bundled Annie into the pram and walked the half-mile through the village to the primary school. Annie howled all the way there, thrashing her body and twisting her angry face as she searched for milk. 'Shh,' Maggie hushed. 'Shh. We're nearly there, baby. We're nearly there.'

Richard was sitting in the office with the other boys, all of them shamefaced and bruised. 'Whatever have you been doing?' Maggie asked, but she didn't wait for the answer. She took him by the arm, apologized to the headteacher, and led him back home.

By the time she got through the door, Annie was howling. She picked her up out of the pram and resumed her spot on the sofa. Richard followed and hovered nervously about the living room, waiting for her to speak.

She was too tired. 'Just go to your room,' she told him. 'I don't want to see you at the moment. I'll speak to you later.'

Obediently, he left. He'd never been good at being on his own. Maggie didn't usually leave him in his room for longer than ten minutes and she'd planned to go up to him soon, but she was so tired, and Annie was so poorly, and she nodded off on the sofa while Annie was feeding.

After a while – she didn't know how long, but it couldn't have been more than half an hour – Richard came quietly back into the living room. Maggie opened her eyes and saw him staring at them both with real contempt.

'She's so boring, that baby,' he declared.

And that was it. That became the thing she based it all on.

21

Fleur

She'd fallen for him too quickly, that was the trouble. He was charming and caring and sensitive and so tortured by his sister's suicide, she'd just wanted to love him enough to heal his pain . . . *Oh, you stupid, stupid, reckless idiot.*

It was the usual story of a deep-soul union; the usual story of a love so strong no one else had ever known anything like it; the usual story of absolute delusion. She still wondered whether he'd believed what he said at the time or if it really had all been an act to seduce her, to render her powerless and get her exactly where he'd wanted her to be. 'Men like this can be very, very persuasive,' her therapist said. 'But it's an act.'

It hadn't felt like an act. Even when she looked back on it, after everything he'd done, it still didn't feel like an act. At the core of him, there was a man capable of deep love. She felt certain of that. He was just so difficult to reach.

'He's impossible to reach,' her therapist corrected. 'It's important that you realize that. Even if that man you have faith in exists, you will never, ever reach him. He's too damaged. He's too damaged and he's dangerous.'

But she had reached him, for a while right at the beginning. They'd shared three months of intoxicating bliss, when she'd never felt so deeply connected to someone, or so cherished. There was a word for it, apparently – for that way he'd made her feel that night when he ran his fingers over her skin, lowered his voice to a murmur and said, with awe and confusion, 'It's like I already know you. It's like I've known you all my life. No one has ever understood me like this. It's as if . . . I know it sounds so crazy, but it's as if . . . as if you complete me, as if I'm finally whole now we're together.'

She could still remember the exact, excruciating sensation of it all being too much, and yet not wanting it to stop, of wanting nothing more than to go deeper and deeper into it.

'I know,' she whispered. 'I know. I feel the same.'

She was aware of her own heart pounding and his breath becoming shallow as they took another step towards losing themselves in the immensity of this connection. They were both frightened, being taken far beyond what they knew, but they were going to stay with it because not staying with it would break their hearts and destroy them.

Lovebombing. That was the word for it, and Fleur had fallen for it as easily as a neglected kitten.

She went to every single one of his shows, no matter where in the country they were. She used up all her annual leave to travel long distances, and when her leave ran out, she started calling in sick. 'I can't do it without you,' he told her, taking her face in his hands. 'I need to be able to look into the front row and see you there and know we'll be going home together.'

There had been something exhilarating about skiving off work and travelling with him to Leeds and Newcastle and Edinburgh. She loved taking her place in the front row of the comedy clubs, hearing the people around her laugh when he performed and then eavesdropping on them as they left, when they said things like, 'He's fantastic. He'll make it big, for sure.'

Fleur felt deeply the honour of being his girlfriend among all these admirers. He used to look at her from behind his mic and give her a subtle, lop-sided smile no one else noticed or knew was meant only for her. She'd always felt she was nothing much – ordinary to look at, average intelligence – but he'd singled her out. There was power in being chosen by a man who could have anyone.

'I'm a loner, really,' he confessed to her when they went to the pub after a performance in Milton Keynes. 'Shier than people think. I've never been happy in big groups of people. I prefer just to have a handful of close friends, people I can have decent relationships with rather than a big crowd to go out on the lash with, you know? But there's something about performing that . . . Well, it just makes me come alive. I don't feel shy then, or embarrassed. I just love it.' He paused for moment and took a gulp of his beer, then he looked at her intently and said, 'But apart from the performing, it's a quiet life that I want. No matter how big or well known I become, I will always guard the life we have together. I want us to have privacy, a normal life. I'm not interested in the parties or the glamour of showbusiness. I just want us to be together, enjoying our little life.'

She smiled appreciative and took his hand. 'It's what I want, too.'

It didn't really cross her mind that he was arrogant, slightly too sure of himself. There were hundreds of up-and-coming comedians treading this circuit with him and only a few were ever going to reach the top. Douglas never seemed to doubt that he would be one of them, not for a minute. Fleur supposed he had to think like that. He wouldn't have a hope of making it if he didn't. Still, she envied him his confidence, that certainty that he was going to become a force in the world.

He said, 'Thank you for being with me, for coming with me on all these tours. I know it's tiring. I know it's . . .'

She silenced him by leaning forwards and kissing his mouth. 'I want to,' she said. 'I want to be by your side all the time.'

'Thank you,' he said. 'I'll make it up to you.'

'I want to do it,' she told him again. 'There's nothing to make up.'

He said, 'I've been thinking about Christmas . . .'

'Me too,' she admitted. She told him, right at the beginning, that she had to be with her mum at Christmas. She'd never spent Christmas away from her, and now Fleur's dad was dead. She had to go home. But she was dreading the days without Douglas.

She said, 'Why don't you come home with me? My mum won't mind. She'll love it.'

Relief washed over his face. 'I'd love that,' he said. 'I've been dreading it. Really dreading the thought of being without you for so long.'

'It might not be the happiest time you've ever had. My dad . . . It's only our second year without him. He used to love . . .'

'Do you think I'm not used to a sad Christmas, Fleur?' His voice was sharp all of a sudden.

'No, of course not. I'm sorry.'

'Because I am used to it, Fleur. For years, Christmas has been a miserable occasion in our house, with my sister not being there. She always wanted to go to Norway . . .'

Fleur cut in. She couldn't help it. 'My dad always wanted to go to Norway! Always. We were planning to go together. We wanted to stay in a log cabin and go husky sledding and ice fishing and see the Northern Lights. Before he died, he apologized to me for not being able to take me.'

Douglas looked at her and nodded his head slowly as he listened, and Fleur had the horrible sense that she was doing something wrong.

22

Maggie

She remembered those last two weeks of Annie's life as good. Very good. It was late October then, before Halloween had taken over the world in the way it had done recently, and when autumn was still cold. The village was preparing for Guy Fawkes Night. A few of their friends were going to be in charge of the bonfire. Bill had volunteered to man the hot dog stand. Maggie rather recklessly said she'd chop the onions ahead of time and then immediately wished she'd kept her mouth shut because why on earth would anyone want to spend hours chopping onions when they had a seven-week-old baby? It felt like more commitment than she could cope with. But still, at least she'd be doing her bit, the way she'd always done.

She'd bought Richard a new duffel coat. He looked like Paddington Bear in it. When she took him to school in the mornings, he liked to push the pram and she would walk beside him and smile at how adorable he looked, so proud of his baby sister.

They were the happiest weeks of Maggie's life.

Annie died on Sunday, 7 November. Maggie could remember the morning in detail, but the rest of the day was hazy and then blank. She'd laid Annie down to sleep in the

Moses basket some time after lunch. Richard had a friend over and they were playing Scalextric in his bedroom. She could hear the cars as they zoomed around the track and spun off to hit the skirting boards, the way they always did.

She headed back down to the kitchen to make herself a coffee and read the paper for as long as she could before the baby woke up, or before Richard and his friend came in wanting biscuits and orange squash. Bill had gone over to the park to help clear up after the previous evening's bonfire party. He'd offered to take the boys with him, but they didn't want to go and Maggie didn't try and force them, even though she would have liked to, even though she loved the idea of quiet for just one hour while Annie slept.

She took her coffee and the newspaper through to the living room. She knew she shouldn't sit down. Sitting down was fatal because it was so hard to get up again. Nevertheless, she did it. She sat down, read the front page of the newspaper and then leaned her head back against the sofa cushions and closed her eyes.

She woke with a start.

Something was terribly wrong. She knew it in every cell, before the thought had even formed. *Why was Annie still sleeping?*

But Annie wasn't sleeping. Annie had died. In the space of one short hour, she'd died.

23

Fleur

The first big warning sign came at Christmas. Before then, there'd been a couple of things that gave Fleur a creeping sense of his jealousy, but she'd been able to shake them off. He moved in with her for a couple of weeks when the lease on his flat expired and then phoned her at work one afternoon, just before she was about to go for a night out with a friend. He told her he felt ill with a terrible stomach ache and was worried he'd need to go to A & E. She cancelled her night out, and when she got home, Douglas seemed fine. He cooked her a meal and they spent the evening eating and drinking white wine and then when they went to bed, he demonstrated that he was a more skilled and considerate lover than he'd been even before now. Afterwards, she lay in his arms and he kissed her gently and said, 'You don't need anyone else. We have each other. You have me.' She'd felt uneasy then, as if the phone call and the meal and the sex had been his way of making a point. *Our life together is so good. I'm not going to let you go out with your friends.*

Everything was normal after that. Her uneasiness faded and she let it go.

On 1 December, he bought her an advent calendar. An

expensive one, with a miniature bottle of wine for each day, and champagne on Christmas Eve. She was delighted. 'I love it,' she said. 'Thank you.'

'We're not just counting down to Christmas,' he told her. 'We're counting down to something even more amazing.'

She looked at him quizzically.

He handed her an envelope. She opened it and there was a Christmas card with an image of a log cabin in the snow at night, the Northern Lights glowing green and purple in the sky above it. When Fleur opened the card, two pieces of paper fell out. She picked them up. They were flight tickets to Norway on 23 December.

'It's just for four nights,' he told her, 'but we're going to do it. We're going to do what your dad and my sister always wanted us to do. I've booked ice fishing on Christmas Eve and husky sledding on Christmas day. It's going to be perfect, Fleur. It's going to be so perfect.'

She stared at the tickets in her hand and was unable to speak.

'What's wrong?' he asked. 'I thought you'd be made up.'

She shook her head. How could she tell him? She'd already told him, but he mustn't have heard her, or he'd forgotten.

She said, 'It's so thoughtful, Doug. So lovely. I want to go, I really do, but would you be able to change the dates to New Year or something?'

His excitement disappeared. 'What?'

'I can't. I can't leave my mum at Christmas. Not now. It's only our second Christmas since Dad died. I thought I'd explained this . . .'

His face took on a hard edge. 'Right,' he said.

'I'm sorry, Doug. I just . . .'

He turned away from her.

'Please understand. I love what you've planned. I do. But I . . .'

He said nothing.

They sat in silence for a long time. Anger and pain were radiating from him, and she had no idea what to do.

She tried again. 'Please, Doug . . .' she said.

He turned around and picked up the tickets from the floor, then he pulled a lighter from his pocket, sparked it up and held the flame to a corner.

'Please don't do this,' she said, as the tickets caught and began to burn. 'Please.'

He sat there, controlling the flame until the tickets had disappeared and there was ash all over the floor where they sat.

Then he stood up and left.

He didn't speak to her for three days after that. He didn't seem angry any more. He simply brooded around the house with a hurt expression, as though she'd wounded him more deeply than she could ever understand. She thought over the things he'd told her about his childhood – how loveless it had been; how impossible it was to please his parents, no matter what he did or how hard he tried – and realized he was feeling her response to his gift as just another rejection from someone he loved, someone he'd been trying so hard to make happy.

She couldn't bear it. All she wanted was to go back to the way things usually were between them, when they were together all the time, when they enjoyed themselves and laughed so much, and when he'd cherished her in way she'd never been cherished before.

They lay in bed after the third day he hadn't been able to speak to her. He'd rolled away from her touch. She waited a while, then said carefully, 'Doug? Can we talk about this?'

He said nothing.

'I'm sorry,' she told him. 'I'm really sorry. I know how much I've hurt you.'

He turned to her with the lost expression of an unhappy child. 'Do you?' he asked.

'Yes,' she said. 'I do. I really do. I understand.'

'What do you understand?'

She didn't answer. She didn't want to spell out her shame.

'What do you understand?' he said again. His voice wasn't angry. It was gentle.

'I understand . . .' she said, 'I understand that all your life, you've tried to please people and they've always rejected you, and now I've done it as well.'

He nodded slowly. 'That's it,' he said. 'That's exactly it. I've felt so hurt by you, Fleur.'

To her horror, he began to sob.

She ran a hand soothingly over his back. 'I'm so sorry,' she whispered. 'I want to spend Christmas with you in Norway. I really do.'

He sat up and cupped her face in his hands. 'Do you?'

'Yes, of course,' she told him, and her heart began to pound with the anxiety of how she could break this news to her mother. 'I'm so happy you arranged it. Will you . . . Will you be able to reprint the tickets?'

His face broke into a smile and he wrapped his arms around her. She leaned her face against his chest and breathed in his familiar scent. Everything was going to be okay.

He said, 'I know I should have thought more about it. I just got so excited. I'll come with you to talk to your mum,' he said. 'I'll help her understand. I'll say it's all my fault. I just was longing to whisk her daughter away for the holiday she's always dreamed of.'

'Thank you,' Fleur whispered. 'Thank you.'

But it wasn't like that when they travelled from Brighton to Dulwich to speak to Fleur's mum. It wasn't like that at all.

'My lovely Fleur!' her mother said, opening the door wide. She was always like that – loud, exuberant in her affection.

Fleur hugged her mother and then introduced her to Douglas. Douglas gave her a bunch of flowers, the way perfect boyfriends did when they were meeting their future in-laws.

Fleur's mother accepted them with a smile and thanks, then she led them both downstairs to the basement kitchen of Fleur's childhood. 'Is it too early for prosecco?' she asked.

'Never,' Douglas said.

They sat at the table and Fleur's mother poured the drinks and handed round bowls of crisps and a plate full of dates wrapped in bacon.

'These are delicious, Martha,' Douglas said.

Martha beamed. 'Thank you. Fleur says the same about you.'

'Mum!'

But Douglas just laughed. 'I'm glad about that,' he said. 'You can never be sure.'

Immediately, Fleur felt herself tense. Was he going to add anything else to that statement? Was he going to talk about how she'd gone out one night after work and he'd whipped himself into a frenzy, convinced she was out on 'one of those nights where women sit around and slag off their boyfriends'?

It wasn't meant to be like this, she knew that. But maybe these tense moments were the things she had to accept in order to have the highs. And the highs were so good. They really were.

And besides, everything was fine. Douglas and her mother were talking to each other like two old friends.

The afternoon went on. They ate lunch at 2.30. Fleur's mother had made her own pasta using the pasta maker Fleur had bought her last Christmas, and she'd cooked a sauce with tomatoes, chillies, olives, capers and anchovies. It was deliciously sharp and pungent.

Then Martha said, 'I've made a special dessert. It's a chocolate orange tart with Cointreau cream. I thought if it was any good, I could make it again for Christmas Eve.'

Fleur couldn't look at her.

Douglas reached for Fleur's hand, held it firmly in his and said, 'Actually, Martha. Fleur and I are going to Norway for Christmas. It's my present to her.'

Martha looked momentarily flustered, then she said, 'Oh. Okay. That's . . . Well, that's lovely.'

'Fleur was so worried you'd be upset.'

'Oh, no. Of course not. I'm not upset. I can go to my sister's, or she can come to me. It's fine. Fleur has always wanted to go to Lapland. It was a dream she and her dad had for years.'

'I know it was,' Douglas said. 'That's why I booked it.'

'Well, that's lovely,' Martha said again.

The tone of Douglas's voice changed suddenly. It had been light and joyful before, but now when he spoke it was low, with an undercurrent of something Fleur couldn't quite put her finger on, but which she didn't like. 'I knew you'd understand,' he said. 'Fleur is an adult now, isn't she? She needs to be free to choose. She's felt such an obligation to you since her father died, but I pointed out that you're an adult as well. Every adult is responsible for their own happiness. You'd never expect Fleur to make sacrifices.'

Fleur looked at her mother and tried to let her know, somehow, that this wasn't what she wanted, that these words from Douglas had nothing to do with her.

But her mother just smiled weakly. 'No,' she said, in a voice that wasn't hers. 'No. Of course not. I'd never ask Fleur to sacrifice anything for me.'

PART THREE

24

Emma

Emma was still awake when Maggie came back to the cabin some time after midnight. She'd been lying in bed, drinking wine and googling more about Meredith Slater. So far, she'd found out the following:

- Meredith Slater had gone missing nearly two years ago.
- She was married to a man named Kevin, who seemed to be someone important in a group of Jehovah's Witnesses.
- She'd been thrown out of the Witnesses. Her husband didn't mention why.
- Her father had just died and her mother was desperate to see her.

When Emma weighed all this up, she could accept that Clover wasn't exactly lying, or that she had at least been honest enough. She'd mentioned having been married, and when they were exposing themselves round the campfire this evening, she'd also spoken about disowning her parents, leaving the Witnesses, not supporting her mother.

She didn't seem to be hiding who she was. She just hadn't told them her real name.

Emma remembered there'd been a Jehovah's Witness boy at her primary school. He wasn't allowed to go to assembly or the Christmas church services. Emma had felt quite jealous of him at the time, but she knew more about the Witnesses now.

From one cult to another, she thought, and wondered if Clover herself was aware of the glaring link between growing up as a Witness and getting wild groups of women together to smash out their feelings.

Now, to Maggie, she said, 'I thought you'd been attacked by the beast.'

Maggie frowned. 'What beast?'

'The beast of Bodmin.'

'Oh, right.' Maggie laughed and climbed into her bed. 'No, I wasn't attacked. Although,' she paused dramatically, 'do you think that could be what we heard in the bushes?'

'No. What we heard in the bushes would have been a ghost.'

'Really?'

'Bound to be. That's what you're all doing, isn't it? Raking over the dead past. It's someone's past, coming back for them.'

'Like their conscience, you mean?'

'Yes,' Emma said. 'It was Clover's conscience, hiding in the undergrowth, ready to pounce if she didn't admit to all her shame.'

'I meant maybe her conscience imagined it there. She's got stuff to feel guilty about.' Quickly, she added, 'I mean, she hasn't. Of course she hasn't. That's not what we're here for, is it? We're not here to judge anyone. But that stuff she let slip about her parents, about disowning them and not being there when her father died, and not going back to support her mother. That's serious.'

'It requires a cold heart and some serious determination. Everything Clover does here is about her warmth and sensitivity, and yet she's turned her back on her family. It makes me think she might not be as warm and sensitive as she makes out.'

Mildly, Maggie said, 'You seem determined to believe this woman is a fake with some dubious ulterior motives.'

'I'm not,' Emma said. 'But look at this.'

She passed Maggie the driving licence she'd found on the ground by the cabins.

Maggie held it for a while and frowned. 'I don't understand,' she said.

'You do, though.'

'You mean Clover isn't really Clover?'

'She's definitely not,' Emma told her. 'And look at this.'

She passed Maggie her phone, open at the blog written by Meredith Slater's husband.

Maggie read for a while in silence. Emma watched as her frown turned to an expression of disbelief.

She put the phone down. 'I don't understand,' she said again.

'You do, though.'

'Are you saying that Clover is actually called Meredith Slater and Meredith Slater is a . . .' She stumbled over the words. '*A missing person?*'

'That's what it looks like.'

Maggie was silent as she took this in. Eventually, she said, 'What should we do?'

'I don't think we can do anything.'

'But shouldn't we . . . I don't know . . . go to the police or something?'

'I've checked. She's not formally registered as a missing person with the police.'

'But that's ridiculous!'

Emma shrugged. 'Not really. The police aren't going to do much about a twenty-two-year-old woman who decides to leave her husband. She clearly wasn't ill. It doesn't sound as though she was vulnerable. There are no kids involved. She's just a sane adult who walked away. They won't be sending out helicopters for that.'

'I suppose not,' Maggie said. Then she added, 'But her family are still looking for her. You don't think . . . You don't think they could have followed her here, do you?' She appeared to be warming to the drama.

'I have no idea. But I'd say this story explains exactly why she was so alarmed when she heard that rustling in the bushes earlier. She must spend her entire life worrying they're going to find her.'

Maggie looked afraid suddenly. 'It might have been them,' she said. 'It might have been her husband, watching, getting ready to pounce. They do that.'

'Who does that? Husbands? My husband has never done it.'

'Abductors.'

'No one's going to abduct Clover,' Emma said.

'How do you know?'

'Well, I suppose I don't know.'

'Exactly. He sounds weird enough in his blog. He seems obsessed to me.' She paused for a moment, then added, 'I do feel so sorry for her mum, though. And her father has just died and she still won't go and see her.'

'I know. It's sad.'

'Didn't she mention this when we were round the campfire this evening?'

'Yes.'

'So she knows exactly what she's doing.'

'Yes.'

Maggie paused for a while. Emma could almost see her trying to talk herself out of being carried along by the mystery and excitement of it all. 'It's not really any of our business. We don't know her story, and I suppose she must have her reasons for leaving and refusing to go back. That's the shame she was letting go of.'

'Yeah,' Emma said. 'By throwing her knickers on the fire.'

'Don't knock it till you've tried it.'

'I'm not knocking it.'

'You are. I can see it on your face.'

'No doctor or mental health professional is going to validate stripping naked and dancing round a fire as a way of releasing years of toxic shame.'

'Oh, but what do they know?'

'Is that a serious question?'

'Yes. Honestly, after my daughter died, I spent years in therapy and I can tell you now that none of it was as effective as watching my fat-lady knickers burn on the fire this evening.'

Emma laughed.

Maggie said, 'It must be weird, growing up as a Jehovah's Witness.'

'I know. And I don't know her full story. I just find it so hard to imagine properly abandoning your family like that, not unless they really are abusive.'

Emma had seen more than her fair share of children with terrible parents. Before doing her PhD and moving into higher education, she'd spent ten years teaching English in a secondary school and she'd had to deal with kids whose parents really hurt them, or didn't protect them, or neglected them, but all the kids ever did was defend and forgive. That same year, she was teaching *Love Through the Ages* to her sixth-form group, and they'd had a long discussion about unconditional love and what it meant. The students, being young and only understanding life through what they'd been told, parroted that old refrain, 'Parents have unconditional love for their children,' and Emma wanted to stop them and say, 'No. This isn't true. It's the other way round. The children I know have unconditional love for their parents. It never stops, no matter how awful the parents are.'

She couldn't say that, of course. These were the privileged kids. They wouldn't have had a clue what she was on about. But her own daughter was a prime example. She'd forgiven Emma for years of neglect.

Maggie said, 'That's true. Even my son hasn't abandoned me. Not fully. He still does his duty.' She sighed, and appeared lost for a moment.

Emma said nothing, just focussed on not fleeing. She often wished she wasn't like this and could face the visceral mess of people's feelings. She just couldn't. If an emotional scene came on television, she had to leave the room. Her kids always said it was because she was going to cry. It wasn't, though. (No one had ever seen her cry.) It was because she couldn't stand it. When *Frozen* was at peak popularity and that terrible 'Let it Go' was always playing everywhere she went, she wanted to rewrite the lyrics. *Keep it in* she thought. *Why will no one ever just keep it in?*

Maggie appeared to come back to the room. She said, 'I just saw Fleur over in the barn when I went over to fill my hot water bottle . . . Oh, damn. I forgot all about the hot water bottle . . . Anyway, she said she was doing a reverse meditation.'

'A what?'

'Well, she made it up. It might not stand up to scrutiny.'

'None of this would stand up to scrutiny, Maggie. None of it. Fleur takes it far too seriously.'

'You're probably right. But it was great, anyway. She said that instead of clearing her mind, she was going to fill it. She was going to fill it with all the memories of her abusive ex-boyfriend and then simply observe him and herself without emotion and then she felt she'd be able to let him go at last.'

'Did it work?'

'It's probably too early to tell. But I decided to try the same thing. I mean, I don't have an abusive ex-boyfriend, but I have . . .' She paused, then finished, 'I do have things I need to let go of. To forgive myself for. To realize I was human, and suffering, and I took it out on someone else.'

Emma nodded, and tried to stay present. There was something wide and confiding in Maggie's eyes and Emma was afraid of what she might reveal. *There's no blood,* she reminded herself. *Just a story.*

'Did it help?' she asked.

'I don't know yet. I hope it helped Fleur.' She glanced furtively around the cabin, as if expecting her to walk in, then lowered her voice and said, 'She said something during that shame release session that I think I've latched on to and become suspicious of.'

'Really? What?'

'She said she needed to work out if she wants to keep the thing he's left her with.'

'Well, it's probably not fifty thousand pounds, is it? It'll be either an STD or a baby. I can't imagine she'd want to keep an STD, so she's probably pregnant.'

'That's what I think as well.'

'And she thought the wisest way of dealing with this pregnancy wasn't to phone her GP, but to come and dance naked round a fire and howl at the fucking moon.' Emma found she was incapable of talking about howling at the moon without adding the word *fucking* to it.

'She probably wants to think about it.'

'Well, I'm sure the moon will shine its light and guide her to the right decision.'

'You're hard on her.'

'She irritates me.'

'But she's pregnant with the baby of a man who abused her.'

'She'll work it out.'

'But if she keeps it, he'll never be out of her life.'

'She needn't tell him.'

Maggie looked shocked. She probably wasn't as

accomplished at keeping things quiet as Emma. She said, 'She wouldn't be able to do that.'

'She would if she tried hard enough.'

Maggie appeared thoughtful for a moment, then she said, 'Can I ask you something, Emma?'

'If it's about my heart chakra, then no.'

'It's not about your heart chakra.'

'Then you can ask.'

'I was just wondering what it is that *really* brought you here. You don't seem very taken with it.'

'I'm not.'

'But you must have had some idea what it was all about.'

'Not really. Clover is very evasive in her marketing. I should have realized.'

'Yes, but even I knew it was going to be full of hippie crap.'

'I came because of my daughter. I needed a break.'

'You said that before.'

'That's because it's the reason I'm here. Every time you ask my reason for being here, it will be the same reason.'

Clearly, Maggie didn't believe her. She said, 'But we're all here for something more complicated than needing a break, aren't we? Fleur's here because of an abusive relationship and maybe being pregnant, I'm here because of my husband's death. Clover's here because, well, God knows what horrors lurk in her past, but no one is this mature at twenty-two unless they've lived a terrible life. So don't tell me you're here for a break. You could have gone to the beach. You must have some secret trauma that brought you.'

Emma drew in her breath. 'This sounds very much like a question about my heart chakra, Maggie.'

Maggie smiled. 'If this were group therapy, we'd all have to tell our stories.'

'But it's not, so we don't.' She saw the expression on Maggie's face and added, 'Look, I'm less open to all this than the rest of you. It's just the way I am. I don't have any desire to strip naked and talk about the most shameful moments of my life with people I've only just met. Or anyone else, for that matter.'

Maggie kept on pushing. 'You mentioned adultery earlier.'

'Yeah. That was the wine speaking. I shouldn't have said anything. Anyway, it's over now, and no one knows about it.'

Maggie's eyebrows shot up in surprise. 'Really?'

'Really.'

Emma felt the old pricking sensation in her eyes, but she was well trained at reining back the tears. Her eye muscles were the fittest part of her whole body.

Maggie backed off. 'I thought today that maybe I'd like to spend the rest of my life coming on retreats, but now I'm not sure. It's quite a lot of work, isn't it? All that dancing and smashing things up, and so much thinking about who you were and who you want to become. It's like school.'

'Did you write down your intention this morning? About the new person you want to become?'

'I did, yes. I said I wanted to become someone without a terrible weight on her shoulders.'

'That's a good one.'

'What did you say?'

'Nothing. Like I said at breakfast, I'm beyond self-improvement now. If the world doesn't like me, it can fuck off.'

'Maybe you don't actually need to be here, Emma. Maybe that's why you're so resistant to it. You're already fairly bold and uncompromising.'

Emma tried to not feel irritated with her. She didn't know what she was talking about and that wasn't her fault. 'Maybe,' she said. 'I'm tired. Shall I turn the light out?'

Maggie nodded. 'Goodnight.'

They slipped into a welcome silence and Emma closed her eyes. He'd been gone for over a year now and there were still times when the pain of missing him was excruciating. That was the trouble when love ended when it had only just taken off. A few more years together and perhaps she'd have been longing to see the back of him. But the way this happened had been cruel, ripping the joy out of her world when everything had so much potential. It was too easy to torture herself with the life that was waiting for them, the one they could have lived if it hadn't been for that passionate, misguided woman.

25

Fleur

After Maggie had left, Fleur blew out the candles and walked slowly back through the darkness to her cabin. She couldn't help casting anxious glances towards the trees and hedgerows that framed the grounds of the retreat centre, wondering who could be lurking there, waiting to reach out and put a stop to all this.

She understood enough about Douglas to know he wasn't going to stay away forever. He'd be back one day to hoover up what was left of her. She needed to stay strong. It was what she'd come here for – to regain her power and make a decision.

It couldn't have been him in the bushes. There was no way. It wasn't his style to loiter, criminal-like. Douglas was more subtle than that. He'd never do anything anyone could prosecute him for, or anything anyone could actually witness.

Back in the cabin, she switched on her lantern and got into bed. She rested her hands on her middle. There were no outward signs of the early life she was carrying. Since taking the test and having the pregnancy confirmed by her doctor, she'd been sick a few times but nothing more than that. She couldn't believe she was in this mess. It was ridiculous. *She* was ridiculous.

She hadn't had a chance to tell Clover about it. Perhaps she wouldn't need to. Perhaps she could make a decision without anyone else's input.

Douglas wasn't interested. She'd been to his flat to see him just after she found out. 'I'm pregnant,' she said. 'It's yours.'

His response, as usual, was pond-calm. 'What are you going to do?'

'I don't know. I thought you might have a suggestion.'

He shook his head. 'No, Fleur. No. You know I'd like to have a family one day, but it's not something I can do like this, not when I've been tricked into it.'

'I haven't tricked you!'

His voice was beautifully gentle. 'Maybe not deliberately. But subconsciously. You're still grieving for your father and the family you used to have. It's natural that you would want to start again and you feel that time is slipping away from you. Maybe you understand now what it was you let go of. How good we were together. How exceptional.'

'That's not it,' she protested. Good God, when would he ever stop? She couldn't stand him when he was like this. It made her wonder what she'd ever seen him, although she knew, of course. She knew exactly what she'd seen him. She'd been bonded to him – ferociously, foolishly – by her desperation for him to always be the man she loved. If he could only be that man, instead of slipping into someone else, someone she could hardly recognize, they'd have had the most amazing life together. Even after they'd separated, she couldn't help wishing, couldn't help hoping that he'd come back, forever changed, and they could walk into that life that was waiting for them.

That was why she'd done it. It was why she'd slept with him that day, three months after they'd split up, when he came over to pick up some things. 'I've been feeling awful about what I did to you, Fleur,' he told her. 'Truly awful. I've been seeing a therapist. I've told him everything. I'm going to behavioural change classes. I'm going to change this time. I really am. It won't be easy, but I'll change.'

She'd fallen for it.

Now he was saying, 'You thought if you could persuade me to sleep with you, you'd fall pregnant and you'd have a powerful hold over me then. A way to get me back.'

She felt like banging her head against the wall.

'But I'm afraid it's too late, Fleur. If I'm going to have a child with someone, it needs to be with someone I can trust. I did love you. I do still love you. If I could trust you, I'd want nothing more than to be with you. You know you're the only woman I've ever loved. But I can't. I can't trust you. Just look what you've done.' He fixed his gaze on her middle and shook his head in contempt.

'So . . . It's up to me what I do? Is that what you're saying?'

'Yes. You can go ahead and have the baby if you want to, but I don't want you to think of it as mine. I won't be thinking of it as mine. It's your child. You made this decision.'

There was no point arguing. He spoke as if he really believed what he was saying, even though he couldn't because no one – no one in the world – could possibly think this was the truth.

'Okay,' she said, and she left and went home.

And now, two weeks later, here she was, still trying to make a decision.

She was thirty-three years old. Of course, she knew women went on having babies into their forties these days, but Fleur was through with men. She didn't want to go anywhere near another one in her life. This felt like her only chance to have a child and she wasn't sure she could give it up.

But what if it grew up to be like Douglas? It was bound to inherit some of his traits, even if she did everything she could to nurture them out. Also, she'd seen what happened to her friends with babies. They were all exhausted, and that was with a partner beside them. She remembered one of her mates saying, 'I know I ought to bollock her for that, but honestly, I am so tired. I haven't got the strength. I'm just going to pretend I didn't see it.' Would Fleur, as a single mother, really have the energy to cultivate a decent human out of Douglas's genes?

Also, if she had this baby, she would never be rid of him. Oh, sure, he said he wanted nothing to do with it but, like everything Douglas said, it meant nothing. Eventually, one day when he was bored or when some other woman had left him and he felt injured, he'd remember he had a child in the world and decide to lay claim to it. She could hear him now. *I'm their dad. It's my right.* Just thinking about the endless possibilities for drama and disaster made her head spin.

But she wanted a family. And now she had one, growing

inside her. She wasn't sure she had it in her to take a couple of pills and bleed it out, coldly, deliberately, painfully, as if having a baby at the age of thirty-three was the worst thing she could ever imagine happening to her.

She felt no closer to making a decision than she had done two weeks ago. She'd wanted to talk to Clover about it, but now she wasn't so sure. She was left with a strange, uncomfortable feeling about the way she'd fobbed them all off earlier with her talk of foxes. It was silly, really. Of course she'd said that. She'd wanted to get on with the evening and didn't need everyone over-reacting to some rustling in the undergrowth. It was just that this retreat was all about trust and honesty and . . .

Fleur shook it away. She was being ridiculous. And really, she had more important things on her mind than why Clover had let slip a lie about a fox.

26

Emma

Emma had forked out for some Healing Touch therapy. It was one of the optional extras Clover offered. 'I'm trained in it,' she'd said yesterday. 'I took a course in Therapeutic Touch Massage a year ago and I combine it with other elements as well. The session is two hours. It includes massage, meditation and spiritual healing.'

Emma could get on board with massage. She could also get on board with meditation. She could see the worth of rooting herself in the present moment instead of always returning to the regrettable past or venturing to the unknowable future.

Also, she needed to be nicer to Clover. Maggie was right. She didn't know Clover's story, or why she'd gone missing.

'Great,' she said. 'Book me in.'

'It will have to be first thing. Before our morning practice. Say, six?'

'Okay,' Emma agreed. The prospect of rising at six for a massage didn't strike her as too awful. She'd gone back to her cabin and googled 'Healing Touch therapy' to see if it existed as a recognized concept. It did. Google told her it was a form of energy healing and there was 'limited research supporting its effectiveness'.

Never mind, Emma thought. She wasn't trying to cure a disease. She just wanted to relax.

Just after six in the morning, she found herself lying on her back on a massage table that Clover had set up in the meditation space. There was a weighted mask over her eyes, towels over her body, and gentle music playing. Clover stood behind her, her hands resting lightly on Emma's chest. She'd made herself a stranger now – distant, radiant and spiritual.

'I want you to take a moment to recall your intention,' she said. Her voice was low and resonant. Emma thought she sounded oddly like a priest.

'Take some deep, clear breaths,' she said, and then she hovered a warm cloth over Emma's face and Emma breathed the scent of lavender.

'Now,' she continued, cupping her hands around Emma's head and holding them there, 'I want you to close your eyes and imagine your crown chakra slowly opening, like the leaves of a lotus flower. As that flower opens, let the healing white light stream in. Let it fill your mind and wash through your body . . .'

Emma couldn't quite manage that. She laughed.

Clover ignored her and reported that she was guiding the light down her spine, through her arms, her belly, and all the way down her legs to her toes. 'And now,' she said, still in that resonant, religious voice, 'as I begin the therapeutic massage of your crown chakra, know that I am with you as you begin your journey. Let your mind go where it will, for it will take you to that part of you that needs most healing . . .'

It was a kind of bliss to lie there on the bed as this

woman cupped Emma's head in her hands and ran her fingers slowly over her scalp, and be told it was acceptable to think of nothing but her last day with Oliver, when they'd woken up early in their Exeter hotel room and decided to drive out to Dartmoor to go hiking. Emma had actually been on research leave at the time, with no reason to travel away from home to the university. She hadn't told her family that. It would have meant she'd have to stop seeing Oliver. Another deception. Another thing she ought to feel guilty about, but didn't. Emma always knew the rest of the world would judge this love as wrong. She didn't. She'd never known anything that felt more right.

They stopped off at the Tesco Express beside the hotel and bought egg sandwiches and a packet of pork pies for a picnic lunch. When they'd first started seeing each other, they used to eat high-class foodstuffs from delicatessens – quail's eggs and celery salt; tiger prawns; expensive water from mountain streams. All of that slowly disappeared. The food had been a luxury to make their time together special, in case they found each other boring and longed to go home. Emma used to imagine Oliver wracked with guilt and wishing himself away from her, so she would simply push a tiger prawn into his mouth and make him enjoy the moment. *He wouldn't be having this at home. At home, he'd be eating a ready-made family lasagne, at best.*

Now, some cheap packaged sandwiches from Tesco and a bottle of Diet Coke did the job. All that mattered was that they were together, snatching the moments they could out of their lives. She'd stopped calling her life with Ben and the children her real life. It made her time with Oliver sound like a fantasy.

It was late March, and they drove out to Dunsford Wood, where hundreds of wild daffodils were blooming beneath the oak trees and the sound of a distant stream reached their ears. Oliver took her hand. They walked for miles, out through the wood and up into the hills and then far onto the barren moorland beyond.

Sometimes, they talked. They talked about nothing much, and then they talked about their families.

'How are the girls?' she asked him.

His eyes lit up, the way they always did when he spoke of his daughters. 'They're great,' he said. 'You know Maisie's got the lead in the school play?'

'Clara mentioned it,' Emma said. 'Good for her.'

'How are yours?'

'I think they're fine. Clara's working so hard. She's always in her room. School have said they expect her to do well.'

Oliver grinned. 'So her mother's illicit affair with the man down the road hasn't affected her?'

'It doesn't seem to have done. Not yet.'

He squeezed her hand. Briefly, she leaned her head against his shoulder.

It had been so easy, that day. Nothing extraordinary happened. They just walked, often in the comfortable silence of two people who knew each other well and had no need to speak. It was always easy, being with Oliver, and Emma liked the person she became when she was with him – calm, easy, good-humoured. She could hardly stand the woman she was with Ben. With Ben, she was quiet, sullen, tetchy, always on edge. It didn't feel like her. When they saw friends, Emma muted herself. She couldn't speak up or have the fun she longed for because Ben was too easily embarrassed.

Sometimes, when she opened her mouth, she could see his eyes close in fear of what she might be about to say. She wasn't even that outrageous, not compared to many people.

They ate their picnic beside the river. Emma scanned the area for a secluded space where they could enjoy a quick outdoor shag before they had to be parted for a week. She could see Oliver doing the same. But it was too much of a risk. There were too many people enjoying the spring sunshine. That was the trouble with Dartmoor.

'We should go to Dungeness,' she said. 'It's the worst place in the world. No one ever goes there. We could have wild sex in the marshes.'

'I'd love that,' he said, and kissed her.

Later, they drove home together as far as Maidenhead, and from there Emma caught a train to Windsor, the town where they both lived with their families and pretended to scarcely know each other.

It was after six o'clock when she walked in. No one greeted her. This wasn't unusual. Jake was sixteen by then, and usually either in his room or out at a friend's house. Clara often stayed late at school for drama or music clubs. They didn't need her, not in the way they used to. She felt it as a loss in some ways, and a liberation in others. Where her head had once been filled with thinking of them and what they needed, it was now full – perhaps too full – of Oliver and when they could next be together.

She hung her coat over the back of a chair in the kitchen and poured herself a glass of wine from the fridge, which she carried through to the living room. Ben was in there, sunk into an armchair, reading a novel. He was always reading. She used to find it attractive.

'Hi,' she said.

He looked up. 'We should talk.'

'Are you sure? We haven't done that for at least ten years. It could be risky.'

Oh, God. Why did she have to be like this? But also, why did he have to be like this? Whatever happened to pleasantries? Why did he just launch straight into that daunting statement, *We should talk*?

'Why don't you sit down?' he said.

She took a seat in the armchair opposite him. He looked serious and it made her afraid. 'What is it?' she asked.

Oddly, she didn't dread the thought that he'd somehow found out about her relationship with Oliver. In many ways it would make life easier if he did know. She didn't like this half-life she lived with Ben, going through the motions of marriage while her heart and mind were elsewhere.

He put his book down. 'I had a phone call from Clara's head of year today.'

Emma's mind started spinning. Clara? Clara had never been a problem before. Clara was well behaved, hard-working, resilient. She got on with things. She was fine.

'Is it something bad?'

'One of her friends – I think it was Lucy – went to talk to her form tutor. She's been worried because Clara has been . . .' He paused and cleared his throat, as if he were struggling to get the words out. 'She's been self-harming.'

'*What*?'

'Yes. They don't know how serious it is. Lucy said she saw Clara's arms when they were getting changed for PE. She was alarmed and asked Clara about it. Clara denied it at first, then confessed. Poor Lucy didn't know what to do.'

'She did the right thing, telling someone,' Emma murmured.

'The school want her to speak to the counsellor, to try and sort it out.'

'Of course. Yes. She needs to.'

Emma was aware that the words she spoke bore no relation to what was happening in her head. Her words were calm and short. In her head, everything was wild.

How had she not realized this was happening? (She knew how.)

Why was her daughter so desperately unhappy?

Was this school stress?

Could it be shame?

Why would she be feeling shame?

Wasn't self-harm something children who'd been abused did?

Clara had never been abused.

Had she?

Of course she hadn't.

Emma would know.

Would she know?

How would she know?

Clara would have told her. Clara always told her if something was wrong.

But why didn't Emma know this had been going on?

She should have known. *She should have known.*

She said, 'Have you spoken to her?'

Ben shook his head. 'No. I thought it was best to take some time and think about it for a while rather than rushing in.'

The way they handled this was going to matter. It could mean the difference between making Clara well and making her worse.

'I think you're right,' she said. Then she added, 'I can't believe we didn't know this. I can't believe we didn't realize something was wrong.'

Ben said nothing. She wondered if he was silently thinking it was her fault.

Her mind slipped away from her again.

She hadn't known something was wrong because she'd been too busy with Oliver. That was a fact, and there was nothing she could do to change it. For over three years now, she'd only been half-present in this life. She showed up to it in the mornings, she saw the children off to school, she made sure they were fed and clothed, but she was distracted. All the time, she was distracted. She was either thinking blissfully of Oliver, or trying to work out if they could somehow fit another couple of hours together into their week, or counting how long it would be until they could live together, get married, launch themselves into life as a couple.

She hadn't given Clara the time she needed. She'd always known Clara was reserved and private. She wasn't the sort of teenager who would ever post about her problems on social media. She recoiled at that sort of thing. 'Oh, my God! Why would anyone tell the world about this?' she'd said once, when some celebrity had talked about their divorce on Instagram.

'Maybe she finds it helpful to read all the supportive comments from her fans,' Emma said, despite the fact that she agreed with Clara. Why would anyone do that?

'Yeah, but still . . .'

Emma knew Clara would keep stress and heartache to herself and that she'd have to look out for them. She used to. When she picked her up from primary school, Emma would study her face in the line as they waited for the teacher to dismiss her, and she'd be able to tell what sort of day she'd had. At secondary school, she'd get the bus home but Emma still managed the same trick. They used the glass French doors most of the time, rather than the front door, and so Emma could watch from the kitchen as Clara walked up the path and she'd look at her expression and have some idea of what might be going on in her head. She couldn't remember now when she'd stopped doing this, or why, but she had stopped and somehow, she'd lost her connection with her daughter.

I expected too much of her, she thought now. *I expected her to be an adult just because she dresses like one and because it suited me.*

Opposite her, Ben continued with his silence.

Clover smoothed a towel over Emma's back and spoke in a gentle voice. 'That's the end of your treatment, Emma. Just continue to lie here for as long as you need. There's a glass of water on the table beside you.'

Emma lay with her eyes still closed and was aware of Clover pulling back the curtain and leaving. She let herself come slowly back to the room, and hoped the morning ahead of her wouldn't demand too much. All she wanted was to go down to the rainforest again, and just lie among the trees, doing absolutely nothing except experiencing peace.

She felt oddly like crying.

27

Maggie

They met in the meditation space before breakfast and Clover performed a cacao ceremony. They all sat on their sheepskins while Clover warmed a pan of water over a small camping stove. She added small discs of cacao and whisked everything slowly with a wooden frother. Apparently, the wooden frother was an integral part of the process. Maggie supposed a blender would be considered too worldly. A wooden whisk connected them more deeply to their ancient ancestors.

Clover whisked that cacao for even longer than Maggie would have whisked egg whites for a meringue. She appeared lost in a meditative state. Maggie looked at Emma and grinned. Emma didn't grin back. She'd just had her Healing Touch massage and looked as though she was about to cry. This seemed at odds with the idea of healing therapy, but Emma was a contrary woman.

Yesterday, Fleur had told Maggie all about the magical properties of cacao. It looked just like hot chocolate, but it had a Mayan connection and was like a mild, natural drug that induced feelings of warmth and high-level contentment that could cross a boundary into bliss. Maggie was entirely up for this experience.

When she finally finished the whisking, Clover poured the cacao into four stone, handleless mugs and passed one to each woman. She spoke in her nurturing voice. 'Cup your hands around these mugs and feel the warmth of this drink. We are now going to move round our sacred circle and state what we are grateful for and what our intention is for this retreat. If it is too private, of course you don't have to say it out loud. But you formed your intention yesterday and we are now going to reinforce it by drinking this ceremonial cacao.'

She looked round at the group. Fleur, as usual, was hanging on her every word and taking it all very seriously. Emma was back to looking suspicious. Her moment of sadness seemed to have passed.

Clover continued. 'I'll begin,' she said. She put her mug of cacao on the floor, then arranged herself into the meditation position with her legs crossed, her back straight and her hands resting in her lap. She closed her eyes and said, 'I thank the Spirit of Cacao and the goddess of the feminine for bringing these wonderful women into my life for this most special weekend, even the two of them who are laughing at me as I say this.'

Maggie shot another glance at Emma. They arranged their faces into expressions of solemnity.

'I restate my intention to continue my journey to liberation, empowerment and enduring joy and to share the gifts of liberation, empowerment and joy with more and more women.'

She opened her eyes, smiled, and sipped her cacao. 'Drink this with intention,' she told the group, then nodded at Fleur.

Fleur said, 'I, too, am grateful for this incredible weekend with these sisters. I am grateful for their warmth, their strength, their wisdom and humour. I restate my intention to let go of my past. It is no longer serving me and I can't carry it with me into my future.'

Fleur sipped her cacao and Clover nodded at Emma.

Emma said, 'I'm grateful for the food, but I would mostly just like the chance to have a massive shit.'

Maggie couldn't help herself. She laughed out loud. 'Me too,' she said.

Clover made the face of an indulgent mother. 'I think we all feel that way. Now, Maggie.'

Maggie said, 'Like everyone else, I am grateful for this weekend. I'd had no idea what to expect, but I'm finding it so valuable. I would like to restate my intention to build my relationship with my son and the grandchild who will be born soon.'

'Thank you, everyone. I now invite you to drop into silence and concentrate on your intention while we drink our cacao.'

Maggie thought about Richard and took the first sip of her cacao. It had a savoury, earthy taste. She was about to remark on it, then remembered they were being silent now. This was a time for reflection, while they waited for the bliss-inducing effects of the cacao to kick in.

She looked around at the others. They all seemed to be obeying Clover's order to concentrate on their intention. She tried to focus on hers.

If you could turn back time, she'd once asked herself, *how far would you go?*

Would she go back to the day Annie died? The night

before? Perhaps she'd go back to that afternoon of the fight, when she'd had to pick Richard up from school, but maybe she'd go further than that. Maybe she'd rewind her life to the years she'd been trying to conceive and she'd just stop. Stop wanting a second baby. Be happy with what she had. Have her tubes tied.

But then there would have been no Annie. And an Annie that she'd had for a short time was somehow better than no Annie at all. Maggie had usually been able to see it that way.

And anyway, it was all just a destructive waste of energy to think like this. She'd always known that. But God, the desire to turn back time was so strong, so overpowering, and so much like banging her head against a wall . . .

Maggie turned her attention back to the present. She hadn't practised her French since she'd been here. She'd have lost her 653-day streak on Duolingo. It mattered less than she thought it would. All this time, she'd been quietly obsessed with it, quickly doing a three-minute lesson late at night, just so she wouldn't lose her streak. Now she didn't care. The French she'd learnt wasn't going to leave her head just because the app said she hadn't practised. She needed to break away from these chains. They were ridiculous. Everything was ridiculous. She had to stop falling for these tricks.

She looked round the small circle of women, each one sipping her cacao and reflecting on her intention, which everyone knew was related to her life's biggest trauma. They'd all hinted at it, or skated round the edges of it, but no one had talked about it in detail. Fleur had lived with an abuser, Clover had walked away from a marriage, Emma had done *something*, although Maggie had no idea exactly what . . . These women were in pain, but they were also in recovery, here to rebuild their strength in the company of other women, to claim their power and stand in it.

Clover put down her mug. 'Has everybody finished their cacao?' she asked.

Everyone nodded.

Clover smiled at them again. 'After breakfast, we will move into our first practice. Yesterday was all about letting go. Today is about welcoming the women we want to become, and I would like you all to change into the outfits that represent your dark feminine essence. Our work today is on moving from fear and pain into joy and power. I want us to take a minute now to close our eyes and connect with our internal feminine wisdom. Feel the strength of our female ancestors rooted in our bodies. We are not weak. We are not submissive. We will not be ruled or overwhelmed by others. Attend to the area of your belly and feel inside you the fierceness of the female.'

Maggie focussed on her belly. She was aware of a fiery sensation beginning to swell. She sat still and let it spread through her body.

'Now stand,' Clover said.

Everybody stood.

Clover's voice was loud and strong, like a call to arms. 'We are not here to be sweet! We are not here to be silent! We are not here to obey! We are here to be strong! We are here to be powerful! We are here to claim our place on the earth and take up space!'

Fleur and Maggie cheered.

'You're too quiet! We are not here to cheer! We're here

to roar! I want us all to take a deep, powerful breath and *roar*. Let me hear you roar!'

Maggie heard everyone around her suck in their breath and hold it for a moment. Then they leaned into the circle and roared.

She felt the earth shift on its axis.

28

Fleur

'Today, we are nourishing the solar plexus with yellow foods,' Harriet told them at breakfast. 'The solar plexus is the chakra of your emotions and when we nourish the solar plexus, we help maintain our emotional health. You'll see you each have a smoothie with pineapple, papaya, satsuma juice and turmeric, as well as warm banana bread with caramelized yellow pears, and buckwheat porridge with mango compote. I invite you all to eat and be well.'

Everyone helped themselves to the food. Fleur sat down at the table opposite Emma. It was the better option than taking the seat beside her. 'Morning,' she said, because it wouldn't do to be rude, although she would have liked to be.

Emma barely looked up from her porridge. 'Morning,' she said.

Fleur had woken up feeling nauseous again. She'd thought she was over it when she crossed the eight-week mark. (Thirteen weeks already! If she didn't make a decision soon, it would be taken out of her hands.) She ate cautiously, afraid of drawing attention to her condition if she had to leave the table suddenly to throw up.

Clover joined them and sat down next to Fleur. 'Good

morning, my queens,' she said, smiling warmly. 'Are we all well rested and ready for today's practices?'

Maggie said, 'I think so.'

Clover looked delighted with the anticipation. 'When we've all finished our breakfast, I'll invite you to go back to your cabins, change into your wonderful outfits and come back to the meditation space, so we can begin our own transformations and witness and honour the transformations of our sisters.'

It sounded incredible. Fleur wanted to be transformed, more than anything else in the world. She wanted to be transformed from someone who still thought with longing about a cruel man to someone who could walk away from him, knowing she would never go back. She wanted to be transformed from someone too weak to make a decision to someone bold and strong and powerful. She wanted to be so many things that she wasn't, and she knew Clover was the person to help her.

On the other side of the table, Maggie was saying, 'I'm worried about my outfit. I spent ages fretting over it before I came here. I asked my husband's advice, but he wasn't interested.'

Emma looked at her quizzically. 'I thought your husband was dead.'

'Oh, he is,' Maggie said.

'But you still speak to him,' Fleur said sympathetically. 'I get that.'

'Well,' Maggie began, 'I think he came back six months after he died.'

And she told them all a story about a cat that had come to live with her, how she'd fed it her husband's favourite food and it knew its way round the house. 'I'm not lying,' she insisted, although she spoke with an impish smile. 'There was one day when I was watching something on TV – I can't remember what, a history programme, probably – and he sat on the remote control and flicked through all the channels until he came to Sky Sports. That was *exactly* what Bill used to do. It drove me mad, but I can tell you now that behaviour that feels intolerable in a husband is surprisingly acceptable in a cat. I think that's why he came back as a cat. He wanted me to love him. I never loved him properly when he was alive. I was too busy being irritated by him. Now I look after him. I'm making up for being horrible when he was a man.'

By the time she'd finished, everyone was wiping away tears of laughter. Emma said, 'What's he doing now you've come away?'

Maggie said, 'I've left the radio on for him. It's tuned to Five Live – you know, the sports station. God, it's boring. I imagine he'll just be lying in the kitchen, listening to the football and waiting for me to come home.'

'Have you left him enough food?'

Maggie shook her head. 'No way. If I leave him all the food he needs for a weekend, he'll guzzle it in one go. He always loved his food, even when he was a man. He put on weight in his last years and he was never slim to begin with. I've asked my neighbour to go round and give him his meals one by one.'

'Very wise,' Emma said.

Fleur said, 'I hope my ex never comes back, not in any form.'

She imagined Douglas as a vicious dog. He wouldn't be a

rottweiler or a pit bull, though. He'd be something beautiful, like a golden retriever or a red setter. Everyone would love him at first, and then he'd show his savage side, but only at home, only in private. He'd start softly – chewing shoes, shredding cushions, gnawing furniture – and then one day he'd launch an attack, pushing his owner to the floor and biting chunks out of their flesh.

The thought made her shudder.

Clover noticed. She reached out and placed her hand on Fleur's arm. 'He won't,' she said. 'He's gone.'

Fleur smiled gratefully. He was gone, but she was thirteen weeks pregnant with his child.

Emma, as if deliberately changing the subject, looked up suddenly and said, 'What's the solar plexus?'

'It's the area in our upper abdomen and it's the chakra that governs our ability to be confident and assertive,' Clover told her. 'It enables us to make decisions from a place of inner wisdom. When we nourish and nurture our solar plexus, we build a strong sense of who we are and our own power. It's the key to becoming a bold, wild woman.' She smiled, as if hopeful that Emma would understand now.

Emma, of course, didn't understand. Or rather, Fleur suspected, she understood perfectly and preferred to simply pretend she didn't. 'Oh, right,' she said. 'My life now makes so much more sense. If I eat yellow foods, I'll become powerful.'

Clover ignored Emma's sarcasm and nodded kindly. 'That's exactly right,' she said. 'You'll find yourself emboldened and more confident, able to stand your own ground.'

'What about flying?'

'Sorry?'

'Will I be able to fly as well?' She spoke so seriously, Fleur wanted to slap her.

Clover did a heroic job of keeping her voice level. Fleur had no idea how she managed it. 'You can always try, Emma,' she said.

'Great. As soon as I've finished this yellow breakfast, I'm going to go out there and find something high I can hurl myself off.'

Clover reached out and touched her arm, 'Please don't do that.'

Emma shrugged.

Clover said, 'How are you feeling after your Healing Touch therapy?'

Fleur was surprised Emma had even tried it.

Emma said, 'Fine.' There was always such a brittle edge to her voice when she said that word.

'These things can be very powerful,' Clover explained. 'Even just sipping cacao can be a strong spiritual experience, but when you combine it with a Healing Touch therapy, it can be even more potent. Don't be afraid if powerful feelings rise to the surface.'

Emma smiled sweetly and looked Clover in the eye. 'I've been meaning to tell you . . . I found your driving licence yesterday. You must have dropped it over by the cabins.'

Fleur could see the colour draining from Clover's face and began to wonder what on earth was going on between these women.

Before Clover could speak, Emma went on, 'I've decided not to take part in this morning's session, so I'll bring it to you at lunchtime.'

Clover cleared her throat. 'Thank you,' she said. 'And

I'm sorry you won't be joining us this morning.' She pushed her chair back and walked away, leaving her breakfast almost untouched on the table.

The atmosphere in the room had soured. For a while, no one spoke, then Maggie said, 'Emma, that was a bit much. I think you've really upset her.'

Emma shrugged. 'I just told her I'd found her driving licence.'

'And you knew *exactly* what you were doing.'

Fleur had no idea what they were talking about. 'I don't understand,' she said. 'Why has that upset Clover?'

Maggie shook her head. 'Never mind.'

Fleur looked from one to the other. 'What's happening?'

Emma leaned back in her chair. 'Clover isn't who she says she is. I found her driving licence and her real name is Meredith Slater. I googled her and found she's a missing person. We don't know who she really is, but she's definitely not Clover.'

Fleur tried to let this sink in, but couldn't. 'Of course she's Clover.'

'She isn't.'

'Well, okay. She might have changed her name, but she's not pretending to be something she isn't. She's genuine in what she does.'

'Maybe,' Emma said.

'Of course she is. I can't believe you just threw that at her, Emma. You don't know her story, or why she's "missing". It could be trauma or abuse or anything at all that you have no idea about . . .'

'I agree,' Maggie said mildly. 'We should at least have

waited until we had concrete evidence that she's a serial killer before confronting her with it. Now she might think she has no option but to murder you, Emma. There's no way she'll be saving you when you decide to hurl yourself off a tall building and see if you can fly on nothing but the magic of yellow foods. You'll be six feet under before you get another chance to howl at the moon.'

Emma laughed, but Fleur was speechless at such open cruelty. She said, 'I can't believe you two.'

'I'm just trying to lighten the mood,' Maggie said. 'No one thinks Clover is bad. She's just not being honest, which is a shame, seeing as that's what she wants all of us to be.'

'She'll have her reasons,' Fleur said staunchly. 'And none of them will be bad.'

'You're very loyal to her,' Emma said.

'I believe in her.'

'Well, that's obvious.'

'I don't know what your issue is, Emma, but you will be the one missing out if you don't do this properly.'

'Do this properly? You mean come on a retreat for rebellious women and then buy into all the bullshit and do everything I'm told? Can you not see that there's nothing rebellious about it? It's just one woman selling her batshit ideas to us and expecting us to lap them up.'

Fleur heaved a deep sigh. She knew Emma's type. It was a type not worth arguing with. Her opinions were fixed and there would be no changing them. She needed to let go of this, to move on and stop wasting energy on this toxic woman.

'I'm going to find Clover,' she said. 'See you later, Maggie. Enjoy your morning off, Emma.'

She left the barn, and found that she was shaking with anger.

29

Emma

Emma couldn't understand this at all. She'd gone for the dubious-sounding but intriguing Healing Touch therapy and followed it up by drinking something that was really just hot chocolate with a Spanish name, and now she could hardly hold back her tears. It was like a return to the earliest days after Oliver, when she'd felt like a gaping wound, when her heart was always racing and she thought she was dying, but somehow she'd still managed to eat breakfast with her family and apologize for the milk being off.

She hadn't signed up for this when she booked the massage. She'd wanted to simply lie back and be soothed.

Afterwards, as they all tucked into their emotionally nourishing buckwheat porridge, she'd been acutely aware of Clover watching her, the way she imagined a woman would be watching her husband if she'd just laced his coffee with poison. Emma could feel movement inside her, the creeping sensation of something about to erupt, but she refused to give in. Clover wanted this, she thought. She was longing to see Emma clutch at her chest and fling herself over the breakfast table like a Victorian madwoman.

Emma, like everyone else, laughed hard at Maggie's story of her cat-husband. She hid it so well – the fact that she was close to madness. She knew, though, that there was no way she could face another awakening exercise. All she could do now was rest.

She was furious with Clover for making her feel this way again.

As she walked towards her cabin, she heard her name being called and turned round. Clover. Of course. She had to fight the urge to hide behind a tree.

'Emma,' Clover said. 'I wanted to speak to you, to check that you're okay.'

'I'm fine,' Emma said.

Her most powerful feeling at the moment was a desire to tell this woman – this child – to fuck off.

'I'm really sorry you won't be joining us this morning. Is there anything I can do to help you?'

God, why was she being so nice when Emma had just been a complete, passive-aggressive bitch? 'I don't think so. Thank you.'

'Okay, but if there is anything, please let me know. The work we do here is emotional, and I'm here to support you if it gets overwhelming.'

'I'm fine,' Emma told her again, then she turned and walked away before Clover could see the tears in her eyes.

When? She asked herself. *When will I ever recover from this?*

PART FOUR

30

Meredith

Meredith was born eight weeks prematurely. Her parents told her the story of how she'd had severe anaemia as a newborn. 'She's poorly,' the doctor said gravely. 'There is a possibility she could require a blood transfusion.'

Her parents refused. To accept the blood of another was against the will of Jehovah. Life was a gift from God, and blood was the force of this gift. Only God had the power to give life. It was sacred; not something for His people to offer or receive. Once blood had been shed, it could only be used for the atonement of sin, and it was only the blood of Jesus that could redeem a creature and save its life. All Witnesses must abstain from receiving the blood of another.

Her father told Meredith this, over and over again, throughout her childhood and beyond. Her mother sometimes joined in, although most of the time, Meredith slowly realized, she simply nodded her silent support.

The doctor, who was no-nonsense in his attitude towards the follies of the over-devout, took her parents to court. The judge ruled that the welfare of the child was paramount and agreed that her parents' wishes should be overridden. Otherwise, Meredith would die, and where was the sense in that? Even at five years old, when her father first told the terrible story of her birth, Meredith could see no reason why Jehovah would have given her life only to take it away a few days later.

She had the transfusion and her parents were devastated. They told the elders at the Kingdom Hall and the elders were kind and understanding. They met with her parents at a judicial committee, listened to their story and saw they were repentant. There was no need for formal sanction or disfellowship. They prayed for Jehovah's forgiveness, but all of them understood that Meredith was tainted and difficult to love, and that the acceptance of another's blood could affect her prospects for marriage.

Meredith understood herself as imperfect in the eyes of Jehovah, her congregation and her parents. She had to spend much of her childhood repenting and praying for forgiveness. The anaemia she was born with didn't disappear as she grew. It became chronic and made her ill. She was a frail child, weak and nervous. Her parents weren't rich and couldn't afford red meat, so at every meal Meredith had to eat liver, spinach and tofu, and drink prune juice. Her mother wouldn't let her leave the table until she'd cleared her plate. 'This is to save your life,' she'd say. And so Meredith would force the food into her mouth and down her throat, always anxious to defeat Death, who seemed to lurk in every shadow, ready to wrap her in his black cloak and whisk her into the night.

She always took tablets but, now and then, when she could hardly walk from the tiredness, when she felt dizzy and her skin turned yellow, she would go to hospital for iron injections. They worked, and she'd feel better. Often, she'd feel better for a long time and could live almost the life of a normal child, apart from the fact that she was a Witness.

Meredith knew that all Witnesses tried to keep their contact with non-Witnesses to a minimum. These worldly people were seen as bad influences. They fought in wars; ended their marriages; watched violence on television; believed it was acceptable to fall in love with members of the same sex; they read novels and magazines that promoted these behaviours; and they lived unholy lives that made it clear the end of days was coming. The people in her congregation said those who wanted to live by God's will should not love this world and its practices. A new world was on its way. They needed to prepare for that.

Meredith thought her parents shunned the world even more forcefully than other Witnesses. Their experience with the doctor and the court had made them deeply suspicious of everyone. They sent Meredith to school, but she wasn't allowed to go to assembly. She would sit in her classroom and draw pictures instead. It wasn't a church school, but Meredith's infant teacher was Christian and liked to inflict her beliefs on the children in her class, so her mother came and picked her up ten minutes before lunchtime to make sure she wouldn't be exposed to her teacher's version of grace. She had to go home for lunch to minimize the time she spent with other children. Afterwards, her mother brought her back to school but then picked her up early so she didn't have to listen to the afternoon prayer or sing the hymn about God protecting them on their way home.

She was exempt from RE lessons. She wasn't allowed to draw or go anywhere near the symbol of the cross. 'Jesus died on a simple stake,' her father said. 'Not a cross.'

Wearing a cross around the neck, as Meredith's teacher did, was a sign of dangerous idolatry.

Because of all this, it wasn't easy for Meredith to make friends. There was a girl she sat next to called Mary who often asked Meredith to go to her house after school. Meredith's mother appeared to consider it and would try and discuss it with her father, but her father always said no, and in the end the invitations stopped. She wasn't allowed to go to birthday parties. Her own birth date, 7 March, was never acknowledged and she used to look with awe and envy on those children who came into school wearing huge badges letting everyone know *I am 6*.

'Pagan,' her father said. 'It all comes from folklore. There's so much nonsense about candles having magical powers to grant wishes, and your birthday giving you a star sign. We must shun this, Meredith. Jehovah condemned folklore and magic. We do not observe the date of anybody's birth, and this is why we do not take part in Christmas. The only important day we must observe is the day of Christ's death, for death and our entry into the Kingdom of Heaven is more important than our birth into this world.'

Meredith had to accept it, and she did. She was a good girl and did as she was told. Occasionally, her mother would buy her a small gift like a flower press or an embroidery set because her family followed the example of God and God was a being who gave good things to His children, such as daisies and rain. Her mother told Meredith it was much more fun to receive presents when she wasn't expecting them than to have everything for her birthday. Meredith was never entirely convinced, but she went along with it.

One year, when 7 March rolled round and Meredith would have been eight, her usual teacher was sick and they had a supply. This supply teacher was young and kind, and she was also so pretty Meredith couldn't stop staring at her. She sat at the front of the class and looked down the register at the dates of birth and then she smiled and said, 'It looks like we have a birthday today. Meredith, would you like to come to the front?'

Meredith shook her head. 'I . . .'

'There's no need to be shy,' the teacher said.

Meredith moved to the front of the room.

'Now, let's all sing Happy Birthday to Meredith, using our best and loudest voices.'

The class sang. Meredith stood in front of the whiteboard and blushed, but couldn't help enjoying it.

When she sat down again, the other children at her table promised her all sorts of things: they would share their sweets with her at break; they'd play with her; they'd use their dinner money to buy her a piece of cake at lunchtime.

Meredith glowed, and knew better than to mention any of this to her parents.

When she was eleven, Meredith started secondary school. Her skirt was longer than everyone else's, falling three inches below the knee rather than one inch above. She was still anaemic, still pale-faced and weaker than her classmates. When they did cross country, she tried to muscle on and not let her weakness show, but after five minutes of running, she became breathless and dizzy and had to sit on the ground with her head between her knees while everyone else flashed past her. *Don't make a fuss,* she'd say to herself. *Just sit here and it will pass*. She couldn't bear the thought of a teacher having to come and find her and lead her back to school, while everyone else enjoyed the drama and sent rumours through school that Meredith had a mysterious illness that was probably deadly.

It had always been difficult for Meredith to fit in, but now it was even harder.

'How come you get to skip RE lessons?' one of the boys asked her during form time, about three weeks into the term. He wasn't like the boys in her primary school. He had a tough edge that Meredith was afraid of.

She couldn't answer. She looked down at her desk.

'I don't believe in God, but I ain't allowed to skip RE.' He turned to the boy beside him. 'Why's she allowed?'

The other boy had been to Meredith's primary school. 'Jehovah's Witness,' he said. 'Not allowed to do anything. Never even had a birthday or Christmas.'

'That true?'

Meredith stayed silent. Eventually, they left her alone but by the end of form time, everyone knew the truth about Meredith.

'We don't want you getting too big for your boots,' her father said. 'You need to learn to run a household, not be filling your head with foreign languages.'

Meredith had just scored 96 per cent in a French test.

'How are you doing in Home Economics?'

Meredith shrugged. 'Okay.'

'That's what I want you to focus on, Meredith. That and art.'

'There's a trip to Paris in the spring. Just for a weekend.

We'd see the Eiffel Tower and Notre Dame and the Sacre Coeur. I was hoping . . .'

Her father shook his head. 'Absolutely not. This new school of yours worries me, I must say. What sort of teacher thinks it's acceptable to take children to a city like that?'

'We'd see the Mona Lisa,' Meredith added hopefully. 'You want me to show an interest in art.'

'We like to see you painting. We don't want you traipsing round foreign art galleries, being exposed to all sorts of dangers. What if Christ returns for Judgement Day and you're in Paris, exposing yourself to the art of false religions? How do you think He'll judge you then?'

Meredith gave up and took herself to her bedroom. She was starting to feel that none of this made any sense.

The time came, as she'd always know it would, when Meredith had to start accompanying her mother on her pioneering work. Her mother was one of the Kingdom Hall's greatest pioneers. She didn't work. She devoted her time to her home, her child and her faith. Her father made sure of it. 'You don't need money,' he told them. 'No one needs a lot of money. Jehovah has always supplied His people with all they need, and we must tell the good news about Him to everyone in desperate spiritual situations. The gays and the wicked . . . They all need to know they can be helped to the right path through God's love. We need to give them hope for the future. This is the work you and your mother will carry out, and it's as important as the work I do.'

Her mother was silent as she moved about the room, preparing for a long Saturday of door-knocking: putting tissues into her handbag, straightening her skirt, brushing her hair.

She picked up a pile of *Watchtower* magazines from the table in the hallway and split them between two carrier bags. She handed one to Meredith. 'There,' she said. 'And have you got your Bible?'

Meredith nodded. She didn't want to do this. She knew exactly what lay in store. She looked down at her neat grey skirt and white blouse and thought how old she looked – like a shorter version of her mother. The girls at her school were into fashion now. She saw them at weekends, waiting at the bus stop so they could go into town, and they'd be dressed in tight jeans with long boots and suede jackets. Some of them wore lipstick and mascara. They looked older than twelve and very pretty, Meredith thought.

'Your father would call them bad influences,' her mother would say as they drove past them. 'You'd better shield your eyes.'

Now they stepped outside into the bright spring sunshine and her mother said, 'We're going to head to Princes Crescent. I did some research and I know that's where a couple of the girls from your class live. Your father says their parents need our help.'

Meredith felt as though her heart was falling through her body. 'Mum, please . . .' she said. 'I wouldn't . . .'

Her mother sighed. 'Come on,' she said. 'The sooner we start, the sooner we'll finish.'

Meredith followed a few steps behind as they headed through the rows of Victorian terraces towards Princes Crescent. Princes Crescent was grander than the old estates. It stood alone on the edge of town, six tall Georgian townhouses overlooking a green. The people who lived there had money, and daughters who could afford to go shopping every Saturday. Meredith's parents saw them as morally and spiritually bankrupt.

They walked up a short path lined on either side by flowerbeds filled with tulips. The front door at the end was much wider and smarter than the door to Meredith's house.

Her mother reached up to the brass knocker and rapped loudly, three times. Meredith took another step back. She couldn't stand this.

Charlotte, a girl from her class, opened the door. She was dressed in deep red corduroy trousers, a black top and a beret that matched the trousers. She looked great.

Meredith's mother looked her up and down. 'May I speak to your parents?'

Charlotte glanced at Meredith but didn't acknowledge her. Meredith thought maybe she didn't recognize her outside of school, in her strange grey skirt and white blouse.

'Mum!' Charlotte called into the house. 'Door!'

A well-groomed woman with a big smile came to greet them. Her smile faded when she saw strangers at the door. 'Hello?'

Meredith's mother smiled. 'Good morning,' she said. 'We are your neighbours. We've been looking forward to this day. We'd like to talk to you—'

'I'm sorry. I'm very busy.'

'I understand. It is very difficult, in these busy times, to make space for—'

'I don't mean to be rude. If you're Jehovah's Witnesses, I have my own religion. I'm not interested in changing.'

'But—'

The door in front of them closed. Meredith's cheeks burned.

They carried on and the reception was the same everywhere. Doors were closed or sometimes slammed; people looked out of their windows and didn't answer; one woman even stood in her front garden and when she saw them approaching, pulled out her mobile phone and said in a loud voice, 'The Jehovah's Witnesses are on their way. Don't open the door.' A man told them to fuck off.

They went on like this for three hours. The only person who talked to them was an old woman who was hard of hearing and kept asking them to repeat what they were saying. 'I am bringing you the good news about Jehovah,' Meredith's mother shouted. Meredith wanted to ask her what the point was. This woman must have been in her late eighties. If she was as sinful as everyone else on the planet, there was no way she could redeem herself in time for Judgement Day.

In the end, Meredith said, 'Do you ever feel like giving up?'

Her mother said nothing, and Meredith began to suspect she'd rather not do any of this.

They walked home and Meredith ate her lunch of liver and spinach. 'It's to keep you alive,' her mother said, as usual, and Meredith realized she was close to tears.

31

Emma

The realization that Clara had self-harmed was one of those moments for Emma. It shocked her, and the force of the shock was enough to sober the intoxication of her love affair and pull her back to her family.

She had to break up with Oliver. She had to. Her daughter needed her, and Emma needed to be fully present at home again, instead of always being only half there. She wasn't sure where or how to end a relationship that had mostly taken place in an Exeter hotel room. She thought maybe they should walk out over Dartmoor again, but then she'd be committed to asking him for a lift to the train station afterwards, and neither of them needed that. A public place, like a restaurant or a pub, would be all wrong. She was going to try hard to not cry, but she had no faith in it.

In the end, it happened in the hotel. Usually, he drove down in time to meet her after her last lecture of the day. It was on *Othello* today, and why tragedy could bring pleasure to its audiences. The irony wasn't lost on her as she spoke about how witnessing flawed characters make bad decisions and then suffer from heartache and loss gave people a safe space to release the darker emotions they might otherwise hold in check. She'd had to pause for a moment to gather herself afterwards, and worried for a while that her students might have noticed. She decided they probably hadn't. They usually only paid attention for the first fifteen minutes of a lecture. After that, they were lost.

She met him as she crossed the car park to the hotel entrance. He'd just arrived. Her heart lurched as she saw him stepping out of his car and walking towards her, a smile of pure happiness on his face, his arms ready to hold her.

She kissed him only lightly. She needed to back off. She couldn't get too into this or her resolve would break.

They checked in and went up to their room. Oliver took off his shirt and draped it over the back of the chair. She turned away from the sight of him.

'Are you all right, Em?' he asked.

She paused before turning round again, and wished he'd put a top on. 'No,' she said. 'No, I'm not.'

She hadn't planned to do it this soon, but what was her other option? Say yes, everything was fine, then spend all evening worrying about how to break it to him?

'Sit down,' she said. 'I need to talk to you.'

He sat on the bed, a look of fear on his face. 'What is it?'

In the corner of the room was a desk with a chair. She pulled the chair out and sat down, keeping her distance so she wouldn't be tempted to touch him when she spoke.

She kept her voice matter-of-fact. 'We found out last week that Clara isn't okay. She's been self-harming and I didn't know about it. I didn't know that anything was wrong and I should have done.'

'Oh, Emma . . .'

His voice was full of loving concern. She had to interrupt him.

'And I had a moment of realization. I've been neglecting them, Oliver. Jake and her. I can't go on with this. I need to go back to my family. I need to be there with her while she recovers.'

He looked bewildered. 'You can't go on with this?' he asked. 'With you and me?'

'That's right.'

'But Emma . . .'

Her voice when she spoke was stronger than she felt. 'Please don't try and talk me out of this. It will make it harder for both of us. It's not what I want. It isn't. I want to be with you, but I have children who are struggling and they need me. This isn't the right time for us.'

He was quiet for a while, then he said, 'I'll wait.'

She nodded. 'If you can, I'll come back. But for now, there needs to be a clean break.'

'Are you sure? You don't think it's a bit extreme? There's no compromise here?'

She shook her head. 'I've thought about it. I've thought and thought about it, but no. This has been a part-time relationship all along, and that's why I've always been so distracted. I'm not really there when I'm at home. I'm always thinking of you, missing you, wishing I could be with you. It takes up all the space in my head. I'm not a teenager any more. I shouldn't be living like this when other people need me. I've always known it but I haven't been able to resist. I've been selfish, and I need to stop. I need to repair the damage I've caused.'

'You're being really hard on yourself, Em. I don't think this is your fault.'

She brushed his comment aside. 'I don't know the reasons behind it yet. Maybe I never will, but my daughter is suffering and I've been blind to it.'

He took a deep breath. 'Okay. I understand. But don't think of this as over. I mean it when I say I'll wait. I'll wait as long as it takes.'

She smiled gratefully. 'Thank you.'

They were silent, not looking at each other.

He looked around the room. 'I should probably go,' he said, 'unless you want to . . .'

She shook her head. 'I don't think we should prolong this.'

He stood up and kissed her chastely on the cheek. 'I hope Clara gets sorted,' he said. 'Get in touch when you're ready.'

Then he picked up his bag and left. It was the calmest, most grown-up separation she'd ever been through. She'd done it. She'd finally managed to resist the irresistible, but as the door closed behind him, she laid her head on the desk and cried.

32

Meredith

When she was sixteen, Meredith's anaemia caused her to faint at school, right in the middle of maths. She knew it was going to happen. Her head began to spin and she felt light as air, and she realized too late that she'd forgotten to take her iron tablet this morning. It would be the worst thing, she thought, to faint in front of everyone, so she bent down to pick up her bag and see if she had any iron in there. Anything would do – a pill, some apricots, a packet of beef jerky. But as she leaned over, it happened. The world went black.

When she came round, she was lying on the camp bed in the first aid room, being tended to by a concerned-looking nurse.

'You poor thing. You just lie there until you feel better. Do you know what caused this?'

'I forgot to take my iron tablet this morning,' Meredith told her. 'I've never forgotten before. I overslept. I was in a rush.'

'These things happen. I've phoned your mum and she's on her way. She'll take you to the GP, get you checked over.'

'I think I'm fine now. Really,' Meredith told her.

'It's never a bad idea to see the doctor, love. Rest and then come back tomorrow.'

She adjusted the bed so Meredith could sit up. Meredith knew what the doctor would do. There'd be a blood test, possibly some iron injections, and strict instructions to take her pills and eat red meat.

The possibility that she might one day need a blood transfusion was always there. Her father said they would fight it all the way next time, to make sure it didn't happen again. Meredith understood this meant that she would die.

Her mother came to pick her up, and Meredith could see her fear. She was ashen-faced and shaking as she led Meredith to the car. 'We'll need to get you to the hospital as soon as we can,' she said.

Meredith strapped herself into the passenger seat and waited for her mother to start the car, but her hands were shaking too much to turn the key in the ignition.

'Are you all right?' Meredith asked.

Her mother gave her a weak smile. 'I'm fine. I want to get you checked by a doctor. Maybe increase your iron. We can't . . . Your father . . . He'd never consent to allowing you another transfusion.'

This was the first time her mother had even hinted that she might not agree with Meredith's father about her health.

Meredith said, 'I don't want to die, Mum. I want to be allowed a transfusion if I need one.'

Her mother cast a frightened look around the car, as if she thought her father might suddenly appear from behind the seats. She wrung her hands together and said, 'I know. I know you don't. I don't want you to, either, but your father . . . he's a devout man, Meredith. The laws of Jehovah are everything to him.'

Meredith paused a while before saying, 'What about you? Are they everything to you?'

'I want to live a good life, Meredith, but sometimes I . . .'

'What?'

She spoke quietly, as if unleashing a terrible burden. 'Sometimes I wonder whether God really demands as much from us as we think he does. Times have changed, Meredith, since the Bible was written. Life is sacred, and I don't think He would really want you to sacrifice your life for Him.'

'Really? Do you really think that?'

Her mother spoke slowly. 'The Witnesses think of themselves as the only true followers, the only true religion, but there are others, Meredith. Other forms of Christianity. They teach about a God who loves and cares for the whole world. A loving God wouldn't want you to end your life if it could be saved. I feel sure of this.'

'Does Dad want me to die?'

Her mother shook her head vehemently. 'No. Of course he doesn't, but he believes in the Kingdom of Heaven and the laws you need to follow to find your place there. If you were to refuse a transfusion, he has no doubt that you would be accepted to dwell with Jehovah. It doesn't happen for everyone. Not everyone makes it. Very few of us will make it, in fact, but if you sacrificed your life for God, your father is sure you would be accepted.'

Meredith fell silent.

Her mother looked her in the eye and said, 'I want you to make an appointment with the doctor. I want you to tell the doctor that you want to be given a transfusion if you ever need one. I've read all about it, Meredith. Your father can't stop them, not if you want to be treated.'

'But . . .'

'And you must never tell your father that I told you. Never.'

'Mum . . .'

'Please, Meredith. Please just do it.'

Meredith sat back in her seat, relieved and astonished. She'd never known her mother felt this way.

It looked like nothing was too serious, the doctor said, but took some blood to be on the safe side. Meredith just needed to remember her tablets and to keep eating iron-rich foods. 'We'll phone you with the result of the blood test. It should be just a few days.'

The results were as expected. Her iron levels were low, but not dangerously low. It was the receptionist who phoned to tell Meredith, while her mother was out pioneering. Meredith listened to the news, then she said, 'Am I allowed to come and see the doctor on my own? Without my mum?'

'You are, yes.'

'Then can I do that?'

'Of course.'

The following week, Meredith sat anxiously opposite Dr Franklin. 'We're Jehovah's Witnesses,' she said. 'And I have anaemia and might one day need a blood transfusion.'

Dr Franklin nodded sympathetically. 'I know,' she said.

'My father has told me he'll do everything they can to stop it.'

'Is that what you would like, too?'

'No. No, it's not at all. I want to live.'

'Then you have every right, Meredith, to say this and

have your wishes respected by doctors. These days, parents can only refuse treatment until their child is twelve years old. After that, the child can make the decision for themselves.'

Meredith said, 'The trouble is, I'm worried my dad will put pressure on me. He'll try and stop me from agreeing to it.'

'In that case, the doctors would be very likely to take the case to court for a judge to decide, and the judge would almost certainly rule in your favour.'

'But what if there's no time for that?'

'It's very difficult, I know. But in an emergency, a doctor would be allowed to overrule the wishes of your parents and perform a life-saving transfusion. This is all certified by law.'

Meredith took this in. 'That's a relief,' she said.

'I'll make some enquires for you, Meredith. You will be able to sign a document saying that, as a young woman of sixteen years old, you consent to a blood transfusion if you ever need one.'

'I don't know. If my father found out . . .'

'It must be difficult, to disagree with your parents on this issue.'

'It is. It's really hard. I disagree with them a lot. I have my GCSEs this year but he won't let me revise. He says exams aren't important and I need to do pioneering work instead. I wanted to stay at school and do A levels, but he won't let me. They've said I need to get a job. A full-time job in a shop or something.'

Dr Franklin appeared to think about this for a moment. She said, 'Do you think you would benefit from having someone to talk to about this? I can refer you to a counsellor who might be able to help you stand up to your parents and carve your own path.'

She spoke calmly, but Meredith could see she was seething underneath.

'Okay,' Meredith said. 'That sounds good. I wish I could stand up to them, but . . .' She shook her head.

'I understand,' the doctor said.

Meredith took her GCSEs and did well enough in them, even though her parents insisted she spent her evenings and Saturdays going from door to door with them, sharing the good news about Jehovah. She had a job for the summer, full time in Boots. It was okay for a week, but after that, it became boring.

Her results were more than good enough for her to stay on and take A levels. She'd wanted to do maths, French and biology, and she'd achieved A grades in all of those.

She tried one more time to persuade her parents to let her stay at school.

'No,' her father said. 'There's no need for it. Higher education just exposes young minds to the views of fallen people.'

'But this isn't higher education,' Meredith protested. 'It's just A levels.'

'And then after that, you'll want to go to university. It never stops, Meredith. You've got yourself a good little job, and it's only until you're married. Then you can stop work and run a home.'

Meredith wished she could say everything she was thinking, about it not being the 1950s any more, about wanting a future she could look forward to, but there would be no point. Her father was never going to budge from this. It crossed her mind to wonder what her mother thought, but it hardly mattered. Her mother would never speak up against her father in front of him, and it seemed she'd only go behind his back when Meredith's life was at stake.

It wasn't fair, Meredith thought, as she lay in bed that night. Her friends were all staying on at school, they had promising futures ahead of them, while all Meredith had was a couple of years working in a shop, followed by marriage to someone her parents would inflict on her from the Kingdom Hall. Her friends had fun as well. They'd started going out in the evenings, and a group of them had even gone to Glastonbury this year. Meredith wasn't allowed to do anything with people from school. She was only allowed to make friends with the girls from the Kingdom Hall, but she found them all so boring and when she spoke to them, she couldn't see what it was that made them acceptable, but not the girls at school. Anyone would have expected them to have halos and angel's wings. They didn't, though. They were just the same as everybody else.

She thought about what her mother had said about this other, more loving God. Although they'd always done their best not to expose Meredith to Him, she'd known He existed. In infant school, the rest of her class had made signs with angels on them and the words *God loves me,* and they'd taken them home at the end of the day. She'd seen posters outside the other churches in town, inviting the lonely to discover God's love. She thought she wouldn't mind having a God like that in her life.

She sat up in bed, and brought her hands together in prayer.

33

Emma

She'd known the first six weeks after separating from Oliver would be hard. She only heard from him once, when she turned her phone on in the morning and there was a text message from him.

Missing you.

She checked and saw that he'd sent it at 1 a.m., which meant it was best ignored. She remembered after she'd had Jake and she and Ben had come up with the rule that nothing either of them said in the middle of the night was to be taken seriously. Emma, of course, gained the most from this rule, as she was the one doing all the breastfeeding and therefore the one most likely to say terrible things. Ben would just open his eyes now and then and say, 'Everything fine?' and she'd usually say yes, but once she took them both by surprise and said, 'No, of course everything's not fine. I've been awake for four fucking years while you've just lain there snoring.' Another time, when Jake had finally fallen asleep after she'd been pacing the floor with him for more than two hours, she crawled back into bed and Ben's snoring started the moment she closed her eyes. She sat bolt upright, feeling wildly on the edge of madness.

'For God's sake, will you stop snoring?'
'I'm not snoring. I'm awake. I was breathing.'
'Stop fucking breathing, then.'

She hadn't meant it, obviously. It was just the middle of the night and people were at their most vulnerable in the middle of the night. She pretended not to have received Oliver's message. He didn't send another one.

She was devoted to making Clara well now. She'd dealt with it as well as she knew how – calmly, without drama. 'The nurse told us we need to lock all the sharp objects away,' she said as she sat on the edge of Clara's bed. 'Do you think we need to do that, or do you think it was a one-off?'

Clara said, 'I think I'll be okay. It was kind of a horrible thing to do. I was just feeling so stressed and I thought the pain would release it.'

'And did it?'

'No. It just made my arm hurt.' Clara smiled.

Emma said, 'The nurse told me about a website. It has some ideas of things you can do to distract yourself if you ever feel like doing it again. Shall we have a look at it?'

'Okay.'

Clara moved up and Emma sat next to her on the bed and took out her phone. She googled the site and they went through the list. She could keep an elastic band round her wrist and ping it; she could hold an ice cube; hit cushions; tear a piece of paper into hundreds of pieces . . . It all sounded so desperate and so sad.

Clara said, 'I'm all right. It was exam stress. The nurse and I worked out a timetable I can follow for all my coursework and revision and I feel better about it now.'

She said, 'I'm sorry I didn't realize.'

'Why would you? I didn't tell you.'

'I should have known.'

'Why?'

'Because I'm your mother. It's my job to know these things. I should have been keeping an eye out.'

Clara turned to her curiously. 'Why weren't you?' she asked.

Three days after his text message, it was all over the news. There'd been a lone terrorist attack on a café in central London. A suicide bomber, thought to be independent of any organization, had simply walked in, ordered a coffee and pulled the trigger. She was a woman in a café frequented by yummy mummies after the school run. Her motive was unclear.

All afternoon, Emma watched the news unfold. It was awful, shocking, but deeply compelling. Everyone in the café had died. Sixteen people, including a baby.

Then Ben came home with Jake, who he'd picked up from rowing club on his way home from work, and he came into the kitchen white-faced and shaking and he said, 'Did you hear about the terrorist attack today?'

'Yes, I did. Awful.'

'I've just heard that Oliver Goodwin was involved.'

'Who?'

'Oliver Goodwin. Clare Goodwin's husband. Their daughter's in Clara's year.'

'I know who he is,' Emma said. 'Is he okay?'

'He's dead. I can't believe it. I know we didn't know him well, but . . .'

Emma let the shock freeze every part of her.

PART FIVE

34

Fleur

Fleur, dressed in her dark essence outfit of black leather trousers and a tight red top with a plunging V-neck, headed across the woodland to Clover's cabin. There were still fifteen minutes before they had to be back in the meditation space, and she needed to speak to her, to check she was okay after Emma's moment of brutal nastiness.

She stepped onto the veranda and rapped on the door.

'Just a second,' Clover called from inside.

Fleur waited, remembering what Emma had said. *Her real name is Meredith Slater and she's a missing person.* Fleur was no expert in missing people, but people didn't go missing for no reason. They did it because they were ill, or they'd had enough. Her mind suddenly slipped back to the previous evening, when Clover had seemed on such high alert to the rustling in the bushes and then put it down to a fox. Perhaps she was as anxious as Fleur about being found.

Clover opened the door, wearing a leopard-print suede skirt that had a classy, expensive look to it, with a black halterneck. She saw Fleur and smiled her usual beautiful, welcoming smile. 'Hello, my love,' she said. 'Come in.'

Fleur stepped inside Clover's cabin. It was identical to her own – two single beds separated by a small table, a rug and a tiny wood burner. On the table was a framed print that read, *Don't look back. You're not going that way.*

'I wanted to see if you were all right,' Fleur said. 'After what Emma said.'

Clover appeared to brush the comment aside. 'Oh, I'm fine. She only said she'd found my driving licence.'

Fleur wasn't sure what to say. Clover probably wouldn't appreciate the fact that everyone on the retreat now knew there was a mystery about her. Cautiously, she ventured, 'It was just that you seemed a bit upset, that's all.'

'Did I? I wasn't. I just remembered something I needed to get ready for this morning.'

She was a master of control, Fleur thought. She pushed it a little further. 'Emma mentioned the name on your driving licence isn't Clover. She said it's Meredith Slater.'

Clover wouldn't meet her eye. 'That's right. Meredith is my given name, but I use Clover these days. For business purposes. There are lots of people in my line of work who use business names. They suit the work better. I always thought Meredith was a bit of a posh name and I don't want to put anyone off. I want to be inclusive.'

'That makes sense,' Fleur said. She thought for a while before taking another step. 'Those noises last night . . .' she began.

'Yes?'

'Was it really a fox? Did you really see one?'

'Why would I invent seeing a fox?'

Her tone was defensive. Fleur backed off. 'Oh, I don't know. Stupid of me.' She decided to change the subject. 'I'm sorry Emma is being so difficult. I admire your patience. Do you still think you'll be able to work your magic on her?'

Clover sighed. 'I don't know,' she admitted. 'She's my toughest case yet. I think perhaps she just isn't suited to this kind of retreat. She's brittle.'

'She's horrible.'

'She has things going on.'

'That's not really an excuse for being so rude to you.'

Clover was quiet for a moment, then she smiled brightly and said, 'But what about you, my love? How are you getting on? I hope you're enjoying your celebration of leaving that man.'

'I . . .' Fleur found her eyes brimming with tears.

Clover gazed at her with loving concern. 'Oh, my sweet queen. What's the matter?'

Fleur shook the tears away. 'I'm sorry. I'm so stupid, and you haven't got time for this. We need to be in the barn soon and—'

'Maggie won't mind. She'll wait. I'm here if you want to share.'

The easiest thing was just to blurt it out. 'I'm pregnant,' Fleur said. 'It's Douglas's.'

'Oh, Fleur . . .'

'And I don't know what to do.'

'Does he know?'

'Yes.'

'And?'

'He wants nothing to do with it.'

'But he could always change his mind. Any time he likes. You know that.'

'I do know that. If I have this baby, I'll never be free of him. But I want a child, Clover, and I'm already thirty-three.'

'Women have babies in their forties these days.'

Fleur looked her directly in the eye. 'You don't think I should have it.'

'It's your decision, but do you remember on our last retreat we worked on ridding ourselves of toxic people and situations?'

'Yes.'

'He's a toxic person. If you have his baby, he will be in your life forever. Or rather, he'll probably be in and out of your life forever, because he'll never stick around for long. Then you'll end up in a toxic situation. With a child. You need to be free of him, Fleur. You do. Having his baby will give him too much power over you.' She spoke with passion, and then as if she'd said too much, she added, 'But it's up to you. I can't tell you what to do. I want to, though. I want to tell you not to have it.'

Everything she said made sense. It made perfect sense. 'But I just don't think I'm the sort of person who can have an abortion. It seems so . . . heartless.'

'Plenty of women with huge hearts have had abortions, I'm sure.'

'Yes. Of course.'

'We need to work on toughening you up. We need to get you into a mental space where you can see this situation objectively. See Douglas for what he is, and see what your life will be like if you can never get away from him. Perhaps you don't really want to get away from him. Do you think that might be it, deep down?'

Fleur felt as though the truth had just come along and stabbed her. 'You should be a therapist, Clover,' she said.

35

Maggie

Maggie was struggling to get into her dark essence outfit. She'd had to use significant force to get the zip halfway up her back, but now it was stuck and she needed someone to come to her rescue. It used to be Bill's job, helping her into an overly ambitious dress that had fitted when she'd first bought it, but now she was left to battle on by herself. Small things like this could still shake the old grief back to life.

Also, the neighbour in charge of feeding cat-Bill had just sent her a text message.

> We had a storm here last night. It has damaged your beautiful roses. I think it must have scared Bill because I haven't seen him today and the food I left last night hasn't been eaten.

Maggie had read the message and sighed. Bill would come back, but she'd worked so hard to keep her roses going through the autumn. Every day, she'd pruned and cleared and watered, and she'd loved drinking her morning tea in the conservatory with Bill, looking out at that last bright reminder of summer. Now one storm had probably wrecked them.

She typed back:

I'm sure Bill will find his way home. Annoying about the roses, but storms are always a hazard in an English garden. I should move to the south of France or somewhere if I want year-round roses.

She turned her attention back to her dress. Where was Emma? She'd be able to help. She'd left the barn before Maggie had finished her breakfast, and Maggie had expected to see her back here, slipping into her dark essence outfit. Emma was the kind of person who could slip into an outfit. She was slim and had long legs. Women with long legs could be more easily elegant that women like Maggie. They could step over low walls and country stiles effortlessly, while Maggie would have to heave herself up and always ended up panting like a dog.

Oh, but then wayward, rebellious Emma wasn't going to be taking part in this morning's activities. Maggie had forgotten about that in all the breakfast-time drama.

She walked out onto the veranda and peered out in the direction of the barn. There was Emma, heading this way, thank God. Maggie felt they must know each other well enough now for Emma to be able to zip her into her dress without it feeling too awkward. Emma was weird, though. You could actually feel her keeping her distance.

'I need help,' Maggie called to her as she grew closer. Emma's head was bent low and she didn't look up. Her shoulders were hunched and Maggie realized they were shaking, as if she were sobbing.

It struck Maggie as being very unlike her.

'Em?' she said. It seemed all right to call her *Em* in these circumstances. It infused her name with a tender concern. 'Are you okay?'

Abruptly, Emma seemed to bring herself under control. Her shoulders stopped heaving, she drew a hand over her eyes and brushed the tears off her face. There were a lot of tears. This hadn't been a gentle weeping.

'Sorry,' Emma said after a minute or so. 'I thought you'd have gone already.'

'I can't get into this ridiculous dress.'

Emma smiled. 'Do you need some help?'

'Yes, please,' Maggie said, and looked at Emma with concern. 'What's wrong?'

Emma shook her head. 'Nothing. I don't know what's happened to me. I woke up delighted I was going to be having a gorgeous massage and now I'm suddenly a wreck. I'll be okay in a minute. Take no notice of me.'

'All right, if you're sure.'

'I'm sure.'

They stepped back into the cabin. Emma took hold of Maggie's zip and yanked it. 'I don't know, Maggie,' she said. 'Can you suck your boobs in?'

'I think that sounds anatomically impossible. You mean lift them up. They come down to my knees. That's what's causing all this trouble.'

Together, they did some pulling and tugging and re-arranging, and eventually the zip was fastened. Maggie looked down at herself. 'It's as well there's not a mirror in here.'

The dress had flattened her breasts. Emma reached up to the shelf above her bed and took down a long black coat, which she handed to Maggie. 'Have this,' she said. 'You'll be fine.'

'I don't think your clothes are going to fit me, Emma.'

'It's loose. It'll be fine.'

Emma helped her into it and did up the buttons at the front. 'There. Your boobs are covered.'

'Thanks.' Maggie paused for a moment and said, 'Are you going to talk to Clover?'

'Oh, I don't know. I probably should. I know I was a bitch. But I need to recover first from whatever it was she did to me this morning.'

'What did she do to you?'

'She made me visualize my crown chakra opening and a healing white light cascading through my body, and I don't know what happened but now I'm a total mess and I can't take any more of this.'

Maggie sat down on her bed. 'Do you want to . . . I don't know . . . talk about what's wrong?'

'I think she's a witch.'

'I think that's extreme.'

'I'm worried about her mother. For your child to just go missing and you not to know whether she's alive or dead . . . That's horrific, Maggie.'

'But . . .' Maggie hesitated, confused, 'this isn't why you're upset. You're upset about something else.'

'Oh, probably,' Emma admitted. 'I probably am. I'm completely predictable. I know exactly what a therapist would say. They'd say my focus on Clover's mother is just another symptom of my reluctance to examine myself. They're full of shit, though, therapists. They mostly just recite textbooks written by someone who studied a few rats.'

'Okay.'

'The thing is, I'm pissed off now. I didn't come here to feel like this.'

Maggie was beginning to feel too hot in this long coat and the dress that was too tight on her chest, but now didn't feel like the moment to start stripping off again. 'Maybe this is part of the healing,' she said. 'Maybe you need to feel wretched again so you can heal and move on.'

'I am *sick* of feeling fucking wretched!'

Maggie backed off. 'Okay.'

Emma sighed. 'I'm sorry. I really didn't mean to shout at you.'

'Don't worry.'

'Do you want to take Clover's driving licence to her?'

'Nope. That's for you to sort out.'

'Okay.'

Maggie sighed. This felt uncomfortable, as if Emma were trying to punish Clover for the fact that she was overwhelmed after the mysterious healing practices. 'You're not . . . You're not going to do anything, are you?' She could see Emma was furious. It hardly seemed fair, and Maggie didn't know her well enough to know whether she could act impulsively, out of spite.

Emma said nothing.

Maggie said, 'Well, if you're staying here, I'll go and join the others.'

'I'm sorry. I'll be fine later. I just need to rest. Recharge my emotional battery.'

'All right,' Maggie said. 'Take care.'

She left and shut the cabin door and deep inside her, a feeling of fear for Clover began to rise.

36

Fleur

Fleur was sitting on a chair in the meditation space, watching the others while they danced. 'You are the masculine energy,' Clover had told her. 'I want you to imagine yourself male, and watch the women in front of you while they dance. There is to be no judgement of how they dance, how they move, what they're doing. You are simply a force of masculine energy, observing.'

What? Fleur thought, but did as she was told. She imagined herself as a man – not Douglas or any of her previous boyfriends, just a man she didn't know – and watched Maggie and Clover while they swayed and turned in time to the music.

She felt genuinely awed by them. They were beautiful, these women. The energy they put in the room was overpowering – feminine, fierce, intelligent, with the slightest hint of vulnerability running beneath it.

Fleur thought, *If I were a bloke, my dick would be hard as rock right now.*

And it occurred to her then that energy like this was a threat. It always had been.

She knew that the trauma of being with Douglas was locked in her body. She could talk it through with her therapist, but it was still there. It was buried in her bones, it was held in the fibres of her muscles. And now, it was real and growing in her womb.

After a while, Clover said, 'Now Maggie, take a seat. Imagine you are the masculine energy. Fleur, come and dance.'

Fleur stood up and stepped into the dance space. She loved dancing. She always had. But in any other place, she'd feel self-conscious knowing she was being watched like this. It wasn't like that here. Here she felt safe and as she danced, she knew Douglas was gone. The music played, and she moved with energy. She had no idea what she looked like and didn't care. No one here was judging her. Her eyes met Clover's and they both smiled and kept moving. Clover raised her arms above her head and whooped.

Douglas wasn't here. He wasn't here to tell her she shouldn't be doing this, she was attracting attention, that some man would come along and take her away from him.

She crossed the floor with abandon, and felt the trauma in her bones begin to shift and release. It flowed through her body and dispelled, then shattered into fragments. She wanted to keep on dancing, to smash that trauma so hard it could never take root again.

But no matter how hard she danced, there was always the baby, growing away inside her.

37

Emma

Emma lay on her bed in the cabin. God, this was ridiculous. Why couldn't she stop crying? Two years had passed since that last day with Oliver, and here she was, still missing him. She didn't really know where this sudden wave of grief had come from. Surely she wasn't meant to buy into the idea that Clover's touch really was healing, or that the earthy-tasting hot chocolate really contained magical properties? Nothing about this felt healing or magical. It had felt ridiculous. Now she just felt wretched.

She'd lost sight now of why she'd ever thought that coming here would be useful. It was a stupid suggestion. Irresponsible. She couldn't possibly excavate her deepest emotions with two half-mad women and their pseudo-spiritual leader. There was nothing safe about this safe space. For all that Clover clearly believed in her practices, she was a fake, a charlatan, pushing people to explore dangerous ground and then lacking any skill to support them when they'd done it. Their well-being was a game to her, and the woman was dangerous.

Emma reached for her phone beside the bed. She wanted to read the rest of Kevin Slater's blog. She wanted to go back to the beginning and find out exactly what had happened.

At the top of the home page was a photo of Meredith Slater. She was undeniably Clover. Since leaving, she'd cut and coloured her hair and lost some weight, but the face was just the same. They'd know her if they saw her.

Finding Meredith

Day 7

Many of you reading this will know that my wife, Mrs Meredith Slater, disappeared exactly one week ago today. Myself and her parents are deeply worried for her safety. If you see her, please get in touch via the button below.

Emma scrolled on. Most posts were more or less the same. One, after she'd been gone for a month, appealed to people to look out for her in Cambridge because they thought she might have headed there, although they didn't say why. There were a lot of posts asking for prayers for her safe return, and others trusting in Jehovah to bring her back when he felt ready.

Slowly, over time, the blog posts became less frequent, then picked up again more recently with the news that her dad was ill.

Finding Meredith

Day 549

My wife, Mrs Meredith Slater, has not been seen by

her family for over a year and a half. There have been no recent sightings of her, but I ask you all to continue your prayers for her safe return. As many of you in the congregation know, her father is now gravely ill and would like to see his daughter before the end of his life. We have shunned Meredith since her disfellowshipping, but we are hopeful that this realization that her father is dying will prompt Meredith to return and repent. We trust in Jehovah to bring Meredith to us as He sees fit.

If you see her, please get in touch via the button below.

It was the refrain he used to end every post. *If you see her, please get in touch via the button below.*

Finding Meredith

Day 562

We are increasing the urgency of our appeal to help find Meredith. Doctors now believe her father has only days left to live. He seems to be holding on because he wants to see his daughter and ask her again to repent so she can be welcomed back as the Witness we all know she is at heart. We all believe Meredith will be heartbroken when she finds out her father has died without her having repented. Please could anyone who has any idea at all where Meredith might be get in touch with me as soon as possible. Someone must have some idea. Were you one of her many friends? Did Meredith confide in you at any time? Did she say she was planning to run away? Did she give any hint at all about where she was going? Any information you have, even if you think it is irrelevant, could help us in our search.

If you see her, please get in touch via the button below.

The words were plaintive. Neither her husband nor her mother had any idea where she was. And now her father had died and her mother was alone, and Clover was refusing to even go and see her. Beneath all this gentle wisdom, she was so hard. Cruel.

Emma read a few more posts. There was a lot of talk of Jehovah and the congregation, which was all alien to Emma and not a world she understood, but at the heart of this blog was grief and bewilderment. No one knew where she was, or why she'd left, and all Emma could think about was Clover's mother – her heartache and fear.

If you see her, please get in touch via the button below.

Emma hit the button. It took her to a contact form. She didn't even have to give her name.

38

Maggie

It was Maggie's turn to watch the dancing. She wondered if she'd looked as powerful and desirable as these other women when she was up there. She hoped so. She'd felt sublime. She still couldn't believe she'd wasted the last forty years of her life not dancing.

If Bill could see her now, she thought, he'd be amazed by her. She wondered how he would see these women, if he were here. He'd be intimidated, probably. The sight was raw. A more confident man would admire it, and perhaps try to get near it. A man like Bill would have shrunk away, knowing he had no chance. Some other man would want to own it. Some other man would rape it.

But here, in this room together, they were safe. The feeling of safety among these women was exquisite. She could be entirely herself here. It felt even better without Emma.

Anything was allowed. Maggie knew that. She knew that if she stood up, walked over to the altar and picked up the pad of paper she knew was there, no one would judge her, no one would mind. So she did.

She didn't have any paints or an easel, so she started sketching in biro instead. It was years since she'd done anything like this. Although they were dancing and not keeping still, she was able to draw them well enough. She wasn't aiming to be exact. She just wanted to capture the energy of them as they span around the room in their black dresses and leopard print.

It was a quick sketch. Clover, her arms waving in the air, and Fleur with her back turned, her leather trousers and long hair in silhouette as she swayed in front of the window, a woman ready to be seen.

Maggie held the sketch in her hands. She'd made them look like witches, she thought. A coven of women, full of spells. She wondered if there was enough energy in this room to clear her past.

PART SIX

39

Fleur

They flew to Norway two days before Christmas. Fleur tried her best to enjoy it. The scenery was magical: deep snow; pine forests; dark, clear skies. They drove huskies, they travelled on snowmobiles to see reindeer; they went ice-fishing in the dark. Every night, they trekked out with a guide and set up camp at the edge of the frozen lake to wait for the Northern Lights. They were lucky. The lights appeared – billowing psychedelic sheets above and all around them.

Douglas was enraptured. He sat behind her and wrapped his arms around her neck. 'Isn't this amazing?' She could see his breath in the air, like smoke.

'Amazing,' she agreed.

And it was amazing. Of course it was, and she knew this was the most loving gift anyone could ever have given her. Douglas knew she'd always wanted to see the Northern Lights with her dad, and now he'd brought her here, and there they were – the Northern Lights in magical technicolour.

But her dad was dead and it was Christmas and she missed him, and Fleur needed to be with her mum. There was an ache in her chest as strong as the day of the funeral.

There were text messages from her mum in her phone.

Merry Christmas, my darling! I hope it's wonderful there. I'm with Auntie Sue and we're pissed on champagne truffles.

She sounded upbeat, but Fleur knew her mother well enough to know this was an act for her benefit. *I'd never ask Fleur to sacrifice anything for me.*

Her mother had phoned a few days after their visit. 'How's Douglas?' she asked, and Fleur could tell she was keeping her tone deliberately casual.

'He's fine.'

'That's good. Have you managed to get out with any friends recently?'

'Not for a while.'

She could hear her mother joining the dots. 'Really?'

'I'm quite busy. I'll catch up with people soon.'

'I hope so. Is . . .' She paused, as if weighing up whether she should say it or not, then obviously decided to go ahead, ' . . . is Douglas okay with you going out?'

'Yes, he's fine with it,' Fleur said. Her mother had always had a strong instinct when it came to Fleur's well-being and Fleur could tell she'd moved into high alert when she met Douglas and he told her about Norway. She couldn't blame her. He'd spoken like a police officer, taking charge of Fleur's life.

'Okay. Good. That's good.'

Fleur changed the subject, but she knew that conversation meant her mother no longer liked Douglas.

After watching the lights for an hour or so, they headed

back through the snow to their log cabin. Douglas didn't speak, and then he didn't come and talk to her like he usually did while she undressed and had a bath. She felt the tension rising in the atmosphere and started bracing herself for a row.

When she stepped out of the bathroom, wrapped only in a towel, he looked up from where he sat in the cabin kitchen and said, 'When we get home, I think you should go straight to stay with your mum.'

She looked at him, unsure of what to say.

'You're obviously missing her. I should never have brought you on holiday.'

He wasn't speaking with concern.

She said, 'I've loved this holiday.'

'You haven't, Fleur. You've been miserable since we got here. I was stupid. It was a stupid idea. You need to spend next Christmas with your mother. I'll go somewhere else.'

'Douglas . . .'

He walked away from her and sat on the fur beanbag by the window, gazing at the snowlight outside.

Fleur went into the bedroom and put her dressing gown on. She didn't want to go and sit with Douglas, but he'd be cross if she went to bed without saying goodnight.

She stood in the doorway that led from the bedroom to the living area and said, 'I think I'll just read my book for a while.'

He carried on looking out of the window. 'Okay.'

Fleur felt utterly miserable. She had no idea where this man had come from, or how to bring back the one she'd fallen in love with. It occurred to her that she would never have fallen for him if he'd been like this from the start, and that perhaps she should leave him. The thought was agonizing. Tomorrow, or the day after, he'd switch again and become the loving, funny, wonderful version of himself that she adored. Then he'd take her soaring to heights of happiness she'd never known before. She thought, *Maybe if I just love him enough, he'll stop being this insecure.*

He was a complicated man with a difficult history. She'd known that from the very start. He'd brought her on this holiday, and she loved him. She needed to stick with this, and in time they would build something incredible.

40

Maggie

The days and weeks after Annie's death went by in a fog. There was a coroner's report, a funeral to prepare and an inquest. The cause of death was unexplained and given as Sudden Infant Death Syndrome. Maggie was aware of the unspoken judgement coming towards her. Healthy babies shouldn't just die. She must have done something wrong. Maybe, despite her smart appearance in court, she had a filthy lifestyle behind closed doors. Did she smoke, they asked? Did she wash the baby's blankets? If she wasn't breastfeeding (she was), then did she sterilize her bottles?

Doctors and other professionals hadn't known, back then, that the way to reduce the risk of this sort of death was to lie baby to sleep on her back. The parenting books and the midwives had told Maggie that her babies should sleep on their fronts.

When they came home from the coroner's court, Maggie took herself up to the bedroom to change out of her suit. She felt drained, entirely exhausted, so she sat for a while on the bed, beside the empty Moses basket. Neither she nor Bill had been able to bring themselves to get rid of it yet. Where would they get rid of it to? They couldn't give it away or sell it. But to throw it out would feel like a violation. It was still there, in their room, by Maggie's side of the bed.

She reached in, pulled out a blanket and held it to her face. For days now, she'd been numb from the shock but there, with that softness against her cheek, she felt the grief coming towards her, a giant wave that would pull her under, that she would never be able to swim against.

She felt, in that moment, the flick of a switch inside her, as the sadness that threatened to crush her turned to rage instead. She had the urge to smash things. There had to be someone to blame for this. Even though she hated them, she understood those men in the courtroom, with their severe expressions and their judgement. A baby didn't just die during a daytime sleep. She was loved, she was healthy, she was fine. She was absolutely fine. Something had happened to her, something Maggie didn't know about and the coroner hadn't spotted.

She knew it. She knew it as clearly as she knew night from day. The paramedics and the doctors who'd looked at Annie were wrong. The coroner was wrong. Of course, they didn't care. Annie wasn't their baby. What reason did they have to get this right?

This surge of angry energy was doing her good. It would spur her on. It was so much easier to feel rage and keep going than to be overcome by grief and give up.

When she looked back on it now, of course it was mad. She couldn't explain it, other than that her loss had possessed her, turned her into someone new and frightening. It would have been better for everyone if she'd just shut herself away, hidden under the duvet for a year or two and re-emerged when the pain lessened enough for her to function.

She hadn't done that, though. Instead, she set to work, trying to find out what had happened to Annie. She needed someone to examine the fibres in the blankets and the sheet in the Moses basket, so she bundled them into a carrier bag and took them to the police station. The officer who was assigned to her was gentle enough, but clearly thought she was insane.

'Annie's death was not suspicious,' he said. 'There is no criminal investigation here.'

She put the bag full of blankets on the desk. 'Can you just give these to one of your scientists or something? Get them to do some tests? I know you can do amazing things these days. Please. I just want to know what happened.'

The officer looked helpless and desperate to get away from her. 'I'm sorry. That just isn't possible when there's no criminal investigation. It's unlikely they would find anything. Cot death is—'

'Then can you give me the name and address of a scientist I can go to myself? I'll pay them. I'll pay them whatever it costs.'

'It's not my area, I'm afraid.'

'Can you find someone whose area it is?'

'I can ask.'

'Thank you.'

She sat and waited for him to go and find the right person. He didn't move. Instead, he stood up and said, 'I'll be in touch.'

'Do you know how long it will take?'

'It should be within the next few days.'

Maggie picked up her bag and went home. She walked

into the kitchen and Bill said, 'I was starting to get worried. Where've you been?'

'I went to the police station.'

'Oh, Maggie,' he said, and put his arms around her.

She knew he was suffering, too. He was suffering just as much as she was. His work had given him a fortnight's compassionate leave, but then he'd have to go back. Maggie wasn't sure how he would bear it.

He released her and said, 'Don't do this to yourself, love.'

'I have to. I have to find out what happened to her. I need to know why she died.'

'I know. I know you do. But sometimes things happen and there are no explanations. It was a cot death. That's what it was. There's nothing you did, nothing you didn't do. It was a tragedy.'

Maggie banged her fist down on the worktop. 'I won't accept that!' she said. 'I just won't. Something happened to her. I'm going to find out what it was.'

He could obviously see there was no reasoning with her, and he was right. He backed away and took himself into the garden. When she looked back on those days, she often wondered why he'd stuck around, why he hadn't just taken Richard and left her. In later years, she asked him and he said, 'It didn't cross my mind.' She still wasn't sure if she believed him. How could it not have crossed his mind?

Because he loved you.

She stood in the kitchen without him and planned what to do next. She was going to solve this. She was going to solve the mystery of her baby's death, even if no one would help her. There was no one more terrifying than a woman grieving for her baby.

41

Fleur

January that year was wonderful for Fleur. The real Douglas had come back to her, at last. He was once again funny, caring, easy to be around, and after three weeks had passed with no sign of the sullen man who'd been too present in recent months, Fleur dared to believe that this was it now: he'd recovered from his depressive state and now he was here to stay.

He had a paid comedy gig at least once a week. Low pay, but at least he was no longer working for nothing. The gigs were mostly fairly local – Hastings, Tunbridge Wells, never further than London – and Fleur went with him as often as she could. She thought his act was improving all the time. There were occasional lukewarm audiences, but that always happened, even to the stars, apparently. Douglas was happy. Thank God.

His gigs were the only times they went out that month. It was too cold, too dark and they were skint now after the Norway trip. They spent most of their evenings taking it in turns to cook, then they'd eat and drink wine and curl up on the sofa with Netflix. It wasn't exciting, but it was easy and Fleur welcomed easy.

The meals Douglas cooked were always extravagant

and took him ages to prepare. Fleur usually warmed up a pizza or a ready-made lasagne. She took no joy in cooking. There was something about following recipes that made her want to rebel. They were too bossy. *Chop the pepper into two-inch squares,* she'd read, and she'd think, *Don't tell me how to chop my peppers. I'm cutting them into one-inch squares and fuck you.*

She explained this to Douglas. He found it endearing.

'Why do you always make amazing things?' she asked him as they sat down to eat his beef goulash, which he'd been cooking over a low heat all day. 'It makes me feel like a lesser person.'

He shrugged. 'Because I enjoy it. Because I love you.'

She blushed. She couldn't help it.

He reached over the table and took her hand tightly in his. 'I do, Fleur. I love you more than you could ever know. I'm so frightened of losing you, it makes me crazy sometimes. Promise me you won't leave me.'

He gazed at her with urgent, frightened eyes.

'I won't leave you,' she said. 'What we have is amazing.'

His face relaxed into a smile. 'Thank you. I don't deserve you. I know I don't. But I'm going to stop being so anxious. I'm going to treat you properly. I'm going to treat you the way you deserve to be treated. All the time.'

She said, 'That day when you burned the tickets to Norway . . .'

'Yes?'

'It really frightened me.'

'I know. I know it did. I'm sorry. The whole Norway thing . . .' He shook his head, as if he couldn't believe what he'd done. 'It was selfish of me.'

Selfish. It was the first time he'd used that word to describe himself. He'd always said he bought the holiday to make her happy.

He carried on. 'I wanted you to myself. You'd already said you needed to go to your mum's but I thought if we went there, I don't know . . . I thought it would just be the two of you, remembering your dad and everything. I thought I'd be an outsider.'

'You wouldn't have been an outsider,' she said. 'Never.'

'I know. I've started seeing a counsellor. He's helping me work on all this. The insecurity and the jealousy. He agreed that I need to. He said it will affect my relationship if I don't.'

Fleur was pleased, and stunned. 'I wasn't expecting this,' she said. 'I'm glad you're doing it. Really glad.'

'I know I have a lot of issues. My parents, my sister . . .'

'I know.'

'But I'm going to sort it out. I can do it with you by my side. I know I can.'

'I know you can, too.'

She was so in love with this man, so full of hope for the future.

Things were back to the way they used to be. They spent their weekends enjoying long lie-ins and morning sex. Then Douglas would put together a brunch – American pancakes, fresh croissants, orange juice he squeezed himself. It changed every week. Often, they would head out to the South Downs or the cliffs around Beachy Head and walk for a few miles before finding a pub with an open fire and stopping there for a beer. They were perfect winter days and Fleur wished she could stop time from moving on and taking them away from her.

'We're like old people,' she said.

'With more sex.'

Douglas seemed to think sex was exclusive to the under-forties.

In the evenings, they'd go home and eat more food, then settle on the sofa and watch films, or play one of the weird, geeky board games Douglas loved and Fleur could hardly understand. As they played, she topped up her wine glass and became ever more hopeless at building her settlements or taking over the world with armies of plastic soldiers.

'Why aren't you more competitive?' Douglas asked.

'I don't know,' Fleur told him. 'It must be because I don't really care.'

He looked bewildered, as if he had no idea how anyone couldn't care about winning.

Finally, in early February, she came off the phone to her mum and said to him, 'Have we got any plans next weekend?'

He shook his head. 'No, I don't think so.'

'Great. Then I'm going to go away. To see my mum.' She wasn't asking his permission. She was a grown woman of thirty-two, and she'd never have expected him to ask her if he could go away to see his family.

Immediately, she saw the dark shadow of jealousy pass over his face. She watched him pause for a while and take time to get himself under control. She wondered if this was a technique his counsellor had taught him.

Then he smiled. 'Okay. That's great. You should see her. You haven't seen her for a long time.'

She smiled, relieved, and kissed him. 'I'll bring you a present,' she said.

Her mum hadn't mentioned Douglas when she invited Fleur to stay. Fleur wasn't sure why, exactly, though she had her suspicions it was all because of the way he'd spoken to her before Christmas. Her mother was tactful enough about it. 'Do you fancy one of our weekends together?' she asked, the question immediately excluding Douglas. 'I'll treat you to tea at Fortnum's, shall I? Make up for some of this winter dreariness.'

Fleur loved afternoon tea. It was one of her favourite things to do with her mother, along with spa days and planning holidays they would never take. 'Sounds great,' she said.

The weekend rolled around. She arrived on Friday evening and they caught up over an Indian takeaway. It was always good to come home, even though her father's absence still made itself known as an ache in her chest. But eating at this table, sitting in this living room, sleeping in her old bedroom filled her with the warmth of familiarity she knew she'd never find anywhere else. She would always be welcome here.

In the morning, they wandered along the South Bank to Borough Market. Fleur bought Douglas a handmade pork pie and a jar of overpriced mustard.

'Very masculine,' her mother remarked.

It was only later, when they'd sat down in Fortnum's tea room and were sipping a high-class sparkling wine that might have been champagne (her mother had ordered it when Fleur went to the toilet) that she finally said what was on her mind.

'I'm concerned about you, Fleur.'

'You don't need to be.'

'I've kept quiet about this for months because I know it's your life and you need to be free to love whoever you want to love, but there was something about Douglas that bothered me.'

'He's fine. I know he spoke to you a bit rudely, but he didn't mean anything by it.'

'I think he's controlling.'

'He's not. He's fine. He admits he had some problems for a while, but he's sorting them out.'

Her mother raised her eyebrows questioningly.

'He gets jealous sometimes.'

'That's what I mean, Fleur. Jealous men are bad news.'

'But he's much better now. He was absolutely fine with me coming away this weekend.'

'The thing is, darling, you shouldn't even be having to say this. It shouldn't be the slightest issue.'

'It's not now. It used to be.'

'It's why he whisked you away for Christmas, isn't it? To keep you alone with him.'

'I don't know for sure.'

'I do. I've seen this sort of man, Fleur. There's a type. He's it.'

'Mum, please . . .'

'Okay. Okay. I won't say anything more. Believe me, we all know how risky it is to interfere with our children's romantic lives. I wouldn't be doing it if I wasn't really concerned about you.'

'I know you wouldn't. But I'm fine.'
'Have you got enough money to leave if you need to?'
'Mum, you said you'd stop.'
'Okay, I'll stop. But make sure you put some money aside and if he ever turns nasty, get out. Don't wait. Just get out.'
'For God's sake, Mum. He's not a wife beater.'
Her mother said nothing.

Fleur lay in bed that night, confused and heartbroken. She could never allow Douglas and her mother to be in the same room together again, not after everything her mother had said earlier. There was no way back from that. It was going to be awkward and difficult now, forever. She began to see a future unfold before her, one where she was forced to choose between them.

She sent a text message to Douglas. *Can't wait to see you tomorrow. Love you.*

42

Maggie

That police officer she'd spoken to never did get back to her with a scientist's number. She mentioned it to Bill. 'Should I phone the station?' she asked.

He was emphatic. 'No,' he said. 'No, you really shouldn't.'

'But—'

'If they had any news for you, they'd have told you.'

'Hmm,' Maggie said. She didn't believe that for a minute. She doubted the man had even tried.

Bill said, 'We need to try and hold ourselves together. For Richard's sake. This is badly affecting him. He's afraid to even come near us. He's just hiding in his room, probably to escape from the drama. We have to try and be strong and carry on.'

'I can't just carry on. I need to find out what happened.'

'We know what happened. She died – tragically – in her cot and sadly, there is no reason for it. It happens. It happens to over three thousand babies a year. No one knows why. It just happens.'

'It does not.'

'Why don't you go upstairs and see Richard, love? He needs us. He needs you. It might comfort you to sit with him for a while.'

Maggie sighed. He was right, of course. She hauled the heavy weight of herself out of the chair and went upstairs. Richard's bedroom door was closed. She knocked. He didn't say anything, so she eased it open and poked her head round.

He was sitting on his beanbag, playing with a couple of *Star Wars* figures.

'Okay if I come in?' she asked.

He nodded.

She sat on the floor beside him. 'What are you up to?'

'Just playing.'

She watched him for a while. He laid one of the figures on the floor and the other one jumped on him. 'What's that one doing?' she asked.

'Killing this one.'

'Why?'

He shrugged.

A thought so awful she couldn't bear it flickered through Maggie's mind. *Don't be stupid*, she told herself. *Don't even go there.*

She pushed it away. It came back. She pushed it away again and said, 'Are you missing Annie, sweetheart?'

'No,' he said. 'I'm fine.'

She nodded. 'Okay, but if you ever feel that you're not fine, you know you can talk to Daddy and me, don't you?'

'I'm fine,' he said again, and wouldn't look at her.

How could he be fine, she thought? How, when his baby sister was dead?

The thought returned, huge and dark and dangerous.

She left the room.

43

Fleur

Her train pulled in to Brighton just after 5 and her heart leaped at the thought of seeing him again. She'd only sent him a few text messages over the weekend and in none of them had she asked what he'd done. It was a point she wanted to make, gently but clearly. She didn't need to know every detail of the life he lived away from her. It was okay for them to be separate from each other sometimes and there was no jealousy.

He was waiting for her on the other side of the ticket barriers, wrapped in his black duffel jacket and red scarf. He greeted her with a huge smile. 'I've missed you,' he said, and kissed her several times on the lips.

'Me too,' she said. 'It's great to be back.'

She took his hand and they walked home through town. The shop windows were full of Valentine's displays. It seemed as though everywhere they looked, there were red balloons; huge, heart-shaped biscuits; rings; necklaces; bracelets. Fleur had never really marked Valentine's Day before. She'd always taken a lightly cynical approach to it. It mostly struck her as a day of intense pressure for those who had partners, and a day of anguish for those who didn't, while the card manufacturers and restaurants cashed in on it. This year, though, she wanted to celebrate. She was with the only man she'd ever truly loved. They'd made it through some difficult times, but everything was better now. Last night, as she drifted off to sleep, Fleur had realized she had no doubts now. She wanted to spend her life with Douglas.

She glanced sideways at him and tightened her grip on his hand. On Valentine's Day, she was going to ask him to marry her.

At home, he lifted the lid on a casserole dish and showed her he'd made a beef and red wine stew with dumplings.

'Oh! I haven't had dumplings for years!' she told him.

'Neither have I. I miss them.'

'I bought you a present.'

'You didn't have to.'

'I wanted to. It's only small. I left it in my mum's fridge. I had to go back for it.'

She caught the brief flash of that old darkness on his face and all of a sudden, her heart pumped a beat too quickly. It was always there, she realized, that nervousness around him.

She pushed it away and reached into her bag for the paper-wrapped pork pie and the jar of posh mustard. 'Here,' she said. 'I got them in Borough Market. It's amazing there – so many stalls, all this amazing street food. There was a crumble stand. You had to choose your base and then . . .' Her voice trailed off as she saw him staring at the pork pie as if she'd just handed him a gun to shoot himself. 'It's a silly thing, really. It looked so nice in the market, but maybe now it's . . .'

'It's fine,' he said, and put it down on the worktop.

Fleur had no idea what she'd done wrong, but clearly this present was unwelcome.

He stood in silence. Fleur felt the tension in her body and couldn't meet his eye.

'So what else did you do with your mum?' he finally asked. 'Apart from go to the market?'

'We went to Fortnum and Mason for afternoon tea. She cooked a couple of meals. We just relaxed, mostly.'

He nodded. 'Did you see anyone else?'

He meant a man. She shook her head. 'No,' she said. 'Just my mum.'

'Cosy. Like old times, I suppose. You and your family.'

His words hurt. It wasn't like old times and he knew that. Her father hadn't been there and she'd felt his absence everywhere. There used to be three of them and now there were only two. No, it hadn't been like old times. It had been like new times, where two grieving people were trying to make the best of things.

She said, 'Douglas . . .'

He banged his fist down on the worktop. 'And did you love it there, without me? Did your mummy love having her precious girl at home? Is that why she didn't invite me? Because she wanted you to herself?'

'Please don't do this.'

'Why didn't she invite me, Fleur? Why wasn't I welcome?'

'You were. You would have been. I think . . . I just . . .'

All of a sudden, he grabbed her hard by the shoulders and put his face in hers. 'I am your family now. Not her. It's you and me.'

Her cheeks were wet with the spit that had flown from his mouth as he spoke.

'Get off me,' she said. 'Get off me.'

He tightened his grip.

She kicked him, hard. She wasn't sure how many times.

'What do you think you're doing?' he asked. 'You've lost your bloody mind.'

'I said get off me.'

'Not until you've calmed down. I can't let you go like this. You're in a state. You're dangerous.'

She could see her keys on the worktop beside her and managed to ease her arm and grab them. Without really thinking about what she was doing, she dragged one down his face. It left a long, red scratch.

He let her go. 'You've assaulted me, Fleur,' he said calmly. 'I'm going to have to call the police.'

'Yeah, right. I'll just tell them what really happened.'

'Will you?' he asked, and he grabbed the knife he used for chopping vegetables, held the blade to his cheek and cut, quickly. It took a few second for the blood to appear.

She screamed. 'What are you doing?'

He picked up his phone and dialled. 'Police, please. My girlfriend is assaulting me.'

She was there in an interview room with two officers, one male and one female, while everything she said was being recorded. They asked her questions.

'Can you describe what happened this evening between you and Douglas?'

She told them everything, including the way he'd grabbed her and held on to her shoulders. She hoped there would be bruises to prove it, but there was nothing.

'You admit that you used a key to assault Douglas?'

'Yes, but . . .'

They wouldn't let her finish. 'Did you then assault him with the knife?'

'No! No, I didn't.'

'Why does he have a knife wound?'

'He did it. He did it himself.'

The officer raised his eyebrows and she could hear his unspoken words. *That seems an unlikely story.*

'We take domestic abuse very seriously, Fleur,' he said. 'Very seriously. Douglas has said he doesn't want this to go to court. Now, there are some officers who would override that wish and have you charged anyway. Because this is your first offence, we're going to let you go with a caution. But if you assault him again – or anyone else, for that matter, or commit any other crime – you will be charged and dealt with in court. Do you understand?'

Fleur felt tears of frustration in her eyes. She'd explained. She'd explained what had really gone on but they wouldn't listen. As far as they were concerned, Douglas had been assaulted. She'd admitted to attacking him with a key and that was all it took for them to assume she'd also attacked him with a knife. He had a knife wound to his face. He said she'd done it and she had no way of proving that she hadn't. They believed him. He was the victim, simply on the grounds that he'd got there first. If she'd phoned and reported it, maybe she'd be the victim. But she wasn't. She was the abuser.

'In order for us to caution you, you need to admit the assault.'

'But I didn't do it,' she said again.

'If you don't accept the caution, we will have to charge

you and send this case to court. I wouldn't advise taking that route. Being a defendant in a trial is very, very stressful, and there is enough evidence here for a conviction. I would strongly recommend that you accept the caution we're offering.'

What else could she do?

They let her go and she went home.

Douglas greeted her at the door. She walked past him. 'Don't speak to me.'

He followed her to the bedroom. 'There. Now let that be a lesson to you.'

'A lesson in what?'

'You shouldn't fight me, Fleur. Nothing good will ever come of it.'

'Right.'

He sat down on the bed and smiled. 'It's on your record now. You're an abuser. They'll never believe you, no matter what sob story you give them.'

Fleur stared at him in disbelief. She had no idea how any of this had happened or how she'd ended up here.

PART SEVEN

44

Clover

Clover had been feeling better after last night's shame-release session, and the guilt over not returning to her family had eased a little. Then this morning, Emma told her she'd found her driving licence and Clover had panicked. For a strange moment, she wasn't sure whether to believe her, even though she couldn't imagine for a moment why anyone would make up something so trivial. When she went back to her cabin, she'd emptied her purse out over the floor and her driving licence was gone from the card slot. She wanted to kick herself for not noticing, because now Emma (of all people) knew she wasn't who she said she was, and all it would take was for her to be curious enough to type her real name into Google and there it would all be. Meredith Slater was a missing person with a family desperately worried, and who desperately missed her.

She had a niggling fear that Emma had already done it and told Fleur. That would explain Fleur's weirdness this morning, and her question about the fox. Clover didn't want to entertain that thought, though. She decided she was paranoid, and pushed it to the back of her mind.

Kevin had fallen silent on his blog. He'd written nothing since he announced her father's death. She wondered if he might update it later with funeral details. The funeral would be held in the Kingdom Hall, attended by the whole congregation, and then he'd be buried at the local cemetery. Everyone would pray, with little hope, that her father could become one of the 144,000 followers who might be resurrected once the Earth was destroyed. Only the most faithful could rule with Jehovah in the Kingdom of Heaven. The rest would simply slip away to dust.

She felt the guilt begin to chip away at her restored sense of well-being again, and her thoughts slipped to her mother, alone and grieving. Her mother had never been alone before. She'd lived with her parents until the day she got married at seventeen, and then she'd lived with Clover's father for the next thirty years. He provided the money and she stayed at home and pioneered for the Witnesses. She'd never, as far as Clover could remember, spent even a night away without him. She'd be lonely now. And poor. How could she live with her husband gone?

Now Clover tried to push the thoughts away as she looked through her camera lens at her two wonderful women. Her old life as a Witness was so distant from this. She could barely imagine it – how she'd had to try forcing others into obedience to the laws of Jehovah. Clover cared nothing for obedience. All she cared about was empowering women to live their most unapologetic lives. It could be hard, though. She needed to pay more attention to her own lessons. *Let go of the past. Be bold. Be brilliant. Be who you were born to be. Don't let anyone hold you back.*

'I want you to strike your most powerful pose,' she told them. 'I don't want to see any pretty smiles. I want to see strength, power, determination.'

They stood outside the meditation space together, and Clover snapped them with her Polaroid camera. Hands on hips; feet wide apart; their gazes fixed towards her, unflinching. These women were shedding their good girls.

Clover used a full Polaroid film. She gave each of them one of the best photos. 'Just look at these,' she said. 'See how powerful you look, how ready you are to take on the world. I want you to take one of these home with you, and if ever you begin to doubt your own power, I want you to look at these pictures and see just how incredible you are. Remember how you felt when you were dancing, remember what you saw when you were watching the dancing. I know we haven't talked about it yet – that's for after lunch – but I bet no one here saw a submissive, obedient girl.'

They all laughed.

'Exactly! Now, put these somewhere safe. Do not lose them. These are your treasures from this weekend. When you leave tomorrow, you will bathe in the feelings of this retreat. I hope you'll be able to bathe in them for a long time. But eventually, as you go back to your daily routine, they will wear off. When that starts to happen, take these photos out from wherever you will keep them, and focus on the images. Remind yourselves of who you became while you were here. Tune into your strength. Tune into your dark feminine wisdom. Own yourself. It's time for lunch now. We'll talk more about your experience during this morning's practice when we head down to the forest again.'

Maggie and Fleur left and headed to the dining space. Clover hung around for a few minutes, clearing things away and thinking of things to say in their next session. Her mind went back to Emma. What if she'd found Kevin's blog, seen the truth about Clover and then contacted him to let him know that his wife was here, stripping naked round a campfire in Cornwall with three other women? What then?

She closed her eyes at the thought of it. *It will be okay*, she told herself. *Everything will be okay.*

45

Emma

Emma wandered over to the barn for lunch. Her mood was wretched. She felt like the only solution was to go to bed, wake up in the morning and start again. It was how she used to deal with the worst days after Oliver. She'd become an expert in how to manage trauma. Maybe she should set up retreats to advise others on it. What would she say? She could write a whole book about it.

- Use your hands. Don't underestimate the power of switching off your mind in order to create something. Draw, paint, knit, bake, cook, sculpt. You'll be surprised how pleasurable it is to create something.
- Sleep when you need to.
- Keep working. Even at your worst, the structure will help you.
- On your worst days, remind yourself you will wake up to a new day tomorrow and it might be an easier day than today.
- Remember that this will pass, even though the way out isn't clear.
- Know that nothing will ever be this bad again.

That was the sort of retreat she needed. Something where the sessions were grounded in practical exercises and wise discussion, not pseudo-spiritual bullshit that left her flailing.

She walked into the barn. The others were already seated at the dining table, and Clover was talking. Obviously. Emma pulled Clover's driving licence from her pocket and dropped it on the table beside her. She touched her shoulder as she passed, in something that would have looked like a caring gesture. She had no idea why she did that, and felt like a filthy hypocrite.

She couldn't meet Clover's eye as she sat down.

'Emma,' Clover said. 'It's good to have you back. Are you ready to join the afternoon session?'

Emma nodded. 'Sure,' she said. She couldn't have just stayed in the cabin, waiting for the drama to unfold.

Harriet brought them their lunch. Butternut squash soup and toast topped with yellow tomatoes and vegan feta.

Clover spooned soup into her mouth, closed her eyes and said, 'I can feel my solar plexus responding to the nourishment.'

There was some murmured agreement. Emma didn't even try not to roll her eyes.

Clover continued, 'I know it's a really intense weekend and we've all done a lot of work, but I hope everyone's feeling reasonably joyful. If not, you will be by the time you've eaten this. The solar plexus is all about feeling joyful and balanced.'

'We're all feeling joyful and balanced, aren't we, ladies?' Maggie said.

'Absolutely,' Fleur said.

Emma said nothing. She wasn't sure what to call this

feeling she had, but it wasn't joy. She thought she should probably leave, not just the lunch table, but the whole retreat.

Clover beamed. 'I'm glad. I want you to bring your swimming costumes to this afternoon's session, please.'

'Never,' Emma said. 'I'm not swimming in that river in September. Or any other month, for that matter.'

'Just bring your swimsuit and see. You know I won't force anyone to do anything, but I want you to be free to change your mind. You might find you want to, and then you'll be missing out.'

'She won't be missing out. She can go skinny dipping,' Maggie said.

'I think you know that's not true.'

'You don't know what change might come over you, once you're under the spell of the rainforest goddess.'

'Not even the rainforest goddess has power over me, Maggie.'

'We'll see,' Clover said.

Emma wished she'd fuck off.

46

Fleur

They had two hours free between lunch and the afternoon practice, so Fleur went back to her cabin to rest. She'd long been a fan of the afternoon nap. It gave her a break from being stuck inside her head.

She lay down on the bed and closed her eyes but today sleep was slow in coming. Her mind was still wired from the dancing, and she felt a terrible combination of energized and anxious.

Beside her, her mobile phone pinged with a text message alert. She reached for it and glanced at the screen. There was no name, only the digits of an unfamiliar number.

Can we talk?

Immediately, her heart started racing. She hesitated for a moment, then texted back.

Who is this?

Douglas

How did you get my number?

I'll explain later. I need to see you.

I'm away at the moment.

When are you back?

In a few days.

Can we talk over FaceTime? Now. Please tell me you haven't had an abortion. I need to see you, Fleur.

Maybe tomorrow. I can't talk now. I'm busy.

I need to be with you. I love you. I've never loved anyone like this. I know I fucked everything up and I know it probably feels like we can't be together now after the incident with the police but I promise, if you let me be with you and let me become a father to our child, I'll go to the police and tell them the truth. I'll have that caution removed from your record. I'll stay with you. I will love our baby. I know I will. I would never do anything to hurt it.

She turned her phone off and put it back down on the table beside the bed. There was no way she could sleep now. Douglas was back, and she was plunged again into the old pit of hope, excitement and dread.

He didn't mean it, she knew that, although that wasn't strictly fair. He did mean it. At this moment in time, he meant it earnestly, with all of his heart. But she'd heard all this before. He'd made so many promises, and nothing ever changed, not for very long. She knew the pattern. She knew it well. For a few weeks, or maybe even a couple of months, he'd be wonderful. He'd be fun, charming, caring, attentive, and she'd be madly, deliriously happy. When Douglas was at his best, Fleur experienced the purest form of happiness she'd ever known, and she longed to hold on to it. She still longed to feel that exquisite joy again.

But then things would change. With no warning, he'd become silent. He'd be upset if she left him for an evening to see a friend, and soon afterwards, he'd do something awful. She forced herself to remember the weekend she went away to Norwich. He said he'd meet her at the station when she came home, but when she arrived he wasn't there. She phoned him several times, sent him lots of text messages, and waited for an hour in case he'd been held up. Then she caught a taxi.

He wasn't there when she got home, either. There was no note, he didn't answer his phone or respond to any of her messages. He stayed away in silence for four days.

When he finally walked through the door, he was grim-faced. 'It's over between us, Fleur,' he said.

'What?'

'You need help. You can't just disappear like this. You left me stranded for a whole weekend, with no idea of where you were, and then suddenly you bombarded me with messages and phone calls, asking where *I* was.'

He held out his phone for her to see. 'Look at this,' he said. 'Over a hundred messages and three hundred phone calls. Some of these are so angry and unpleasant. I can't live like this, Fleur. I can't. You need help.'

'But you knew. You knew where I was. You were going to meet me at the station and . . .'

He shook his head. 'You're remembering things that didn't happen. You're remembering conversations we never had. I was so worried when you weren't here. I was frantic. You had me out on the streets, searching for you. I just can't do this.' He thrust his phone into her hand. 'Read these messages. Is this normal behaviour? To rant and rave at someone for four whole days? To leave angry voicemails, demanding to know where I am, when you were the one who disappeared? I was afraid to come home, Fleur. I was afraid of what would greet me when I walked through the door.'

They went on like this for hours, with her telling him what had really happened, and him insisting that she was delusional, until she began to question her sanity, began to wonder whether those conversations she remembered so clearly hadn't really taken place.

She knew the word for it now. Her therapist had told her. *Gaslighting*.

He was never going to change. She had to accept it. If she went back to him, he would drive her to madness.

An hour after his messages, she took herself for a walk through the rainforest, where she could breathe clear air and hide in the canopy of oak trees. The sun was out, but she was aware of the chill of autumn and pulled her jacket tight around her.

She understood what had turned Douglas into this hurt, damaged man. His parents were cold, unloving people. They disapproved of him, wanted him to become someone he wasn't. He said it was because of their childhood that his sister had taken her own life, and his grief for her was intense. Fleur had always believed that if she loved him properly, the way he ought to have been loved all his life, then they'd be able to work together to make him well. She told him she'd go to therapy with him, said she'd do everything she could to support his journey to becoming the wonderful man she knew he was capable of being. She meant it. She meant it with every part of her, but he was never able to stick with therapy for long enough.

'I'm afraid of it, Fleur,' he confessed. 'I'm so afraid of revisiting that old stuff. And also . . . I don't want to face up to the things I've done, and the way I've treated you. I'm frightened to unpick it.' He'd looked up at her with helpless, frightened eyes and she sensed that he was being honest, that this was the closest she'd come to seeing the reality of the sad man beneath the abuser.

But what if the promise of a child was the spark he needed to drive himself back to wellness? What if he committed to change, and then changed? Fleur knew there would be no miracles, that it would take time, but what if he eventually began to like himself enough to stop hurting her?

She had no doubt that Douglas had it in him to love a baby. He would never, ever want to harm a child. He wouldn't be capable of it.

They could have a family together, and live the life she knew they both desperately wanted.

PART EIGHT

47

Meredith

Meredith was seventeen and her parents had linked her with a boy from the Kingdom Hall. His name was Kevin and he looked about fourteen, although everyone said he was twenty and Meredith supposed that must have been true.

She'd been going out with him two evenings a week for a year. Usually, they went to the cinema or the Italian up the road for a meal. She liked him. She did like him, but she didn't think she loved him. There were times when she tried to imagine having sex with him and couldn't. She was grateful for the rule about no sex before marriage, although if she married him, there'd be no getting away from it.

Her father thought she should marry him. He was an Elder at the Kingdom Hall, even though he was so young. Being an Elder had nothing to do with age. It was to do with commitment to Jehovah. Kevin was as committed to Jehovah as anyone could be, and of course this pleased Meredith's father, who worried she might one day stray from the Truth and that Kevin could keep her safe.

He'd given her booklets about marriage. Mostly, the booklets seemed to be telling her not to expect too much. There was even one called *How to Survive the First Year*.

Now she was faced with a choice – to live with her parents for even longer, or to marry Kevin, who she liked but didn't love. If she didn't marry him, her father was bound to find someone else for her, and what if he was worse? She also wasn't sure she had it in her to start all over again, getting to know a bloke whose main personality trait was loyalty to Jehovah.

There was nothing wrong with Kevin. He was kind, decent, hard-working. He wasn't devoid of a sense of humour, either. He just didn't set Meredith on fire, but the marriage booklets seemed to think this was an unrealistic expectation born from watching Hollywood movies, and Hollywood movies were a sign they were living in the end of times.

All she should really expect from marriage was companionship with someone tolerable. Maybe, she thought, that was all anyone should expect. High expectations only led to disappointment and were the reason for the divorce rate.

She should probably just marry him and make the best of it. Her parents said they'd been saving every week since Meredith was born and they had money so she and Kevin could buy a house one day, but they'd need to top it up. They'd have to rent a one-bedroom flat for a year or two, until they had enough for a family home. Then Meredith would be expected to have a baby. The future was laid out for her, a straight road that stretched on to the horizon, without a single bend or surprise.

Her only other option was just to live here with her parents. Her father would go to work in the office every day, Meredith would go to her job at Boots, and her mother would go pioneering. Then they'd all come home and sit at the table for supper, and say grace and talk about what was going on at the Kingdom Hall – the events that were coming up, the newcomers who'd been picked up by pioneers, the people who'd behaved badly, the Witnesses who were at risk of being disfellowshipped.

It was boring. Life with Kevin might not be exciting, but it had to be better than this.

'We'll have to tell him the truth,' her father said one night at supper.

'What truth?' Meredith asked.

'About your birth.'

Her mother pursed her lips and said nothing.

'Okay,' Meredith said.

'You need to be prepared for it to be unacceptable to him.'

'We can explain that it wasn't our choice,' her mother said.

'And we'll just have to see how he takes it.'

Meredith forked mashed potato into her mouth in silence, and wondered if there was any other option. For years, she'd dreamed of running away from here, finding her own place to live, starting a new life away from the Witnesses. But every time she tried to plan it, she didn't know how to leave. She had no money, that was the trouble. She knew she could get a job, an easy job in a shop or an office, but she'd need money before that if she was going to rent a room somewhere. She'd looked up rental prices online. London was out of the question. Rent became cheaper the further north you went, but even in Huddersfield or Newcastle, she'd need about £1,000 to set herself up, and she just didn't have that.

She wondered now whether that was why her mother stayed, too.

Meredith wanted to talk to someone. She remembered the doctor who'd said she could be referred for counselling, but Meredith knew about waiting lists. By the time she had an appointment, she'd have likely been married five years and probably have two babies and maybe also a case of long-term clinical depression. Besides, what could a counsellor do? Their only real power was to nod and ask, 'How does that make you feel?' They wouldn't be able to enter her father's head and change the way he thought.

She needed to talk to someone who could help her. The only person she could think of was her mother but, as always, that felt impossible.

For a few days, Meredith thought about how she could approach her, but no way felt like the right way. She wondered if she should just sit her down, woman to woman, and ask her mother if she'd really wanted to get married all those years ago and if she had, if she still wanted to stay married, and whether she wished she'd ever had a choice in the matter. But when she pictured the conversation, the people talking were not Meredith and her mother. They were another, completely different mother and daughter pair.

In the end, she decided the only thing she could do was just blurt it out, so one afternoon, as she stood in the kitchen while her mother washed a burned cake tin, she said, 'I don't know if I want to marry Kevin.'

Her mother sighed and dried her hands on a floral tea towel that hung off the handle of the oven. 'He's a good man.'

'But I don't . . .' Meredith faltered. She couldn't talk about love or desire with her mother. 'I don't think I can spend my whole life with him. My whole life! Doing nothing but being Kevin's wife.'

'Sit down, Meredith,' her mother said, and pulled two chairs out from the kitchen table.

Meredith was expecting a lecture. She was expecting her mother to tell her she had to marry Kevin because there were no other choices for female Witnesses. They had to run homes and be the centre of their families.

Instead, she said, 'I understand, Meredith.'

Meredith looked up, surprised. 'Do you?'

'Of course I do. I know you think I'm naive, that I just accept this life without question because it's the life I live and I say nothing about it. But it isn't true. It used to be. But after you were born and you had the transfusion and your dad and I had to agree with the Elders that we'd never consent to your having another one, and that we'd let you die . . . Well, that changed things for me. It changed the way I felt. You dad and I . . . We never . . . It's never been . . . Things aren't . . .' She gave up, and let Meredith fill in the blanks. 'What I mean is, I know there's a world out there that you've been exposed to, and I understand the appeal of it for someone like you. There's excitement out there. Possibilities. Why wouldn't you want to explore that at your age?'

'I thought you said it was all evil.'

'If you remember, you'll know I've never said that. Only your dad has ever said that. I've rarely said anything.'

'You don't agree with him?'

'Not always,' her mother admitted.

'Are you . . . Are you happy?' Meredith asked.

'Me?'

'Yes.'

Her mother sighed deeply. 'This is the life I've always lived. I don't know what another life would look like. Your dad has always looked after me. I've never had to work. He's provided me with everything I need. I don't ask for more than that.'

It hardly sounded like happiness to Meredith. She said, 'I don't know whether I want the same life as you.'

Her mother looked helpless. 'I don't know how to help you get another life, if that's what you're asking.'

Meredith felt her eyes fill. 'There are ways,' she said. 'You could let me go back to school, or maybe college . . .'

'Your father would never allow that.'

'What about all that money?'

'What money?'

'The money for Kevin and me to buy a house.'

Her mother looked shocked. 'That wouldn't be possible. Your father has worked hard all your life to save that money for when you get married. He wouldn't give it to you so you can go against his rules. He just wouldn't. If I so much as went near the subject, he'd think I'd lost my mind. There's no question of it, Meredith.'

Meredith gazed at her hand while she spoke. 'What if you didn't ask him? What if you just gave it to me, and I left?'

'Left?' her mother asked, as if she didn't understand the meaning of the word.

'Yes.'

'You want to just take the money and live by yourself?'

'Maybe not by myself exactly. But I could find a house share and go to college. Do my A levels. Go to university. Or something else. Anything else.'

Her mother had been stunned into silence, and Meredith had no courage left to speak further. She just let her words hang in the air between them.

Eventually, her mother said, 'I can't imagine what the consequences would be when your father found out that I'd done that. And as for you, you'd be disfellowshipped, and . . .'

'I don't care if I'm disfellowshipped.'

'Maybe not now you don't, but one day you will.' The colour began to drain from her face as she thought about it. 'If you left here, Meredith, I wouldn't be able to see you again. The Elders would cut you out, and they wouldn't allow me to visit you. And neither would your father. You can't do it. Don't do it. Please, Meredith. I know it isn't easy, but it might not be that bad. Kevin is a good man. He'll take care of you . . .'

'I don't want to be taken care of, Mum.'

'I know. I know. You've been born into different times and it must feel very old-fashioned. You won't be helpless. Your husband will always be the head of your family, but try and think of yourself as the neck. You can turn that head any way you want.'

'Like you do?'

'No, not like I do. But you're stronger than me, and you'll do it. You can make this life work.'

I can't, Meredith thought. *I can't and I won't.*

48

Maggie

The early hours of the morning were the worst time. It was then that the angry darkness descended and took her over.

She replayed the day of Annie's death over and over. The baby had been fine – completely fine! – all morning. Maggie had laid her on her playmat in the kitchen and put the finishing touches to the portrait of her she'd been working on for the last few days. She was copying it from a photo of Annie sleeping in her lap. In the picture, the only part of Maggie that appeared was her hand. It showed her wedding ring, and Annie's hand curled over her finger. She liked it. She liked the way it captured the love of their family and the baby at the heart of it. She'd painted one of Richard at the same age and planned to hang them side by side on the landing.

Obviously, like always, she'd painted in short bursts that morning. Annie would grow restless and want to feed, so she'd put down her paintbrushes and attach the baby to her breast, doing what she could to the portrait with one hand. She'd learnt to do everything one-handed again. It was just what happened when you had a baby.

At 12.15, Annie had fallen asleep so she took her upstairs and laid her down in the Moses basket, following the advice to settle her on her tummy. She remembered thinking how Annie took up nearly all the space in the basket now and it wouldn't be long before they'd need to move her to a cot, and then she passed Richard's room and heard him and his friend Thomas playing as she went back downstairs.

Two hours later, Annie was dead. The only people who could have gone near her in that time were Richard and Thomas. There was no one else around. That was it. The only possibility.

She didn't think Richard would ever have hurt her deliberately. She thought they'd likely been playing a game. Maybe they'd picked her up and handled her too roughly. Maybe they'd done something with that boyish roughness of Richard's – squeezed her too tightly, perhaps; she couldn't think what, exactly – that had made it hard for her to breathe. Maybe when they'd put her back in the basket, they'd put the blanket over her head and she'd suffocated.

The thoughts were wild, uncontrollable and convincing. They took up all the space in her head as she tried to seize the most likely possibility and pin it down. She knew well enough how close she was to the edge of madness. She could feel it. The energy of her mind was electric.

She reached for the glass of water beside the bed and heard Bill stirring. 'You okay?' he asked. He worried about her, though she knew his own nights were anguished as well. She had to pretend not to hear him whenever he took himself downstairs so he wouldn't disturb her with his sobbing. Maggie couldn't comfort him. It was hard enough trying to keep herself afloat.

'I'm all right. Not a fan of the night, that's all.'

'No.'

She said, 'I keep going over it in my head.'

'I know you do.'

'She was fine. She was absolutely fine when I put her down.'

'I know she was, love.'

'So what happened?'

'It was a cot death, Maggie. We know that.' For the first time, she heard impatience creep into his voice.

'The only people who were upstairs when I left her were Richard and Thomas.'

Bill said nothing. She imagined him trying to get to grips with what she was suggesting, and finding it unthinkable.

She said, 'I know they wouldn't have done anything deliberately . . .'

Bill snapped the light on and sat bolt upright. 'You're not suggesting—'

'Maybe they played a game with her, handled her too roughly or something.'

'For God's sake, there was an autopsy, Maggie! Every part of her body was examined by the coroner and there wasn't a mark on her. No one touched her.'

'Then why isn't he upset? Why's he in his room all the time, hiding?'

'He is upset. He's in his room all the time because he can't handle being around us. He is the reason we need to keep going. I've been trying to say that to you since it happened.'

'Last week, I asked him if he was sad about Annie and he said he wasn't. He said he was fine.'

Bill put his face in his hands in exasperation. 'He was

saying that because he doesn't want you to worry about him when you have enough to deal with. It's nothing to do with not caring. He's a kid, Maggie. He's eight years old. He's your son. I can't believe you would even think this.'

There was no point saying anything more. It was going to fall on wilfully deaf ears. Everything she said fell on deaf ears, but it didn't mean she was wrong.

Bill said, 'Don't ever mention this to him. Please, Maggie.'

'Okay.'

'I think maybe we should go and see a bereavement counsellor. This obsession with finding out what happened isn't doing you any good. It's going to destroy you if you keep it up.'

A bereavement counsellor. A stranger. A professional she would have to sit with and talk to, who'd tell her she was losing her mind. 'I'm not ready for that, Bill,' she said.

He took her hand in his and looked at her seriously. 'Please don't say anything to Richard.'

In the morning, she walked Richard to school for the first time since it happened. She didn't feel ready to see people again and face the onslaught of sympathetic faces, or the discomfort of people who couldn't bear to be around her, or the stares from those who simply wanted to see what a woman whose baby had died looked like. She did it because she had to, because Bill was right. Richard needed her, and she needed to hold herself together for him.

He slipped his hand in hers. The simple tenderness of it made her want to lie down on the ground and weep. She couldn't bear it. She turned her thoughts to the fact that he'd been upstairs when Annie died. It hardened her heart, made her furious, and meant it was easier to put one foot in front of the other.

The usual morning crowd was gathered at the school gates. Maggie was aware of the ripple that went through them as she arrived. *Here she is, the woman whose baby died.*

She kissed Richard goodbye and watched him head into the playground to join his class.

One of the braver women came up to her. 'Hello, Maggie,' she said. 'I'm so sorry.'

Maggie forced a smile. 'Thank you.'

'If there's anything I can do. You know, if you need a break and want someone to take Richard off your hands, please just let me know.'

'I will.'

The woman seemed to have run out of things to say. She looked slightly helpless, then said, 'She was such a sweet baby.'

'Thank you,' Maggie said again.

The woman touched her arm briefly, then said, 'I'd better go. I need to do the food shop this morning.'

Maggie nodded and made her escape, and felt so jealous of that woman and her boring, normal life.

At home, she dragged her easel out of the understairs cupboard and tried to go back to painting, but what was there to paint now? Not Annie. Not anyone in her family. Her family had been ripped apart. She arranged some fruit on the kitchen table and tried a still life. It would be easy, she thought – a couple of apples, a banana, a jug of water. That would do. A way to ease herself back into it. She started with a few strokes of green, but the fury inside her began to swell. Where was the point in painting an apple? Where was the point in any of this? She hurled her paintbrush across the room, then she hurled the apple across the room as well. It smashed, its skin splitting open and the white flesh bruising the wall. She threw the other one as well.

She was mad, she knew that. She was completely, completely mad.

She raged herself into exhaustion and spent hours afterwards asleep. It was after two o'clock when she woke, and Richard would be home soon. He usually walked back from school with the children from next door. She had no idea where Bill was. He'd left early this morning and she hadn't seen him since. He was probably trying to escape from her. She couldn't blame him.

She made herself a cup of tea and tried to summon the energy to prepare for Richard to walk through the door, his shoulders hunched and his eyes fixed to the ground. She needed to make him a glass of orange squash and give him a couple of biscuits from the jar, the way she always used to when he came home from school, but it was too hard and all she wanted was to be left alone.

She knew she mustn't mention Annie to him. She knew it. It wasn't going to do anyone any good. Even if she asked, she'd never get a truthful answer, and then Bill would find out and be furious with her.

Bill should bloody well be here, she thought. He'd probably gone walking. That was what he usually did when life or Maggie became too much for him. He shouldn't have left her that day, not knowing what she was thinking and how close to the edge she was.

She went through the motions of making Richard a snack and set it down on the table, ready for when he came in. She was going to sit with him for a while, ask about his day, show an interest, be a good mother.

The front door opened and he stepped inside.

'Hello, love,' she called.

He didn't say anything, but she heard him taking off his shoes and dumping his bag on the floor.

He slouched into the kitchen.

She made her voice sound as bright as possible. 'Sit down, sweetheart,' she said.

Obediently, he took a seat at the table and she sat opposite him.

'How was your day?'

'Fine.'

'That's good. Did you see Thomas?'

'Yeah.'

'How is he?'

'All right.'

It was hard work. She took a deep breath and said, 'Do you remember the day that Annie died, Richard?'

He entwined the fingers of both hands and began to fidget nervously. 'Yeah.'

'I put her in her basket to sleep. You and Thomas were playing with your Scalextric in your room. Do you remember that?'

He shrugged.

She tried to keep her tone calm, but it was hard. She caught the angry edge to it as she spoke. 'Did you, at any point, go and see the baby as she slept? Did you touch her? Pick her up?'

He wouldn't meet her eye. 'We went to look at her, but we didn't touch her.'

Maggie's heart began to pound. 'Really?'

He nodded.

'You didn't pick her up?'

'No.'

'Why did you go and look at her?'

He shrugged.

'Why?'

He was silent.

'*Why*, for God's sake? *Why* did you go and look at her?'

'I don't know!'

'Was she alive when you looked at her?'

'I think so.'

'What do you mean, you think so?'

'I don't know.'

He started to cry. He was beside himself, but she couldn't stop.

'Was she alive when you saw her?'

'Yes.'

'Right. So what happened after you saw her? Why was she dead by the time I next saw her?'

He started to shake, but said nothing.

'Did you hurt her, Richard?'

She took his silence for guilt.

'Did you?'

'No.'

'You need to tell me the truth.'

'I didn't.'

'I think you did.'
'I didn't.'
'You and Thomas were the last ones to see her alive.'
'I didn't do anything.'

She kept on. She kept on and on. When she looked back at the woman she'd been on that day, she wanted to reach back through time, drag her from the table and send her away somewhere – anywhere but there. But she couldn't. It was too late and the damage had been done in those five brutal minutes.

At the weekend, Richard went to stay with Thomas. He started to spend most of his time there. When he did come home, he only wanted to be with Bill. They did gentle things together – watched TV, learnt wood carving, read *The Hobbit*. Sometimes, Maggie would try and talk to him but he was afraid of her now. He spoke when he had to, but he kept his distance.

49

Meredith

They were married three months after her eighteenth birthday. Ceremonies at the Kingdom Hall held no legal weight, and Meredith was hoping she could talk everyone into the idea that there would be no need to have an official ceremony at the registry office as well.

'Isn't it enough that we'll be married in the eyes of Jehovah?' she said. 'That's the important thing.'

Kevin clearly thought she'd lost her mind, but he chose his words tactfully. 'I'm delighted you see it this way,' he said, 'but we need to be legally married as well. Otherwise, what will happen to our children? In the eyes of the law, they will be illegitimate.'

Meredith didn't care. She'd known people at school whose parents lived together without being married and they were exactly the same as everyone else. She said this to Kevin.

Kevin was unimpressed. 'I think you know that while they might have *appeared* to be the same as everyone else, God will have frowned upon that union and when Judgement Day comes, those children will be—'

She couldn't bear to hear any more. 'Okay, okay,' she said. 'We'll do it properly.'

In the end, they had a small service in the registry office with only their parents and two witnesses present. Meredith went through the whole thing feeling dissociated from her body. She watched from somewhere outside herself as she pledged her commitment to Kevin and signed the register.

She did the same when they were married a week later at the Kingdom Hall. An Elder named Francis, who'd known Meredith all her life, talked on and on for nearly forty minutes about how the Bible would help them to a happy marriage. They needed to follow God's rules about commitment; to sacrifice their own wishes to please the other; they needed to make time together a priority; they needed to guard against desire for another; they needed to work hard; and above all, Meredith needed to accept that her husband was now her God-appointed head.

('But don't worry,' her mother had said. 'The man is the head of the family, but the woman is the neck and she can move that head any way she wishes.')

Meredith made her vows and felt dread in her stomach. *I need to get out of this*, she thought. *Somehow or another, I will get out of this.*

They moved into a tiny flat on the edge of town, with one bedroom, a living room and a kitchen that was only big enough for two cabinets and an oven. Kevin's full-time wage from Homebase was only just enough to cover the rent, food and bills, even though he was a manager. Meredith said, 'We need the money. I want to work.'

Kevin battled with the idea of having a wife who worked, rather than staying at home and involving herself only with the Kingdom Hall and pioneering. The wives of the other Elders spent all their time arranging coffee mornings, Bible study meetings and maintaining the Kingdom Hall. They had no need to earn money; 'God will provide the necessities of life, and we have no need for more.'

Meredith thought they must all be miserable and, besides, God didn't provide the necessities of life. Anyone who looked beyond their own front door could see that.

In the end, they agreed that she should work three days a week. The rest of the time, she'd be out converting the sinners and bringing them to salvation.

Her spare time was restricted, even more than it had been when she lived with her parents. Kevin refused to allow a television into the house and she couldn't download the Netflix app to her phone because he controlled all their money. Even iPlayer was out of reach. They had no TV licence and someone in authority was bound to catch her if she lied.

'Kevin, I'm bored,' she told him. 'I am so bored, I'm going to actually die from it.'

He was sitting on the sofa beside her, poring over his notes for his next service at the Kingdom Hall. 'You can read this for me. Tell me if you think it's okay.'

She was sure she'd heard of some frustrated Victorian woman once who'd smashed her brains out against the rocks. She was beginning to feel a remarkable kinship with her. 'No, thanks,' she said. 'I'm sure it's fine. Can we just get a TV?'

He laid his papers down in his lap and looked at her seriously. 'You know we can't.'

'Why not?'

'Because we need to keep ourselves separate from the moral contamination of the world, and the television is full of it. So much violence, and now there's even homosexuality. Men kissing each other. Women kissing each other. We can't have this in our house, Meredith.'

'What about on Sunday nights? Sunday nights are just costume dramas, or things about farming and the countryside. Documentaries about Yorkshire.' She'd had a conversation about this once with one of her friends at school, about why Sunday-night television was so boring. 'It's because people tolerate things on Sundays that they wouldn't tolerate the rest of the week,' her friend had said, and Meredith could see the truth in it. Even so, she'd love the chance to watch a dramatization of some old Victorian novel right now.

'No,' he said.

He must have seen the disappointment in her face because the next day, he came home from work and handed her a carrier bag full of books. 'I don't want you to be bored,' he said. 'I thought you'd enjoy these.'

She opened the bag. Inside it were ancient copies of old romance novels with titles like *A Man of Complexity* and *The Forgotten Husband*. The covers all had pictures of strong, dark-haired men holding fragile-looking women in their arms. She stared at them, one by one. There was nothing here that interested her.

'Thanks,' she said.

'You're welcome. Now, I need to finish my planning for tomorrow's Bible Study. What time were you thinking of dinner?'

She shrugged. 'Whenever you're ready,' she told him. 'I can prepare it for whenever you like.'

She took herself to the kitchen and started chopping onions to disguise her tears.

Pioneering was changing. Someone important had decided door-to-door work wasn't working and instead they needed to set up stands in town centres and catch people as they passed by. They'd thrust *The Watchtower* into their hands and pray for them to read it and be saved.

Meredith was paired with a younger girl called Joni. She was sixteen and had just left school and Meredith was meant to help her grow in pioneering confidence. She had no intention of doing that. She wanted to guide Joni away from all this, to stop her from doing what Meredith had just done.

For an hour, she just observed her. Joni seemed lively and intelligent and capable of more than this. Her attempts to engage the sinners in conversation also struck Meredith as half-hearted. Most people simply walked past.

Joni said, 'What do you think our hit rate is? How many souls do you think we've saved?'

'None, Joni. I think we've saved fuck all.'

Joni only looked momentarily shocked, then she smiled. 'Really? None?'

'If we have brought anyone into the cult – because it is a cult, you know that, don't you? – we'll have ruined their lives. We won't have saved them.'

'You don't . . . believe in this?'

'No. I think it's all rubbish and I'm trapped in it. I've been trapped in it since I was born.'

'Wow.' Meredith's confession seemed to have liberated something in Joni. She said, 'I do find it boring. Really boring. All those services. And I didn't think my friends at school were sinners. I was jealous of them. They had a lot more fun than I did.'

'There's an alternative out there.'

'Yes, but wouldn't you be afraid of it?'

'No. I used to be. I used to think that if I made friends with someone outside the faith, I'd become wicked and when The End came round, I'd be cast out. But I understand now. It's brainwashing. We've been brainwashed. None of it is true. They were convinced Judgement Day was coming in 1914, then 1974. They planned for it. They expected it, but those years came round and guess what? Nothing happened. The world went on just as it always had. It's bullshit, Joni.'

'What are you going to do?'

'I'm going to get out. I'll find a way.' She picked up a pile of *Watchtower* magazines and said, 'How about we throw these away and find something else to do?'

'Really?'

'You don't have to.'

'I think I should stay. For a while.'

'I think I'm going to go. Just for half an hour. Would you mind?'

'No, I suppose not.'

'Thanks. I'll come back. I won't leave you for long.' She began to walk away, then went back and said, 'I probably shouldn't have said all this. You won't tell anyone, will you?'

'Of course not.'

Meredith couldn't imagine Joni having the guts to tell her parents and stir up conflict. They both knew the Elders would come down hard on her for speaking like this. She'd be expected to repent for weeks.

She set off up the road and past the community centre. There was a sign outside. *Free introduction to yoga and meditation. Just walk in.*

She walked in.

Meredith had heard of yoga, of course, but her understanding of it was fuzzy. She thought of it as something young travellers did on beaches in Thailand, or a form of gentle exercise for older women who didn't have it in them to go to the gym any more.

Her teacher was a middle-aged woman called Sam, with muscular calves and an air of serenity. 'Welcome,' she said when the group of six was seated on the blue yoga mats. 'Welcome to my Introduction to Yoga class. Before we begin our first exercise, let me tell you a little about this ancient practice. Yoga is not just a physical discipline. It is also mental and spiritual. We exercise the body, and we quieten the mind. We aim to integrate the body, mind and spirit and, in doing so, we come to realize that we belong in a universe in which everything is connected and we are all of us part of a much greater whole. When we practice yoga, we feel peaceful, relaxed and connected to the universe.'

Meredith felt the stirring of something deep inside her, something like excitement.

'We will begin with the simplest and most basic yoga pose. Please sit cross-legged on your mats with your hands on your knees, palms facing upwards and your spines as straight as you can make them,' Sam said. 'Now, I would like you to close your eyes and inhale to the count of four, focussing on your breath.'

Meredith did so.

'Now hold the breath for four, and then release the breath for four. As you continue to breathe, be aware of your connection to the divine power. Some of you might already think of this power as God, others might come to think of it as simply an unseen power that is higher than ourselves, or you might have your own ideas about what the divine power is. It doesn't matter, but I hope that as you develop your commitment to yoga, you will come to feel yourself joined to the universal spirit and part of a greater whole. This connection, together with your psychical and mental well-being, will lead you towards inner peace and tranquillity.'

Meredith sat still and breathed, and felt herself letting go of Jehovah and something wiser and more thoughtful taking His place.

50

Maggie

For years afterwards, they muddled through. Most of the time, Richard was pleasant enough to her. He'd insist he was fine and that he'd been unaffected by her hatred during his childhood. She never believed him, although she wanted to. How could he have been fine?

Then all of a sudden, there would be moments as he grew older when he'd have an outburst of anger and remind her of everything she'd done wrong. She could never pull him up for his bad behaviour – staying out too late, not phoning to let her know where he was – because if she did, he'd bring up the past. 'You're in no position to tell me how to live,' he'd say. 'No matter what I do to you, no matter how much I worry you or frighten you, it will always be nothing compared to what you did to me.'

She'd try and latch on to that and talk to him about it, but he'd shut down. In the end, she stopped saying anything because the reminders of the past were unbearable.

For years, she'd only ever had fragments of Richard. Now she dared to hope that things might change.

51

Meredith

Meredith had been married to Kevin for a year and every day was boring. They woke up at 7.30, had breakfast together, then Kevin would leave for his job at Homebase. Meredith would either go to work at Boots, or if she wasn't working she'd pick up her pile of *Watchtower* magazines and stand on the street with Joni, being ignored or stared at by normal people with normal lives. On Saturdays, they had tea with her parents. Her mother had taken to examining Meredith's belly the minute she set eyes on her, to see if she was pregnant, no doubt. There was no chance of that. Meredith had endured two months of sex with Kevin and now, every night, she did everything she could to avoid it. For the first time in her life, she was grateful for her anaemia. A wan face and a flash of weakness could get her out of a lot.

Kevin didn't seem to mind too much. He was nervous and inhibited in the bedroom. Meredith could tell he thought God was watching his every move, ready to damn him to everlasting shame if he attempted anything other than ten minutes in the missionary position. 'If you're ill, you need to rest,' he said. She rested. She'd have rather done anything than look up at a face she wasn't even attracted to while he thrust away on top of her and grunted. It made her feel sick.

She wasn't lying about the illness. She was feeling weaker than usual and knew her iron levels were low. After Kevin left for work that morning, she phoned the hospital to talk to them about it and they told her to come in so they could check her over and see if she needed to take iron intravenously. 'Come at one, if you can wait that long,' the receptionist said.

She agreed, and went into town to meet Joni at their usual spot. It was November now, and cold. She said, 'I'm not sure I can stand here for three hours.'

'I can't either.'

'Let's do an hour, then get coffee.'

'Is there no yoga for you today?'

'No. The teacher's got a cold. But I am well on my way to Enlightenment, so it's not crucial.'

Joni grinned. 'Cool. When you've reached Enlightenment, will you teach me?'

'Definitely. You have to start by not ending up like me – married to a man you don't like very much because your parents told you to.'

'I'll try,' Joni said, but she sounded doubtful. Her parents had already made her leave school. Marriage would be their next attack.

'I wish there was a quick and easy way out of this.'

'Me too,' Joni said. 'This isn't how I want to spend my life.'

'I might just leave.'

'Run away?'

'No,' Meredith said firmly. 'I'm an adult. It wouldn't be running away. It would be leaving. Leaving a situation I'm not happy with. When I was younger, I saw a counsellor and she told me I needed to try and stand up to my parents.

I never managed it. But what she did say is that if I could, I should try and earn my own money so I could put some aside and get out if the time ever came when I needed to. She called it an escape fund. You need a minimum of about a thousand pounds so you can pay a deposit and the first month's rent on a flat. I've been to a lettings agent. I reckon I'll need a bit more than that, but it's not as hard to rent somewhere as I thought it would be.'

'Do you think you'll really do it?'

'Yes, but at the moment I don't have much. Bloody Kev takes all my money.'

The unfairness of it brought her blistering rage to the surface and made her dizzy. She stumbled to the edge of the pavement and sat down against a wall.

'Meredith, are you okay?'

Meredith tried nodding but her head was heavy as rock.

She heard Joni shouting for help, then nothing.

She woke up in hospital, a nurse beside her and a needle in her arm, connected to a bag of blood.

'What happened?' she asked.

'Your iron levels were dangerously low. You passed out. Your friend called an ambulance and they got you here. We couldn't get your iron levels where they needed to be, so we're giving you some red blood cells. They'll perk you up.'

She nodded weakly. 'Thank you.'

The nurse looked serious for a minute. 'We phoned your husband to let him know. He came straight away with your father. You probably know they are against you having a transfusion?'

'Yes.'

'You might remember that a few years ago, when you were sixteen, you signed a document giving your consent to a transfusion if you ever needed one to save your life.'

'Yes.'

'Unfortunately, your family weren't aware of this.'

'No.'

'I'm afraid they've gone off in search of a solicitor who will declare you mentally unfit to make your own decisions regarding medical treatment.'

Of course they had.

'But in the meantime, we've begun the transfusion to save your life.'

'Thank you.'

'We've checked your records and you've never been diagnosed with any kind of mental illness or intellectual impairment, is that right?'

She wanted to scream *Of course that's bloody right!* but she didn't have the strength for it, so she just nodded.

'Well then, your family are going to have a serious struggle on their hands to find a lawyer who will support them.'

'My family are mad,' she said.

She didn't hear from Kevin or her parents that day and she didn't bother to contact them herself. She imagined they were still frantically looking for lawyers, or calling emergency meetings at the Kingdom Hall to decide what should be done with her. They'd expect her to repent. She wasn't going to repent. If she didn't repent, they'd have her disfellowshipped and they'd all be expected to keep their distance from her. She wondered if they'd have to send her away and thought it sounded blissful.

Joni came to visit her in the evening. She brought a giant bar of Dairy Milk and sat in the chair beside her bed.

'I'm sorry I scared you,' Meredith said.

'It's fine. I'm just glad you're okay.'

'You know they gave me a transfusion?'

Joni gasped. 'Seriously?'

'Yep. Kevin and my dad are losing their shit.'

'Have you seen them?'

'No.'

'What about your mum?'

Meredith shrugged. 'I don't know. I know she wants me to live. A couple of years ago, she told me to sign the document saying I consented to a transfusion if I needed one, but she forbade me to tell my dad. She's afraid of him. She's never said so, but I can see it. I hate it. I hate that he does this to her, and I hate that she's too weak to resist him.'

'What do you think he'll do?'

'I think he and Kev will have me disfellowshipped.'

'Maybe that can be your way out.'

'Maybe it can. I'm not going to repent. I'm not sorry. If I'd done what they wanted, I'd be lying in a morgue right now.'

Joni shuddered. 'Don't say that.'

'It's true, Joni. Don't you see? This mad religion demands that they let me die. They would have let me die.'

'I know,' Joni said. 'I know.'

She went home on her own. No one came to the hospital to pick her up. She braced herself for the fight the minute she walked through the door.

Kevin was there. He didn't look at her.

She went through to the bedroom and lay on the bed. She tried to read, but couldn't concentrate.

Eventually, Kevin came and stood in the doorway. 'You had a transfusion,' he said simply.

'Yes,' she said. 'If I hadn't, I would have died.'

'You signed a document none of us knew about to say you consented to a transfusion. You did this two years ago.'

'I did.'

She watched as he brought his fury under control. 'You didn't tell me this before we married.'

She shrugged.

'That is an act of grave deceit, Meredith. It goes against one of our most sacred doctrines. I am an Elder at the Kingdom Hall . . .' He was so furious, he nearly choked on his words. 'I wouldn't have married you if I'd known you had done this.'

She looked straight at him. 'Then un-marry me,' she said.

'I can't. It's forbidden. But we held a meeting last night, with your parents and the other Elders, and it was agreed that if you don't repent, you will have to be disfellowshipped and it will be my duty to shun you until you repent enough to be welcomed back into the community.'

'You're going to have a long wait, Kevin. I value my life more than I value the doctrines of this bloody religion.'

Her words had rendered him speechless. He left the room. She wondered if he was going to be sick. She wondered how she could get out of this. She wondered where her mother was.

They were all against her now. All of them. The Elders met at the Kingdom Hall to discuss the issue, and Meredith refused to go. 'I won't be made to feel as though I've done something wrong,' she said.

They had her disfellowshipped. Her parents wouldn't speak to her, and Kevin only said the bare minimum he needed to to get through the day. He ate his meals separately, sitting on the floor in their tiny kitchen. Meredith moved out of the bedroom and onto the sofa, and no longer had to feign illness to avoid sex.

The situation was impossible. She knew it couldn't go on. She lit candles, and asked the divine power for help.

A week after she was disfellowshipped and while Kevin was at work, Meredith went down to the lobby to check the post and found a small white envelope with her name on it. The handwriting belonged to her mother.

She took it back up to the flat and sat on the sofa to read it.

> M, I've taken the money out of the loft where we hid it. It's under our bed. Take it and go. You need to do it today. Dad will be home at 6 and I am out all afternoon. Key in the usual place. Don't write or phone.
>
> Be safe, my dearest girl. I will be thinking of you all the time and hope we can be reunited one day soon.
>
> Mum

PART NINE

52

Clover

It was another bright afternoon, so she took them back down to the rainforest studio, yoga mats under their arms and swimming bags over their shoulders. The forest was the most gentle, beautiful but powerful setting at the whole retreat centre. It did everyone good to be here.

They sat in their usual circle and Clover opened the session by saying, 'Welcome again to this wild and natural space. Before we start, I'd like you to think for a moment about what the word *wild* means to you. You do not need to wait for me to call your name. Just speak when you feel moved to speak.'

There was a long period of silence while the women reflected.

To Clover's surprise, Emma spoke first. 'I suppose for me, it's the opposite of *tame* and it makes me think of how we all feel we have to tame ourselves, and tame other people, too. We aren't wild enough in our day-to-day lives, perhaps. I can admit that if I experience or witness wild emotion, I feel very uncomfortable with it. I try and tame it. Maybe I shouldn't. Maybe I should be more wild.'

There was some murmuring agreement, some nodding of heads. It was the most honestly Clover had ever heard

Emma speak. She tried not to look too pleased. This wasn't school. There wasn't meant to be a right and wrong. But she loved what Emma had just said. Most of all, she loved the fact that Emma herself had said it.

Then Maggie spoke. 'This feels quite wild. I know we're not doing anything revolutionary like throwing ourselves in front of horses or gluing ourselves to the road, but there's a quiet wildness here.' She looked round at the group. 'We're four women of various ages, and we're here, in a wild environment, being our most natural selves. Is that what wildness is? Being more natural. Being more *you*. Perhaps *daring* to be more you. Maybe that's where the wildness comes in.'

Clover felt like clapping. These women were good.

Fleur said, 'I used to think of my ex as wild. I described him that way. He was untamed. The wildness Maggie and Emma have described is a wonderful wildness, a good wildness. But maybe wildness can be dangerous, too.'

They all agreed. It was true, Clover thought, although the conversation had gone in slightly the wrong direction.

She said, 'Like all things, wildness has its shadow side. If we look around, we see all this beauty in the natural world, but of course we know nature can be brutal, too. But perhaps we, as decent people, are at our best when we're our most authentic. Our wildest selves. Maybe we need to learn to not push against wildness so much. I invite you now to close your eyes and sit in quiet contemplation as you think about this. Let the idea of being true to your wildness take shape in your mind and also your body. Welcome the idea of wildness into your heart, your muscles and your bones. Let it sit with you for a while.'

She allowed five minutes to slip away.

'Slowly bring yourself back to the space. Feel your body on the forest floor, and become aware again of the sounds around you. When you're ready, open your eyes.'

They all opened their eyes.

Clover reached into her bag and pulled out her sacred stone, a large rock of raw crystal she'd bought from a travelling healer in Appleby last year. She clasped it as she spoke. 'Our time together isn't over. We have more to do this evening and in the morning, but I'd like us to use this time now to share our stories if we would like to. Please don't panic about this. It is, as always, completely up to you if you would like to share or not. Soon, I will pass round this sacred stone. If you would like to speak, hold the sacred stone and know that the powers it holds within it will help you to find your voice. If you don't want to speak, simply pass the stone to the next person.'

She paused for a moment and cleared her throat. 'This isn't a practice I do on every retreat,' she continued. 'It's something I do when I see that the women here have connected and when I sense they have a story to tell. I, too, have a story to tell. I am moved to tell it because I want to foster a spirit of trust and openness here, and I am concerned that you might feel you have reason not to trust me.'

Fleur said, 'There's no one here who doesn't trust you.' She looked round at the group. 'Is there?'

'Absolutely not,' Maggie agreed

Clover looked at Emma, who just shook her head, uncertain.

Clover smiled. 'Thank you. But I just want to explain, to

put right anything that might have gone wrong.' She took a deep breath in and said, 'You might know I used to be a Jehovah's Witness. I came from a very strict family and my parents arranged a marriage for me to a man I didn't love. I left that marriage and I also abandoned my parents. I suffer from chronic anaemia. I can usually control it with iron pills and diet, but sometimes it gets quite bad and I have to go to hospital for injections. There was also one time in my life, a couple of years ago, when my iron levels became so low, I was dangerously ill and the only way to save me was through a blood transfusion.'

She could see Emma hanging on every word.

'My father and husband had always said I should never consent to a transfusion because it is against the law of Jehovah. They believed very strongly that I should die rather than receive treatment. My mother disagreed, but never had the courage to stand up to them. She told me what I needed to do so that doctors would save my life, but I had to pretend she'd played no part in it.'

She paused again. Emma looked away.

'I wanted to live. When I was sixteen, I signed a paper to override my parents' instructions. My mother knew I'd done this – it was her idea – but my father didn't. So when I became ill, I received a transfusion and was disfellowshipped from the Witnesses. This meant my husband and parents had to shun me until I agreed to repent and return to the truth. In order to repent, I would have to apologize for receiving blood and also sign a document refusing such treatment in future. So if I wanted to see my parents again, or stay married to my husband, I had to agree that I would die if I ever became ill again.'

She saw Emma put her head in her hands.

'I wasn't prepared to do that, so I had to leave. I had no money. The last I ever heard from my mother was a note telling me where their life savings were and that I should take them and get away. She said nothing else, but I knew the laws of the Witnesses said she had to shun me for either the rest of my life or until I repented and could return. The idea of me living my life as a non-Witness is unbearable to my father, and so my mother has to pretend it's unbearable to her, too. She has never been a strong wild woman. My father always wanted to find me, to force me to repent. Because of this, I adopted a new name. I haven't made it legal yet, but I will. My real name is Meredith Slater. I'm telling you this only because I somehow managed to drop my driving licence yesterday and one of you found it. I didn't want anyone to think I was on the run from the law or something. I'm not. I'm on the run from a religion that wants to kill me.'

Everyone sat in shocked silence as they took this in.

Maggie was the first to speak. 'I'm really sorry you've been through all this,' she said.

Fleur said, 'You know I just have the utmost respect for all that you are and all that you're doing to help other women.'

Emma, predictably, said nothing.

Clover said, 'Now, I'm going to pass the sacred stone to the goddess on my left. Maggie.'

Maggie said, 'I don't have a story I need to tell, but I will say that I'm worried about my cat. He went missing last night and isn't home yet, so if you could all ask our feminine ancestors to return him to me, that would be good.'

There was a moment of silence while everyone communed with their goddesses.

Maggie passed the stone to Fleur.

Fleur opened her mouth, as if ready to tell a long story. 'You probably all gathered that I was once . . .' She shook her head, suddenly unable to continue. 'I'm sorry,' she said.

Clover was disappointed. She'd wanted Fleur to tell them about Douglas and her current predicament so that if she was still thinking about having the baby, they could all gently talk her out of it. She couldn't say anything now, though. Her job wasn't to force anyone.

In silence, Fleur passed the stone to Emma. Emma held it for a while. 'I'm not . . .' she began, then started again. 'I'm not very good at this. I've never been very good at speaking from my heart. Actually, I've never really been sure I even have a heart, to be honest. I don't really know . . .' She paused and took some deep breaths, as if to gather herself. Then all of a sudden, she shook her head, stood up and was gone.

Clover gazed at her circle of openness in disbelief. This hadn't been the plan at all.

53

Fleur

They sat beneath their rainforest canopy in silence. No one seemed to know what to do. In the end, Fleur said, 'Should someone go and see if she's okay?'

Clover said, 'No. I don't think that's what she wants. This is all too much for her. We should probably leave her alone.'

'Okay.' Fleur wasn't sure why Emma had come here. She scorned nearly everything they did, and yet she seemed more vulnerable than anyone. 'What do you think is wrong with her?'

Maggie picked up a fallen leaf from beside her on the ground and started pulling it apart, carefully, to expose the skeleton. She said, 'I think things have come up for her. She wasn't expecting it. It's all to do with a man she can't get over.'

'Do you think she'll be all right?'

'Course she will. We're all all right in the end, aren't we? She'll be fine. But honestly, she's so repressed. She said herself she can't cope with emotion. She has to hide from it.'

'Don't be too hard on her,' Clover said.

Maggie seemed to ignore her and carried on. 'From what she's told me, she had a whirlwind affair with this bloke and then when it all went wrong, she was devastated but she had to pretend everything was fine. She couldn't cry. She's kept it in for years.'

Quietly, Fleur's heart went out to Emma. She said, 'That's sad.'

Clover agreed. 'If things are being awoken in her now, while she's here, that's a good thing but it's probably also very difficult.'

'She can't deal with it,' Maggie said. 'She's angry. She's really angry that she's being forced to feel things she doesn't want to be feeling. Told me she's sick of feeling wretched and it's not what she came here for.'

Some kind of understanding, or realization, seemed to make itself known to Clover and it showed on her face. 'She's angry?'

Maggie nodded. 'Furious. She was crying this morning after her Healing Touch treatment – really crying, not just the odd tear – and when she realized I'd seen her, she managed to bring herself under control. Just like that. And then she said she was angry because all she'd wanted was a massage and she ended up feeling like she'd been to a funeral.'

'She said that?'

Maggie waved her hand in the air, as if accurate quoting were a trivial matter. 'No. Not exactly. But it was what she meant.'

'Was she angry with a person or just with her situation?'

Maggie looked slightly uncomfortable. Fleur knew what was coming.

Clover seemed to know, too. She said, 'She's angry with me, I think.'

Maggie nodded. 'I don't think she means it. She's just . . . I don't know . . . I don't want to say childish, but maybe she is. She can't cope with her feelings so she's lashing out.'

'That's okay. She just needs to work through this. She'll be all right.'

Fleur admired that about Clover. She didn't become defensive or angry. She could simply see the situation for what it was and accept it, knowing it would pass. Besides, she could obviously see the weekend was working on the others. Maggie and Fleur were thriving here.

Clover's voice brought her back to the moment. She said, 'Let's move on from Emma for now. What I want you to do is reconnect with the conversation we had earlier about wildness, and what wildness means to you. Close your eyes and take a moment to remember what you said, what other people said, and focus on what resonated for you.'

Being more natural. Being more you. Perhaps daring to be more you.

'Now,' Clover said. 'Gently open your eyes.'

Fleur opened her eyes and looked at Clover and Maggie, and thought how tranquil they seemed.

Clover smiled. 'What do you think? Are you ready to open up to the wild woman within you?'

'I am,' Fleur said.

'Yep,' Maggie said.

'Okay, then we're going to go down to the river and we're going to baptize our new, wild selves. I invite you to change into your swimming costumes, or you can go naked if you prefer, and together we'll go and swim in that beautiful, clear water.'

She looked at them, as if to gauge their reactions. They were already reaching into their bags.

They stood up and Clover led them through the forest to a pool that had formed naturally in the river. At one point, the bank had eroded and they could simply wade slowly through the shallows until it became deep enough to swim in. Further along, the bank was high and grassy and the water deep. 'It's safe to jump,' Clover told them.

She jumped. They heard the splash as she went under, then a gasp as she came up to the surface again. 'It's lovely,' she said. 'Come in and join me.'

Maggie said, 'I'm not jumping. At my age, jumping could easily dislodge an internal organ. I'll just walk in.'

Fleur said, 'I'll come with you.'

She walked with Maggie down to the shallows. Maggie stepped out confidently, just until her ankles were covered. She turned back to Fleur, 'It is cold, but it's okay. I'm just not going to think about it and go.'

She strode out until the water was past her knees and then launched herself forwards and started to swim. Clover cheered.

Fleur stepped forwards into the cold. She swam out to the others, her skin and her senses more alive than she'd ever known. It was hard to tell whether the sensation was pain or pleasure.

'Splash your face with the water,' Clover said. 'It will help you get used to it.'

Fleur did as she was told.

Maggie was grinning widely. She said, 'I never, ever would have thought this was me. I can't believe I've done it.'

Clover wiped a tear from her eye. 'My wonderful goddesses,' she said. 'Join hands and on the count of three, we're all going under to baptize ourselves as wild women.'

They joined hands and counted together. 'ONE! . . . TWO! . . . THREE!'

And down they went, into the ice-cold river.

54

Maggie

Maggie headed up the hill out of the rainforest and followed the path to her cabin. She was wearing only her swimming costume, a towel wrapped loosely over her shoulders. She felt cold, but in a good way, as though the water had cooled her, right down to her soul. An emotional cooling, she thought. She could have done with it when Annie died. It might have soothed her white-hot rage, and restored her sense.

It hadn't only cooled her, though. It had invigorated her. She'd never had this much energy in her life. She felt like she could take over the world. The last time she'd felt anything like this was when she'd been so determined to solve the mystery of Annie's death, but that had been more of a demonic possession than a genuine feeling of energy. This was good. Healthy. She felt alive. She felt a part of the world.

She felt like she could phone Richard.

She opened the cabin door and let herself in, expecting to find Emma lying on her bed, sobbing. The cabin was empty. Maggie looked up at the shelf above Emma's bed, where she'd been storing her clothes. It was empty. She bent down and peered under the bed for Emma's suitcase but that had gone, too.

She sighed, and felt sad. Emma was missing out on a lot. Of course, Maggie wasn't stupid enough to think this retreat was for everyone, but she couldn't help thinking Emma might have come round to it, if she'd given it a chance. But Emma was a mess, Maggie thought. She could hardly cope with any feeling stronger than a mild irritation at having to get out of bed in the morning.

She should probably tell the others they were one wild woman down.

First, she sent a message to her neighbour.

Any sign of Bill?

The reply came back immediately.

Not yet.

Maggie felt the hard ache of worry begin to form in her stomach. Bill had never run away before. She wondered if he was cross with her for abandoning him. He'd never been this highly strung when they were married.

She stepped out of the cabin and saw Clover and Fleur walking up from the rainforest. They'd been swimming for longer than Maggie had. Their bodies were more used to it and it was safer. Also, her skin was paper-thin these days. The water could probably find its way in and dilute her blood, or at the very least, her heart could conk out.

Clover looked up and saw her, and she and Fleur

immediately stopped talking. They seemed to share secrets, these two. Maggie was going to be more aware of that now Emma had gone.

'Are you okay, Maggie?' Clover asked.

'Emma's gone.'

'Gone?'

'Yes, I've just come back to the cabin and she's not there. She's taken all her things.'

Clover was silent, then she heaved a regretful sigh. 'That's such a shame,' she said. 'I'm sure she'd have made progress if she'd given it one more evening.'

Fleur said, 'Maybe she just isn't ready to face whatever it is that upsets her.'

'Or maybe she is. Just not in front of other people. She's private, isn't she? She doesn't like to be seen.'

'She can go so far,' Clover said. 'Last night, round the fire, she took some small steps. I think she might have gone further if she'd given it a chance.'

'Shall we try and find her?'

Clover shook her head. 'We can't keep someone here against their will. That's not what this is about. I want to free women, not trap them.'

'Well, you're freeing this woman,' Maggie told her brightly to make her feel better. Clover smiled. 'Thank you. It's a shame. I said to Fleur yesterday that Emma probably needs this more than anyone, but that's why she can't cope with it.'

Fleur reached out and put a hand on Clover's arm. 'Don't dwell on this,' she said. 'You've done such good work with Maggie and me.'

'And with Emma,' Maggie pointed out. 'The fact that

she's been so upset and had to walk away is proof of that. You may never know what this has opened for her.'

'Thank you, my wild women,' Clover said, but she looked troubled. Maggie wondered what she was thinking.

55

Clover

Clover went back to her cabin to rest and warm up before dinner. She was feeling invigorated from the swimming and from witnessing the transformations of these wonderful women. Every time she led one of these retreats, she loved the new group more than the last. But she was disappointed about Emma, about the fact that she hadn't been able to reach her.

'The work you do is so important,' Fleur said to her earlier. Clover believed it. She believed in nothing more than helping women empower themselves. She wished she could reach more, the ones who truly needed it. She wished she could have reached her mother. Maybe one day . . .

Her phone beeped with the sound of an incoming text message. It was Joni.

> Hi, love. I was just thinking about you and wondering how you are.

Clover read it a few times before responding. It felt like a sympathy message, but unless something was going on that Clover was unaware of, Joni couldn't possibly know that Clover had already found out about her father's death.

She decided to give nothing away.

> Great, thanks. You?
>
> I'm fine. Is now a good time for me to call?
>
> Not really. I'm at work.
>
> When is a good time? I need to give you some news.
>
> It's difficult. I work away and it's really intense while I'm here. You can just tell me by text. It's all right.
>
> It's not really the kind of news for a text message. Are you sure I can't just call?
>
> I share a room.

This wasn't true. As retreat leader, it was important to keep some kind of distance between herself and her clients.

> I don't feel happy telling you by text.
>
> Just tell me. It's fine. I take all responsibility for my reaction.
>
> I need to let you know that your dad died yesterday. Your mum and Kevin have been desperate to get in touch with you.
>
> Thank you for telling me. It's okay. Did you tell them you're in touch with me?

No.

Thanks.

Are you okay?

I'm fine. You don't need to worry about me. I'm living a good life.

Are you going to contact your mum? I think she'd appreciate it.

I'll think about it.

Do you want me to let you know about the funeral?

Yes, please.

I'll message you as soon as I hear.

Cool. I need to get back to work now. Thank you for telling me xxx

Okay. Speak soon xxx

At least she'd had it confirmed. Her father's death had actually happened. It wasn't just an attempt by her family to make her feel guilty enough to repent and go home.

She wanted to divorce Kevin. She was single and planned to stay that way, and she certainly had no intention of marrying anyone ever again, but the thought that she was still legally bound to Kevin bothered her. The trouble was, if she wanted a divorce, she couldn't avoid some sort of contact with him, even if it was just through a solicitor.

She needed to look into it. A solicitor wouldn't need to tell him where she lived.

Perhaps she should send her mother a card. *Sorry for your loss. Meredith.*

56

Emma

Emma's train was just pulling into Plymouth. Every carriage was packed. The last two trains from Penzance to London Paddington had been cancelled and now everyone was crammed into this one, standing in every available space, blocking the doors and the toilets with themselves and their bags. Emma, luckily, had managed to grab a seat at Liskeard but there were still over three hours to go. She couldn't bear it. She'd never coped well with being swamped by people.

She'd texted Clara as they left Bodmin Parkway.

Retreat too much for me. Coming home. I'll call you when I'm leaving London.

Clara's response was prompt and concerned.

Are you okay?

I'm fine, but it was all mad. Too much forest bathing and smashing cushions. Not enough wine.

Clover's story kept playing in her head. *My parents and husband had always said I should never consent to a transfusion because it is against the law of Jehovah. They believed very strongly that I should die rather than receive treatment.*

If her husband came to find her, if Clover went back to him, then her life would be at risk. It had never crossed Emma's mind that her reasons for abandoning her family were so serious. She'd thought of her just as a child; a moody, overgrown adolescent with no idea how good her life was, and who'd walked out so she could punish her mother. Really, she had no basis for this belief, other than the fact that she didn't like Clover and thought she was a fake.

It was the guilt that made her stand up and leave that sweet, sharing circle in the rainforest. She couldn't bear it once Clover had told them. She had to get away. Let the rest of them think she couldn't handle her emotions. Let them think she couldn't cope with having her grief-memory split open in front of them.

In fact, Emma could cope with that. She was fine with it now.

She checked the time on her phone. Just after seven. She'd messaged Kevin as soon as she left the retreat, told him Clover had gone again and she didn't know where. He hadn't replied. Maybe he didn't read her message. Maybe he didn't believe her.

It might not be too late, she thought. If she got off the train now, here in Plymouth, she could be back at the retreat within an hour.

She stood up. The train doors were about to close. She grabbed her bag from the overhead rack. 'Excuse me,' she said, pushing past people, not caring if they thought her rude or careless as her bag banged against them in her rush for the door.

'Excuse me,' she said again. A young man moved aside for her and she stepped out of the train onto the cool, empty platform outside.

57

Clover

Emma's absence made itself felt when they ate dinner that night. There was no one there to question the purpose of what they were doing, no one to pull them out of their intensity with a sarcastic remark. Oddly, Clover missed her. Retreats needed a balance of personalities.

When they'd finished, Maggie said, 'What's happening this evening, Clover? Will it be another wild night round the campfire?'

'That's what I'm planning.'

Maggie, who looked as though she'd shed her skin and was ready to fly, said, 'Excellent!'

They gathered their things and headed outside to the fire pit. Clover lit the fire, then set up a deckchair for Maggie. Fleur set her bag down beside the same rock she'd sat on last night, then Clover noticed as she took a step towards the fire, her hands clasped behind her back, and watched the flames as they grew. She bowed her head slightly and Clover saw her lips move. She turned away, knowing she was witnessing this woman in a moment of private prayer that had nothing to do with her.

After a while, Fleur stepped back from the fire and turned to everyone with a smile. 'There,' she said. 'I'm done.

I came here to make a decision. It was the hardest decision of my life, but I've done it now and I know it's right.' Her voice wavered as she spoke and she wiped tears from her eyes.

Maggie reached out and embraced her. 'Well done, my wild woman,' she said.

No one really knew what Fleur was talking about, although Clover could see it was to do with Douglas. She needed to catch up with Fleur properly, find out what was happening.

'Okay, my goddesses,' she said. 'Let's take our seats for our final circle time of the day.'

They all sat. Clover said, 'I'd like to do this slightly differently today. I'd like someone else to start the conversation. So Maggie, can you share with us how you're feeling at the moment?'

'I'm feeling a mixture of things. I'm elated to have come here and met this wonderful group of women, and to have done this work together, but I'm disappointed that we've lost Emma.'

'I think we share that disappointment,' Clover said.

Fleur nodded. 'We do.'

Maggie said, 'I also feel worried, if I'm honest. I'm worried about Emma. About what she's done, or might do.'

Clover shared that anxiety, too, though she wouldn't admit it.

Fleur murmured her agreement as well. She said, 'I felt from the beginning that Emma was a dark force here.' She paused. 'Well, maybe that's too strong, but I felt she could perhaps be a toxic presence, maybe without even meaning to.'

'I think we can all agree that this wasn't the right environment for Emma to address the issues she faces. But what about you, Fleur? Our time isn't over yet. We still have the rest of this evening and tomorrow, but how are you feeling about your time here so far?'

'Oh, I feel great,' Fleur said. 'Thank you, Clover, for providing us with this space, and this time.'

'You're welcome. I, too, feel elated with this weekend. You two have been brilliant goddesses to work with. I feel certain that Emma will be okay. She'll find her own way through. Now, I hope you can agree that we still have much to celebrate tonight. You will know by now my belief that you can never have too many circle times or too much dancing . . .'

She pulled her phone out her pocket and hit the button on her Wild Women playlist. Maggie and Fleur cheered.

She continued, 'We are here in the privacy of this retreat centre, high up in the middle of Bodmin Moor. This weekend, I hope we have all forged bonds of deep trust with one another and we know that nobody here is judging us. For this reason, I invite you all to dance with true joy and abandon. No one is watching. We are sacred sisters, joined by our experience of the weekend. We understand the desire to be joyful, to be free, to be seen for all that we are. Know that your body is a place of goodness, a place of power, a place of pride. It does not need to be hidden.'

Maggie said, 'Are you telling us we're dancing naked again?'

'Only if you want to, Maggie. That is my only rule. You must never do anything you are uncomfortable with. But I do invite you to consider the spiritual benefits of nakedness.

Being naked allows you to grow more comfortable with your body. We are able to experience ourselves positively when we're face to face with our nakedness, especially in a non-sexual setting. Being comfortable in your own skin, and being comfortable seeing others in theirs, fuels a sense of calm and peace with bodies in their natural state. There is no shame in being seen, and when you are naked, you can achieve your fullest expression.'

She allowed her words to settle for a while.

Maggie said, 'I'm sure this is true.'

'Then I hope you'll dance,' Clover said. She loved this part, when the hard, transformational work was done and spirits were high.

She turned up the music and the dancing started. She knew from experience that women became emotional at this stage of the weekend. They were proud of themselves, and full of a joy and comfort in each other's company that often tipped over into ecstasy.

She believed in what she'd told them about nakedness. She believed it was the only way anyone could achieve their full expression, and she wanted these women to come out of their heads and know themselves in this moment, rooted in their bodies.

She knew she would have to go first and she was fine with that. She peeled off her top and her bra, flung them in the air over her head and went on dancing.

Fleur and Maggie followed.

The music went on. She'd chosen this playlist on purpose – a collection of bold, powerful songs by bold, powerful women. They were designed to inspire and it worked. Clover, Maggie and Fleur were naked now, moving around the fire, their arms in the air, whooping now and then, liberated and joyful.

Clover was aware that Fleur was crying. She met her eye and smiled at her. Fleur laughed and said, 'I don't know why I'm crying! I'm really happy!'

'Me too!' Maggie shouted.

They carried on dancing, cheering, crying. Clover could feel the connection with their feminine ancestors, the ones who'd suffered and fought for this.

She wasn't sure when she became aware of the lights of the car as it grew closer and then pulled into the parking space in front of the barn. When she did, she simply said, 'Looks like we have visitors, my loves, but carry on. Carry on. There is no shame here.'

They carried on.

Maggie said, 'They'll get an eyeful if they come over here.'

'Let's give them an eyeful!' Fleur said.

Clover cast a glance towards the car and the figures coming out of it. They started walking purposefully over the ground towards the group of women dancing by the fire.

Clover closed her eyes in dread. She knew who these people were. She knew before she even saw their faces.

Kevin.

And her mother.

58

Maggie

Maggie noticed that Clover had stopped dancing. She was standing exposed, the flames from the fire rising at exactly the height needed to illuminate the neat strip of her pubic hair.

'Clover?' she asked. 'Are you all right?'

Clover shook her head. 'It's my mum. My mum and my husband. They're here. They've found me.'

Maggie looked in the direction where Clover's gaze was fixed and saw a man helping an older woman across the grass towards them. She looked back at the women standing naked by the fire while the music played and thought, *Emma. Emma did this.*

The man spoke first. 'Meredith.'

He stood in silence as he took in the scene. Fleur laughed. Maggie put it down to nervousness, and her not having a full grasp of the situation.

'Meredith,' he said again. 'What on earth is going on? We've come to get you. We've come to take you home.'

At last, Clover found her voice. 'I'm not coming home,' she said. 'I've left you. I have a new life now.'

She was utterly defiant in her nakedness. She didn't even try to conceal it.

Her mother looked frightened. 'What is this life you're living, child?'

'This is my work. It's what I do.'

Kevin said, 'This isn't work. This is filth. It's absolute filth, Meredith.'

Fleur was the first one to speak in defence of Clover. 'This must look crazy to you, I'm sure,' she said. 'But we can all promise you this isn't filth. Clover . . . I mean Meredith . . . she's a wonderful, wonderful woman and she does good work . . .'

Maggie thought it fortunate that Fleur seemed to have struck the language of the Church at exactly the right moment. *Keep going,* she thought. *Keep on with the stuff about good work.*

'. . . we are all so grateful to her for what she's done for us.'

Clover's mother, who obviously wasn't prepared to listen to anything a naked woman was saying to her, turned back to her daughter. 'Please come home with me, Meredith. I need to talk to you. There are things I have to tell you.'

'Mum, listen . . .'

Kevin interrupted. 'I am your husband, Meredith! You made a vow to stay with me until death. Do you not understand what that means?'

'I will be ending our marriage, Kevin. Divorce exists. I don't have to stay with you until death.'

Maggie admired the way she stood so calmly in her power, just as she'd said they all should. It would have been so easy to crumble in the face of this conflict.

Her mother said, 'Will you at least talk to me?'

'Yes, of course I will, Mum. Of course I will. I have

nothing to say to Kevin, but I want to talk to you. Why don't you stay here tonight? There are spare cabins . . .'

Her mother looked relieved and grateful. 'Thank you. I'd like to—'

Kevin suddenly reached out and hauled Clover up and over his shoulder. 'We're going,' he said. 'Right now. You're leaving this life, Meredith.'

Clover screamed as he carried her towards the car.

59

Emma

She'd called a taxi from the train and it was waiting for her at the station.

'Emma?' the driver asked. 'Up to the retreat centre on the moor?'

'That's right. I'm in rather a hurry,' Emma told him.

'I'll go as fast as the roads will let me,' he said.

He pulled away. 'I take a lot of people up to the retreat centre,' he said. 'I've always wondered what goes on there. Seems a right mix. There's always a fire going. Lots of walkers, I hear. They come for the mystery of the stones, so I'm told. Others come for the wildlife.'

Emma tuned him out. It was dark now. She wondered if Kevin was there yet, if he'd taken Clover away, back to the life that would kill her.

The rounded a bend and the retreat centre came into view. She could see the smoke from the campfire already. She pulled some cash out of her purse and thrust it into the driver's hand. An unfamiliar car was parked beside her. *Kevin*, she thought. He was here.

She grabbed her bag and jumped out. She could hear people shouting, the voices of panic. Then she saw the figures in the darkness, and the silhouette of a man with a woman's body slung over his shoulder. Like a murder, she thought. But the body was flailing.

It didn't take long to work out what was going on. Emma knew she couldn't fight this man. None of them could, not on their own.

She did the first thing she could think of, which was to abandon her bag on the ground, run into the barn, grab a knife from the block in the kitchen, and slash the tyres of the unfamiliar car in the car park. She heard the hiss of air as the tyres went down and all she could think was, *Please let this be the right car.*

Then she ran towards the fire and the man coming towards her with Clover, who was screaming, 'Put me down! Help me! Help!'

'Clover!' Emma shouted. 'It's going to be okay. Just hold on.'

She ran on towards the fire. Maggie and Fleur were standing there naked with a woman Emma supposed was Clover's mother. They all looked terrified.

'Emma!' Maggie said. 'What are you doing here?'

'There's no time for that now. We need to help Clover. I've slashed his tyres. He won't be able to get anywhere. Call the police, Maggie. We just have to keep him here, stop him taking her away.'

Without even thinking of what she was doing, Emma grabbed a large stick from near the fire, turned round and ran after them. Maggie rooted for her phone. Fleur grabbed another stick and followed Emma.

'Put her down!' Emma yelled, and she jumped in front of him.

He was laden with the weight of Clover and had to stop.

'If you don't put her down,' Emma went on, 'I will use this.' She held the stick in both hands, and hoped it looked threatening.

Together, she and Fleur formed a barricade in front of Kevin and moved wherever he moved.

'Keep this up,' Emma instructed Fleur. 'He'll tire eventually. And yes, we've called the police. You can't just come here and take a woman.'

'She's my wife.'

'It doesn't matter who she is, you absolute prick of a man. You can't just take her.'

Fleur said, 'There are laws. If you do this, the police won't see it as a man taking back his wife. They'll see it as kidnap and you'll be banged up.'

Maggie strode towards them. 'Police are on their way,' she said.

Clover's husband sighed and put her down. Clover stood up and gazed at them gratefully.

'This isn't the end, Meredith,' he said. He called over his shoulder to Clover's mother, who was following behind. 'Come on,' they heard him say. 'Let's leave this for now.'

Clover's mother said something they couldn't hear.

Kevin said, 'I'll pray for you, Meredith. For all the good it will do.'

He started walking away just as the blue lights of two police cars lit the retreat centre.

60

Maggie

The police were there for hours. Two of them drove Kevin away for questioning. The other two took statements from all the women, including Clover's mother.

When everything had died down, Clover led her mother to a free cabin so she could stay the night and they could talk. Maggie, Emma and Fleur returned to the fire and Emma brought it back to life. She was visibly shaking.

She said, 'I'm sorry. It was me. It was me who told them she was here. I thought they should know. I didn't realize how serious it all was, and when Clover told us, I felt awful. So I left. I ran away so I wouldn't have to face it, but as the train got further away and I knew Kevin was probably getting nearer, I had to do something. I had to try and stop it. I couldn't get hold of him, so I came back.'

Fleur said, 'You shouldn't have told him.'

'I know that.'

Maggie said, 'Maybe some good will come of it. Maybe she can make up with her mum now.'

Fleur said, 'Her mum is probably in there with her, trying to persuade her to go home with her. They're desperate for her to repent and go back to the Witnesses.'

'She won't do that,' Maggie said. 'I'm sure she won't. Look how far she's come.'

'But she feels bad for her mother. Don't underestimate that kind of guilt. And it's hard. I think she'd like to see her mother, but the Witnesses won't let her speak to Clover when she's been disfellowshipped.'

'So her mother has a decision to make,' Maggie said. 'Her daughter or her religion.'

'And we all know which one she will choose. She made that choice. She made it years ago.'

Emma said, 'We can talk her out of it if she does decide to go.'

'She won't go,' Maggie said. 'I'm sure of it. If she goes, it's suicide.'

61

Clover

Clover and her mother were each sitting on a bed in one of the free cabins. It was odd, seeing her again after so long. She said, 'I'm glad to see you, Mum.'

Her mother wrung her hands. 'I've missed you. I've missed you terribly, but I knew you had to leave. I've been worried about you, too. I had no idea where you'd gone. I had to just have faith that you could look after yourself.'

'I've been fine. It was hard at first, but that money helped. I wanted to thank you for it, but I knew I couldn't contact you. But I am so grateful.'

Her mother sighed. 'I need to tell you something, Meredith. It's about your father.'

'I know. He's dead. He died yesterday.'

'You know?'

Clover nodded. 'I found Kevin's blog. A while ago now. I've followed it now and then, and when he said Dad was ill, I followed it every day.'

'I hoped you might. I hoped you might find it somehow. I wanted to somehow communicate with you. It was why I said I wanted to see you. I hoped you'd get in touch, knowing he was gone and you could.' She paused, then asked, 'Where do you live, when you're not here?'

'I have a flat in Bristol. I teach yoga and Pilates and I run workshops for women.'

'I've missed you,' her mother said again. 'I'm not supposed to talk to you. I'm supposed to shun you.'

'That's up to you.'

'I don't want to. I'd rather have you in my life, but Jehovah . . .'

'I don't think He'll mind.'

'Maybe not, but the other Witnesses, the Kingdom Hall . . .'

'Perhaps they don't need to know. You could always come and see me in Bristol without telling any of them.'

Her mother appeared to seriously consider this. 'Yes,' she said. 'Now your father's gone, it'll be easier. I suppose we're both free now.'

Clover caught her eye, and they laughed.

62

Maggie

They stayed up till the early hours, and in the morning Maggie woke up exhausted.

From the bed opposite, Emma said, 'My God, I can't believe what we've all just come out of.'

'I know. What a drama.'

'Poor Clover.'

'Can I ask you something?'

'Sure.'

'Are you all right?'

Emma took a deep breath. 'I am. I'm okay. Being here has been hard for me. Really hard. There are things I need to work on, I know that.'

'Do you think you will?'

'Yes, but probably in private. Probably not in a situation like this. But I am really sorry for what I did to Clover. I was angry with her. I shouldn't have done it.'

'But you put it right, as well as you could.'

'Yes.'

'And maybe it will have done her some good. Got her back on good terms with her mother. It's important. Family is all anyone has, really.'

'I hope that's right. I hope it does help her. I'm going over to get a cup of tea. Do you want anything?'

Maggie shook her head. 'I'm okay. I'm worried about Bill. I need to check in with my neighbour.'

'He'll turn up,' Emma said, then got out of bed, pulled her dressing gown on and left the cabin. Maggie was aware of not having joined in yesterday's confessional, but she just hadn't been able to do it. She could never admit what she'd done to her son.

She sighed. Everyone else seemed to have made such progress here, but what had she done, other than have a good time?

She picked her phone up from the bedside table and checked her messages.

> Bill still not home. Food untouched. I've called in on all the neighbours and no one has seen him.

Maggie typed back:

> Thanks for looking. If he's not back when I get home, I'll put some posters up.

She scrolled through her contacts for Richard's number and hit the call icon.

He answered after just a few rings. 'Hi, Mum,' he said.

'Hello, love. How are you?'

'Fine. We're fine. We've just been shopping for things for the baby.' He sounded excited.

Maggie's heart leaped. 'What did you buy?'

'Everything,' he laughed. 'Everything. A pram, a swinging crib, a bath, blankets, sleeping bags, some black-and-white toys. Did you know they can only see in black and white for a few weeks?'

She did know. 'Really?' she said. 'That's incredible.'

'We bought some books as well. Oh, and a little hat and some newborn babygrows. They're so small. I can't believe a person will ever be small enough to fit in them.'

'How much was it all?'

Richard floundered. He hated talking about money, probably because he hardly had any. He worked in the arts. 'Oh, I'm not sure. About a grand. It was the pram that cost so much.'

'Let me pay for it.'

'Mum . . .'

'Please. I'd like to.'

'Really?'

'Of course.'

'It would be a huge help.'

'I want to be a help, Richard,' she said. 'If you'll let me.'

She felt the weight of his silence as he took in the significance of what she'd said and everything she hadn't said, too.

Eventually, he said, 'We'd like that.'

63

Emma

Clover was the last one to the breakfast table in the morning. When she walked into the barn, everyone cheered.

She sat down and started helping herself to the food: wholewheat banana pancakes; fruit salad; soya yoghurt. This food was miraculous, Emma thought.

'Thank you so much, my queens, for what you did last night.' She looked directly at Emma. Emma smiled awkwardly. 'Thank you, Emma, for what you did. I know you weren't acting entirely out of concern and that you were angry with me, but I do know you were seeing this from my mother's perspective, and it has turned out to be good. My mother and I have talked, and I think we're going to stay in touch. It's against the teachings of Jehovah, so it's a big deal for her. She's rebelling.'

Everyone cheered.

'And what about Kevin?' Maggie asked.

Clover said, 'I don't want him in my life. He's gone.'

Maggie smiled, 'We would never have let him take you away. Never.'

'Especially not without your clothes,' Emma added.

Maggie said, 'I think after last night, I can safely say I am now at ease with my own nakedness and also quite comfortable around other people's. So you achieved your aim, Clover.'

Clover said, 'Not quite, my queens. Emma hasn't been baptized yet.'

Emma laughed. 'I'm not swimming in the river in September.'

Maggie said, 'Oh, but you should, Emma. You really should. I can't believe I'm saying this, but I plan to do it every day from now on.'

Emma had to say something. 'We'll see.'

Clover said, 'After breakfast, before we end this retreat and our time together, I want to treat you all to a sound bath. I want to bring some calm back to your bodies and minds before you leave today. Last night's drama wasn't the traditional ending to one of my retreats. I think you need a sound bath.'

'A what?' Emma asked.

'A sound bath. It will help bring you back to a state of focussed relaxation after what happened yesterday.'

'But what is it?'

'It's a therapeutic, meditative experience. You will bathe in the sounds and vibrations of different instruments.'

'Like violins?'

'No. The instruments are more primal than that. We use crystal bowls, gongs and chimes. You'll see. The sounds will wash over you and take you into a state of deep relaxation, unplugging you from the world and bringing peace and harmony. It can be easier than traditional meditation because you don't have to concentrate. You just lie down and listen.'

'Okay,' Emma said, and hoped it wasn't going to be like

the Healing Touch therapy, when all she'd wanted to do afterwards was cry.

'It's nothing to fear,' Clover said. 'So when we've finished our breakfast, we'll go to the meditation space. I've already set it up.'

Emma hoped she wouldn't have to focus on clearing her mind of all its content, that she'd be able to let her thoughts wander wherever they chose. She wasn't quite ready to forget Oliver yet, although she was aware of that deep sadness beginning to lift and disperse, instead of hanging like a weight from her heart.

'It sounds great,' she said. Then she reached over and placed her hand over Clover's. 'I'm sorry I doubted you,' she said.

Emma finished her breakfast in silence. The flavours were deep and delicious. It was impossible to eat this food absent-mindedly, the way she'd eaten everything else for years. The tastes rooted her in the moment. She wasn't able to drift away and become only half-present. She needed to harness this when she went home.

When they'd eaten, Harriet came and cleared their plates and they all went over to the mediation space again. Clover had laid the yoga mats on the floor and on each one was an eye mask, rather than the usual blindfold.

'I want you to lie on your back on your mat and cover your eyes with this weighted mask. It will help you block out the external world, and the heaviness of it will aid your relaxation.'

She pulled the curtain across the space again for privacy. Emma couldn't see what happened next, but the room filled with a low, resonant chime, followed by another of a different pitch, and then another. Something like a continuous, melodic hum joined in the background, then more chiming and later, music.

Emma focussed on the grief-ache in her chest and let the sounds begin to ease it. She didn't try pushing the memories away when Clover banged the gong again and the echo took her straight back to the church and Oliver's funeral, The clock had struck eleven. Emma saw herself on the pew with Ben beside her, leafing through the order of service when behind her, the church doors opened and the vicar strode down the aisle.

'I am the resurrection and the life . . .'

Emma closed her eyes as Oliver followed in his coffin. She couldn't bear it. She knew that behind him, his wife and two children would be walking slowly towards their seats at the front, grief-stricken and shell-shocked, the objects of everyone's sympathy and horror.

She hadn't wanted to come today. She'd wanted to stay at home, shut herself away and sob. She had no idea how she was going to hide the depth of her grief from everyone else. If she gave into it, they'd all think she was mad. She could imagine the small-town talk afterwards, the gossips speculating on the overwrought friend of the family who couldn't control herself and had wailed harder than his wife. 'There's something going on there,' they'd say. 'Apparently, she wasn't even a close friend, just an acquaintance, really.' And between them, they'd turn the evidence over and over and say, 'Maybe, *maybe* they were having an affair.'

There was no way in the world Emma could let anyone even begin to suspect the truth. Protecting his family had been too important to Oliver. It would devastate him to think they'd found out after he died, knowing his betrayal heaped more suffering on them and tainted all their memories. She couldn't do it – not to him or to them. She had to hold herself together and go to the funeral with Ben so that Oliver's family could see how many people liked and respected him and how shocked and sorry they all were about the suddenness and brutality of his death.

But God, it was hard. She opened her eyes again and stared at the coffin, now at the front of the church. She tried to imagine him lying inside it, and wondered what they'd dressed him in. Was he wearing his old blue Levi's and Liverpool FC scarf? Or had they put him in a suit? She hoped not. She hoped he was dressed casually and comfortably, the way she always thought of him.

The vicar moved through his speech and then Oliver's wife stood at the front to read a poem. Emma couldn't listen to it. She was heavy with guilt and shame and envy. She longed to be the one up there declaring her love for him, while everyone else gazed in silent sympathy and resolved to make her a meal and leave it on the doorstep so she didn't have to summon the energy from her bones full of sorrow.

After the service, the funeral directors would be driving him to the crematorium. There would be no guests, not even family. No need for any of that. They'd all been invited to his house for the wake. Emma and Ben had said they wouldn't go. Emma had work to do, and she wouldn't be missed. They weren't close, after all.

She stood up for the singing. She felt as if she were dressed in armour, weighing her down. She tried not to think how long this would go on for, how she was going to grieve and grieve for months and years, and keep it hidden from everyone around her.

Eventually, the service came to an end and everyone had to file past the coffin on their way out though the doors at the far end of the church. People stopped to place a flower, or to reach their hands out and touch it. Emma walked stoically past without looking. She felt that if she did, she'd lose all control and hurl herself against it, crying and wailing like Heathcliff after Catherine died.

Haunt me, Oliver. Come back and haunt me.

His wife and children were standing just outside the door, shaking hands with everyone as they passed. Emma kissed each of them on the cheek. 'I'm so sorry,' she said. 'I didn't know him well, but I do know he was a wonderful, much-loved man.'

His wife smiled at her. 'Thank you, Emma,' she said, and Emma walked away.

A few weeks later, she read in the local paper that they'd scattered his ashes on Dartmoor. It was a place he'd loved to go with his family.

64

Fleur

The easeful sounds of the music and the chimes had sent Fleur far away. They'd opened some hidden part of her she'd never been to before, a part that probably hadn't existed until Douglas came into her life. Now, as the sounds washed over her, she felt as though she were drifting above her body, watching the memories unfold beneath her, and seeing herself for what she was: not a victim, but a survivor. A warrior.

She revisited one of the good days with Douglas. They'd gone to London as tourists and taken a canal boat from Little Venice to Camden Lock, drifting through a part of the city she'd never known existed, full of tranquil gardens and weeping willow trees. They spotted warthogs and giraffes as they passed London Zoo. They'd ogled at beautiful houses that had been fought over at property auctions between Madonna and Paul McCartney. When they stepped off the boat in Camden, they'd bought their lunch from a Venezuelan street vendor and eaten it on a bench by the canal with hordes of other people – Fleur had never seen so many people – who'd come to soak up the atmosphere of the crazy world of Camden Market. Afterwards, they spent the afternoon shopping for vintage vinyl and in the evening, they went to a bar and drank too many beers and listened to live music.

A perfect day. It had been a perfect day. The next day was good, too. And the next. All the days had been good after that, for a long time. It was nearly two months before Fleur went to Norwich and everything changed again. In those two months, she'd dared to hope they were over the worst.

She thought about that day now, and added a baby to it. She imagined the two of them drifting down the canal, holding one another's hands with a baby between them. The baby was smiling because the baby would be happy. The baby's two parents adored it. Douglas had taken one look at the baby after its birth and the devotion of fatherhood healed him. He understood now that someone truly needed him and he had to stay well. When he bought his vintage vinyl, he played it on the record player at home and sang David Bowie songs to his child because of course he would be committed to developing good taste in music.

While the sounds kept playing, the memories kept coming back. The good days, the bad days, the trust and the destruction of it. She began to understand what she needed to do.

She had one chance at this life. She mustn't throw it away.

65

Maggie

Maggie didn't want this sound bath to end. It had been one of the most tranquil experiences of her life, to simply lie back and absorb the gentle sounds as they chimed around her. She wished this sort of thing had been fashionable when Annie died. It might have saved her. It might have saved everyone.

In this odd state somewhere between sleep and wakefulness, she was able to let the thoughts and memories drift lightly back to her. They didn't carry their usual force. Often, when she recalled those first years after Annie's death and the way she'd behaved, she felt as though the shame of it would crush her. The excuse of having been a grieving mother didn't seem enough, although that was what Bill said on the rare occasions that she mentioned it. 'You need to forgive yourself, love. It happened, and we can't change it. You were mad with grief.'

It took so much work to undo her certainty that Richard had somehow been involved in whatever had happened to Annie. To Maggie, it made such sense. Annie had been fine when she laid her down to sleep, Richard and Thomas were the only people upstairs, and she was dead two hours later. No one else had even been near her. For everyone to tell Maggie over and over again that he hadn't done it just wasn't enough. She'd never been so sure of anything in her life. To her, it seemed like the only possible explanation.

They all decided Maggie needed careful handling. Bill didn't let many people near her, and every Tuesday he took the morning off work and drove her to a bereavement counsellor. The counsellor guided her to talk through trauma and anger. The trouble with Maggie was that she couldn't shake the anger, no matter how hard she tried. Rumours drifted through the village and came back to her. She'd gone from being an object of pity to a monster.

She watched from the sidelines of her life as Bill took over the bringing-up of Richard. The two of them set up a father-and-son football club in the village. Maggie wasn't entirely sure what they did there, but it used up all their weekends. Other villages got involved as well, and there were matches every Sunday and eventually a league. Their village ended up top of the league one year and Bill and Richard were presented with a trophy of appreciation at the village hall.

Maggie was never able to pinpoint exactly when it happened, but it did happen, slowly, as the years passed and her sanity was restored. She began to understand that sudden, unexplainable deaths did happen sometimes and there wasn't anything anyone could do. One afternoon, when Richard and Bill were out, she took the coroner's report from the folder where they'd filed it away so many years ago, and she read every word of it. Annie's body when she died had been perfect. There was no bruising, nothing at all to suggest anything other than an innocent, tragic death.

And then she found out about the research being done into cot death, and how lying babies to sleep on their backs could make all the difference. She began to address it with her counsellor. 'I needed someone to blame,' she said.

'Bereaved people often do.'

'I think, deep down, I've always blamed myself but I couldn't cope with it, so I lashed out at . . . at my son. Of all people. He was only eight years old. I know it affected him. He had years of thinking I blamed him, years of coldness at my hands.'

'But he's had his dad, hasn't he?'

'Oh, yes. Yes, his dad has been brilliant with him all this time. I think he threw himself into saving Richard. It gave him something worthwhile and meaningful to do, while I just lost my mind.'

'It's not uncommon for bereaved parents to feel that they're losing their minds, Maggie.'

'Yes, but there's a difference between feeling it and actually doing it. I truly lost mine. I must have had no grip on reality at all.' The thought of it amazed her.

'Do you feel that you can talk to Richard about it? Now he's a bit older, he might be able to understand more.'

Maggie sighed. 'Possibly. It's difficult. He's fourteen now and he's pleasant enough around me, but we don't have the closeness he has with his dad. Nothing like it. I can't blame him for that, of course. I think he's still scared of me. He's scared I might lose it again and start shouting terrible things at him. He's a good lad, he really is. He goes to school, behaves well, does his homework . . . but sometimes he just has a phase where he totally ignores me and I have no idea how to get him back. I know it's my fault.'

'Then perhaps that's where you need to start,' the counsellor suggested gently. 'Start by saying you're sorry. Say you know it will take time, but you'd like to repair your relationship. It will be something that needs to be taken at his pace, not yours.'

'I know.'

'But you could try it.'

Maggie tried it. She made Richard a hot chocolate when he came home after school and said, 'Can I talk to you, love?'

He looked nervous, but interested. 'Yeah.'

'Will you have a seat? It's difficult to talk properly standing up.'

They both sat down at the kitchen table.

'I want to apologize to you. For the things I said to you after Annie died. I know you would never have hurt her. I know that. I'm so sorry I said what I said, and I'm so sorry I've . . .' She almost couldn't get the next words out, but she forced herself, 'I'm sorry I haven't been a good enough mother to you.'

He looked embarrassed.

'I'd like to work at making it up to you, if you'll let me.'

'Okay. I mean, it's all right, though. I've been okay.'

'I know you have.'

'But yeah, it'd be nice to have you around a bit more.'

'I'd like to be.'

He grinned. 'But not if you're gonna be mental.'

'I won't be.'

'You're really scary when you're mental.'

She smiled. It was a start.

66

Fleur

After the sound bath, Clover said, 'I think we could do with some cacao this morning. It will help bring you gently back to the present following whatever you experienced during this session.'

She started whisking. Maggie and Emma took their places on their sheepskins. Fleur said to Clover, 'How are you feeling?'

'Grateful,' Clover told her. 'Grateful and free. I'm so glad my mum came. She's still over in the cabin but I said she could join us if she wants to.' She looked at Fleur with concern. 'How are you feeling?'

'Okay.'

Clover nodded. Fleur sensed that she wanted to ask more questions, so she turned her gaze to the floor. This was too private to talk about now. The turmoil she'd been drowning in for months was beginning to ease and the feeling of absolute certainty that she'd made the right decision was like being washed in relief.

She sat down on her sheepskin with the others while Clover went on whisking. Clover's head was bent low, and Fleur wondered whose spirit she was calling on.

Clover handed each of them a stone mug and placed

the jug of cacao in the centre of their circle. Then she sat down and said, 'It was an eventful night last night. I want to thank you, my queens, from the bottom of my heart, for the care and strength you showed me. And for your power.'

No one seemed able to find the words in response.

'I would like us to drink this cacao in honour of all of us, and to form our intention to all that we are.' She reached forward for the jug and poured the steaming liquid into her mug. 'I thank the spirits of our ancestors for helping us find our dark feminine strength this weekend.'

She passed the jug to Emma. As she poured her drink, Emma said, 'I celebrate having been brought here this weekend to find these women. I know I look like the retreat's only failure but I'm not. I know what I need to do now.'

She passed the jug to Maggie. 'I thank the dark feminine divine for finding me.'

She passed the jug to Fleur. 'I celebrate our freedom from entrapment.'

They drank in silence.

When they'd finished, they set their mugs down on the floor and Clover said, 'I now close this ceremony.'

She gathered the mugs and moved them to the side of the room, then sat back down. 'This morning, I want you to create your souvenir of our time here. I invite you all to write a letter to yourselves, in which you remind yourselves of the journey you've been on this weekend – what you've learnt, who you've become, the decisions you've made while you've been here and how you plan to take this experience into your future. I will hand out an envelope to everyone and when you've finished your letter, place it in the envelope, seal it and address it to yourself. I will then post these to you in the future. Whatever you write is completely personal, to be read only by you.'

She reached behind her for paper, pens and envelopes and handed them round.

Fleur picked hers up and started writing.

67

Clover

She watched as they wrote their letters. Each one of them was crying softly and Clover knew their trauma was finally shifting and becoming a foundation for power.

One by one, they put their pens down and dried their eyes.

Clover said, 'And now, we will go into our final practice of the retreat. Please come and stand with me and form a circle.'

They stood together, the four of them. Their bond now was tangible.

Clover said, 'We are each going to take it in turns now, at any point when we feel ready, to step inside this sacred circle of women and make our affirmation. You will think of the thing you have achieved this weekend and you will state it. For example, you might state *I am powerful* or *I am radiant*. Then the rest of us will repeat this statement back to you, three times. Okay?'

They all nodded.

Clover said, 'There is no rush, and there is no order in which we need to do this. If no one is standing in the centre of the circle, we can simply silently absorb the energy within it. Be aware of the power, the healing, the essence of all that we are that is being held in this sacred space, and let it enter your bodies and minds.'

They all stood for a while, in quiet and easy reflection. Then Maggie stepped into the circle. 'I am forgiven,' she said.

'You are forgiven,' they repeated.

'You are forgiven.'

'You are forgiven.'

She stepped back.

'Thank you.'

There was another silence, longer this time. Clover was deeply aware of the energy in the space. It felt electric.

Fleur stepped into the circle. 'I am strong,' she said.

The voices echoed.

'You are strong.'

'You are strong.'

'You are strong.'

She stepped back.

It was Clover's turn. 'I am free.'

She listened to the voices as they chimed all around her.

'You are free.'

'You are free.'

'You are free.'

Emma stepped in. 'I am at peace,' she said.

'You are at peace.'

'You are at peace.'

'You are at peace.'

Clover stood back and looked at the women around her. She knew she'd done good.

68

Emma

It was time to leave. The others were all involved in an extravagant, emotional goodbye in the barn, so Emma made her escape quietly and went back to her cabin to collect her bag. She couldn't do what they were doing – the hugging, the tears, the insistence that a form of magic had taken place this weekend and now everyone's trauma was healed. It wasn't that she didn't want to believe it. Perhaps it was true for Fleur and Maggie, and now Clover as well. It was just that Emma still felt she had a long way to go. She wasn't ready to start celebrating. Her life would still be waiting for her when she went home: her troubled daughter, her dying marriage, her secrecy around Oliver that meant she'd been living a double life for so long now that she hardly knew how to stop.

There were things she needed to do. She counted them on her fingers.

1. Talk to Ben. Tell him about Oliver.
2. Talk to Clara. Tell her about Oliver.
3. Stop pretending.
4. Apologize.

She sat on her bed and dialled a taxi number. They told her they were five minutes away. Really, she should go into the barn and say goodbye. It was the polite and right thing to do, but she couldn't stand it. Besides that, they pretended not to, but they all hated her for what she'd done to Clover, even though things had turned out well in the end. They easily couldn't have done, that was the point.

She picked up her bag and carried it out to the parking area and waited. The taxi pulled up. She climbed into the back seat so she wouldn't be forced to make conversation with the driver. God, she felt so bad leaving like this again after everything she'd done.

She leaned forwards and spoke to the driver. 'Could you just beep your horn a few times as we leave?' she asked. 'I haven't said goodbye and feel I should.'

'No problem,' he said, and beeped obligingly.

Immediately, the rest of them appeared at the doorway to the barn. They smiled and waved at her, as if they were the Railway Children.

She waved back, and then the taxi turned out onto the main road and she was on her way, at last.

69

Fleur

Fleur slung her backpack over her shoulder and walked away from the retreat centre, back over the moor towards Bodmin Parkway where she would catch her train.

It was cold now, and the sky heavy with the threat of rain. The moorland surrounding her was vibrant, purpled all over with heather. A woman at a fair had sold her some heather once, told her it would bring her luck. She put her bag down and stopped to pick some, tucked it into a buttonhole in her jacket.

When she knew she'd left the retreat behind her, she pulled her phone out of her pocket and turned it on. There was a message from Douglas.

> When can I see you? This is urgent, Fleur. Please speak to me.

She didn't stop walking as she typed her reply.

70

Maggie

It was four o'clock when Maggie finally walked through her front door. The house felt very quiet after her weekend. She put her bag down in the hallway and set about finding Bill.

In the kitchen, his food bowl was still full. She called his name a couple of times and listened for his mewling. Nothing.

She walked back to the living room and checked under the sofas. He wasn't there. She went upstairs and looked under every bed and inside every cupboard, still calling for him, but there was still no Bill. She checked both bathrooms and the downstairs toilet.

Posters, she thought. She'd need to put posters up around the village with his face on them. *Have you seen this cat?*

Finally, she opened the back door so she could head out to the greenhouse to see if he was in there, hiding from her or sulking.

The doorstep was covered in rose petals. Pink, white, yellow . . . All the roses she'd spent the summer pruning and caring for to ensure they continued into autumn.

She stepped out into the garden to check the damage from the storm. The rose bushes were beyond the patio, bent over by the rain, with just a few, sad-looking petals left on their stems. She gazed from the bushes to the door. No wind could have done this. Bill must have picked up each fallen petal in his mouth and taken them there.

A gift, she thought. *A goodbye.* He knew she was okay now and didn't need him to hold her here any more.

She took a deep breath and headed back to the house.

ONE PLACE. MANY STORIES

Bold, innovative and
empowering publishing.

FOLLOW US ON:

@HQStories